Annika's Aurora

Nighthawk Search and Rescue Book 2

Amanda Zook

To those who battle the darkness, you will find the light within.

"Keep your face always toward the sunshine and shadows will fall behind you."
~Walt Whitman

IF YOU OR SOMEONE YOU KNOW IS HAVING THOUGHTS OF SUICIDE, CALL THE NATIONAL SUICIDE PREVENTION LIFELINE AT 1-800-273-TALK(1-800-273-8255), HELP IS AVAILABLE.

"Life is a storm, my young friend. You will bask in the sunlight one moment, be shattered on the rocks the next. What makes you a man is what you do when the storm comes."

Alexandre Dumas

"It is when you are going through the most difficult chapter of life that your hero is revealed, and how beautiful it is when you finally realize

you have the strength to save yourself."

Dodinsky

"And in the end we were all just humans ...
drunk on the idea that love, only love, could
heal our brokenness."

F. Scott Fitzgerald

"She never seemed shattered; to me, she was
a breathtaking mosaic of the battles she's
won."

Matt Baker

Chapter 1

ANNIKA SCREAMED LOGAN'S NAME one second before the discordant crunch of metal, but by then, it was too late.

Annika Northrup could only sit helplessly as the world went into slow motion. Logan wrenched the steering wheel hard, and she hoped they would swerve enough that the collision didn't kill them all as the eighteen-wheeler drifted into the oncoming lanes. The clank and clatter of metal annihilating metal reverberated in Annika's ears. A piercing scream echoed in the air, which she belatedly recognized as her own.

Annika prayed. Prayed for the lives of her two best friends. Jamie, her twin brother, and Logan were the most important people in her life. She'd never survive if she lost them. Especially Logan, the boy she'd been in love with since fifth grade when he made rainbows for her using a glass prism ruler. The man she ached for with hope that one day would see her as more than a best friend.

This was not how it was going to end for them. It just couldn't. As the jeep rolled, metal crunched, and glass pinged, the last hours of their idyllic day together rushed through her mind before her head was slammed into the doorframe, and darkness consumed her.

Earlier

The trio of friends had been enjoying their last bit of freedom together. It was the summer after high school graduation, before they all headed their separate ways. With the top of the Jeep Wrangler removed, they were flying down the old farm road loving the late summer breeze as it whipped through the open vehicle.

In just a few short days, Annika would be heading off to college with her twin brother Jamison, who sat up front in the passenger seat. Annika sat in the back behind Logan Cain, the driver and their best friend. His eyes, Annika noticed, constantly searched for her in the rearview mirror as he drove. Each time their eyes met, an electric shock shot through her system, causing her heart to pound erratically in her chest.

The three had been nearly inseparable since elementary school when a skinny kid asked if he could sit with the twins at lunch one day. Their bond had been instant, and they often joked that Logan's presence in the Northrup family turned the twins into triplets.

All the Northrups loved Logan like he was one of them. Especially their mother, Johanna, who showered Logan with an abundance of motherly love since his own mother had been locked up for dealing drugs before ultimately succumbing to those same drugs. With no father that he knew of, Logan lived with his grandmother, whose attitude toward him was more harsh than loving. Because of it, he spent most of his time with the Northrups.

Since Logan was headed off to Navy boot camp the next day, the three of them had spent their last day of freedom together. Annika had tried hard not to let her moroseness ruin the time they had. But she couldn't shake the dread of losing Logan.

She'd had numerous talks with Logan about his decision to join the Navy. For purely selfish reasons, she didn't want him to go. While she was proud that he wanted to serve, she worried something would happen to him, especially if he succeeded in his goal to become a SEAL.

She broke down once, overcome with fear for him. He had held her as she cried the worst of her worry out, but his mind was set. Since nine-eleven, he'd spoken often of his determination to serve; a compulsive need to do good for this world. It was his way of giving back for all the Northrups had done for him over the years. His way of seeing to their protection, but Annika wanted *him* protected.

Jamie, for the most part, had been good with Logan's decision. While he was sad to say goodbye to his best friend, he was incredibly proud. He couldn't wait for Logan to kick some terrorist ass overseas. Annika got the feeling that Jamie wished he could join Logan, but his heart problems prevented it. For once, Annika was grateful for the hours spent in the hospital as the doctors tried to fix her brother's heart.

As their last day together progressed, Annika shoved her sadness away, listening as Foreigner played through the car's sound system and the wind whipped her hair into a frenzy. She tried to tame the long blonde locks into a hair tie, but the air rushing through the jeep ripped the strands out of their confinement repeatedly.

They stopped next to the river to enjoy a picnic lunch that Johanna had packed for them. They sat for hours, reveling in the breeze that swept up the river; their talk centering around everything and nothing.

Annika leaned against Logan's shoulder as they sat in the shade of a tree, a book in her lap, soaking up every last moment she had with him. She wished she could freeze time, never wanting the idyllic day to end.

Logan hummed softly, a Foreigner song, his favorite group. His voice had always filled Annika with a sense of security. A place where she'd felt safe and protected. She had wanted to take shelter in his voice. To crawl inside and allow the timbre of his deep tones to surround her.

"How did Abby take the break-up?" Jamie asked Logan. He stood at the river's edge, skipping stones he'd collected in the pockets of his cargo shorts. His favorite Grateful

Dead shirt sported wet spots as the stones plunked into the river in front of him.

Jamie had never been very good at skipping stones.

Logan groaned. "Not good. I think she was expecting to someday become a Navy wife. Especially if I made the SEAL teams."

Annika giggled. "She does have a thing for men in uniforms. But then who doesn't?" She'd eagerly anticipated seeing Logan in his uniform for the first time. If he looked half as good as he did in his shorts and favorite Foreigner t-shirt ... Annika savored that mental image.

"Ah, so the truth comes out," he teased. "You like a man in uniform too, huh? Well, I'll have to make sure to send you a picture of me in mine to make you drool."

"Ha ha. I'll just show it to Abby. She'll be so jealous!" The disgruntled look on Logan's face made her giggle.

"Glad you cut her loose," remarked Jamie. "You didn't need that type of baggage."

It was Annika's turn to groan. "Ugh, that Abby. I think she'd worked her way through most of the student body before settling on you. I don't know why you fell for her."

Logan shrugged. "She's hot!" Annika punched him in the arm.

"She may be hot," Jamie threw another stone which plunked in front of him, splashing more water onto his clothes. "But there was nothing between her ears."

"Who needs brains when she's got a mouth that ..." he broke off laughing when Annika shoved him.

"Is that all that matters to you? Is that all you want from a girl? If she can give good head, she's a keeper, is that it?" As the only girl in the group, she felt the need to stand up for all womankind, even the vapid Abby. Not to mention that she was incredibly jealous. She'd watched for years as Logan made his way through all the girls in their school, never once looking at the one girl who could love him for who he was and not what he could give her.

Logan held his hands up in surrender as she threatened to punch him again. "No! No, of course not. I only look for a woman with brains, not a great set of ..." he held both hands up in front of his chest suggestively.

Annika shoved him again, but as he fell backward, he grabbed her. She tumbled with him, ending up sprawled across his chest. Their eyes met, and the laughter died. Her stomach jolted, and her body heated. There was a tingling between her legs that was hard to ignore, and her nipples had hardened. Staring down into Logan's dark eyes, she wished she could lean forward and kiss him.

She'd been feeling those electric jolts more and more often whenever Logan touched her. It was scary. She didn't want things to be awkward between them. If he knew she'd developed more romantic feelings for him, it might push him away. She never wanted to lose him like that.

She rolled off and lay beside him on the blanket, her head on his outstretched arm, hoping no one noticed her aroused state. Jamie came and laid down on her other side. She grabbed his hand as together they quietly watched the clouds roll by, the tranquility of the afternoon settling over them.

"Okay, lay it on me, Sunfire," Logan said. He was talking, of course, about Annika's penchant for quoting literary greats. Annika's dream was to be a literature professor someday and, never without a book, she always had a quote for every occasion.

"Well, let's see," Annika began. "There's the usual 'parting is such sweet sorrow.'"

Both men groaned, remembering having to struggle through *Romeo and Juliet* in tenth grade. They would never have made it through if Annika hadn't interpreted it for them, tutoring them through the entire play. She even made them sit through Leonardo DiCaprio's movie in hopes that they'd get a better sense of the story if it were played out for them to see. They hated it.

Annika laughed at their reaction. "Okay, not a fan of Shakespeare. I get it." She thought for a moment, then remembered a nice one she'd read once. "'Never say goodbye because goodbye means going away and going away means forgetting.' J.M. Barrie."

"You are an endless supply," Jamie remarked.

Annika shrugged. "I like words."

"Yeah, but where do you keep all those words?" wondered Jamie. Annika smiled at him.

"What's that from?" Logan asked.

"*Peter Pan*."

Jamie groaned. "Seriously! A kid's book! That's the best you've got for us?"

"Some of the best quotes come from children's books," Annika stated.

"'How lucky I am to have something that makes saying goodbye so hard,'" Logan quoted.

Annika smiled. "Milne. Nice. See, Jamie. Children's books. Winnie the Pooh is very wise."

Jamie snorted. "Whatever."

Logan's thoughts were in turmoil later that day after they had enjoyed dinner at a favorite hangout of theirs. The trio sat listening to the band while he dwelt on that moment by the river when Annika lay across him ... *Fuck. What was that?* That needed to stop happening.

Something intense passed briefly between them. Annika was like a sister to him, a best bud. He could *not* be having *those* types of feelings about her. He hoped that Jamie hadn't noticed his reaction, praying his shorts were baggy enough to hide his erection.

And even as she lay tucked against his side, he could still feel her with every fiber in his being. He'd concentrated very hard on squashing his raging hormones as her fruity scent drifted over him. He could still smell her even now as they sat side by side, listening to the band. Something citrusy. How could one scent be such a turn-on?

He shifted uncomfortably in his seat, willing his hard-on to go away, but he couldn't stop himself from stealing glances at her. The girl he'd known for most of his life was growing more beautiful by the day. Her long blonde hair lay loose past her shoulders and was wind-blown from the ride in his jeep. He found it extremely alluring. She wasn't one to wear much makeup, so her skin was smooth and flawless. There was once a word he read that described her skin perfectly—alabaster. Like pure white marble carved from the heavens.

Christ. Now he was spouting poetry. It was bad enough he'd spent last night trying to find the perfect quote for Annika. He must be losing his mind, or there was too much blood flowing to other regions. He shifted in his seat again.

Annika caught him staring at her and smiled, causing his heart to skip a beat. She reached over and squeezed his hand. He turned his over and laced their fingers together, not wanting to break contact. Relishing the feeling of her hand in his, he gently stroked his thumb across the soft skin. An image of stroking other parts of her skin popped into his mind, and his dick throbbed. He ruthlessly pushed those thoughts aside.

Annika was a hand holder, often holding hands with both Logan and Jamie. Christ, how he was going to miss that. He suddenly felt very sad to be leaving tomorrow. But also extremely grateful to be able to share these last few hours with her. And Jamie.

Jamie. His best friend. His *brother*. Logan owed him so much. He'd been there for some of Logan's darkest times. From dealing with his mother's incarceration when he was very young to when he'd found her on the floor in the bathroom where she had OD'd shortly after she'd been released.

Jamie was the first person he'd called after nine-one-one. Rushing over, he'd sat by Logan's side through the whole awful ordeal. He'd quietly packed up a few belongings and brought him home. The Northrups, of course, had welcomed him as a son. And they'd all stood by his side as his mother was lowered into the ground. Their tears for the boy and not for the dead woman.

As the band ended their last set of the night, the trio stood, knowing their time together was ending. They were quiet as they left the bar. Annika, being Annika, grabbed both boys' hands as they walked to the jeep. She swung their arms back and forth, attempting to add some levity to the moment.

He'd promised them he'd come home as often as he could, but the twins were soon going off on their own adventure; they would both start at Purdue in a few days. Annika wanted to be a teacher. Jamie was "still exploring his options," which was code for: he had no idea what he wanted to do with his life. But Logan wasn't worried. Jamie was smart, he'd soon find his way.

Logan held the car door open for Annika but stopped her before she could get in. "'There are no goodbyes for us. Wherever you are, you will always be in my heart.' Gandhi." Another quote he'd spent far too much time looking up just for her.

Her luminous blue eyes widened in surprise then melted as the words registered. She kissed him, a quick kiss, on the lips. "Thanks for spending your last day with us. It was just what we all needed." She turned her face away suddenly and hurried into the jeep. Logan knew she was trying to hide her tears from him, and his heart clenched for the pain he was causing her. But it was just like Annika to hide, her feeble attempt at protecting him. She didn't want to make this any harder on him than it was already.

He was distracted. That was his only excuse. He'd been distracted by the feeling of her soft lips on his. He'd been distracted by the sheen of tears in her eyes. Distracted by thoughts of a future he dreamed of having with Annika.

The truck was on them so quickly after Annika's scream; there was nothing Logan could do as it hit them, sending the jeep rolling over and over down an embankment. A tree t-boning the passenger side stopped their momentum and Logan's world went dark with Annika's name on his lips.

Chapter 2

Fifteen years later

December

Logan Cain's thoughts were a jumbled mess. For some reason, he couldn't let it go. The rush of the water. The pleading eyes. The anguish. It all played in slow motion continuously in his mind. And each repetition ended the same way—in failure.

The woman had been desperate to live, and he'd been too late to do anything but watch as she slipped away. He'd failed again. He'd lost another life, and it hit just as hard as his failure that night before boot camp, even though the woman was a stranger to him.

Do not *go there*. If he wallowed in that grief again, he might not come out of it. He needed to focus. There was a job to do, and his Nighthawk teammates were counting on him.

After leaving the SEALs, Logan had joined Nighthawk Search and Rescue, an organization developed by Graham and David Whitaker. Not only did they assist with rescues wherever they were needed, but the brothers had also built a large facility where they trained organizations looking for instruction and certifications. First responders came to Nighthawk from everywhere to improve their rescue operations. Logan, being former Navy, focused on training those groups on water rescues. Living by the Great Lakes made that type of training necessary. Though the Coast Guard covered the lakes, for the most part, there were numerous waterways that led into the lakes.

One of the largest of those was the St. Joseph River which Logan was currently navigating. He stood at the helm of one of the rigid inflatable boats, or RIB, that they used in training for water rescues, trying, with no success, to forget his memories.

"Yo, Logan!" Graham called to him. "You in there?"

He shook himself back to the present. "Yeah, sorry."

"You okay?"

"Yeah. Why?"

Graham grinned at him. "You just blew past the dock."

Fuck. Logan looked behind him. Sure enough, the Nighthawk docks were rapidly disappearing behind them. Turning the wheel, Logan brought them quickly about as they all leaned into the tight turn. Graham and his brother David stood behind him laughing.

Jude Riker and Atticus Mobey, nicknamed Finch, were in the stern packing away the supplies they had used for training, laughing their asses off as well. He'd take a ribbing about this one for a while and he would good-naturedly put up with it, as they all did when teasing and jokes started among the close-knit group of men. The teamwork among his SEAL squad had been decent but lacked the close camaraderie he'd found with his Nighthawk family.

After tying off the RIB, Graham pulled him aside. *Shit.* Here came the ass chewing for getting distracted. It had been a rookie mistake. One he hadn't made since his first weeks at boot camp. He had to get his head in the game, or he'd very likely lose everything he'd worked so hard for.

"Listen," Graham started. "I know that last mission was rough. Losing Mrs. Petersen was tragic; the entire team has been affected by it. But it seemed especially hard on you." He held up a hand to silence Logan when he was about to deny it. "I can also tell you are not ready to talk about it. I completely understand that. But the team needs your head here. Why don't you take a few weeks off? It's nearly Christmas. Go spend some time with your family. We don't have any groups scheduled until after the holidays. It's the perfect time for you to disappear for a bit. I may just do that myself." Graham *would* relish a long weekend away with his girlfriend, Natalie. Especially after the last getaway they'd planned had been canceled when the Nighthawks were deployed to help evacuate people from a flood in Wisconsin.

His boss needed time away with his girlfriend since, while the team had been working, an employee and friend of the Nighthawks had attempted to kill Natalie by pushing her into an old abandoned well. Natalie had been trapped for three days before they'd realized she was missing.

But somehow, Graham knew. He'd been out of his mind with worry on that SAR trip since he couldn't get ahold of her. By the time Monday rolled around, and Natalie didn't show up for work, Graham was frantic to get home. They raced back just in time to save her from that pit before she succumbed to hypothermia.

But Graham wasn't offering Logan time off so he could have a romantic getaway with a girlfriend. Logan didn't have anyone. No family either, but he hadn't shared that with any of his teammates yet.

"Are you letting me go?" He'd always feared that he'd fail to live up to the men on the Nighthawks team. His failure with the Northrups was always with him. And now he had this new failure with the woman in the river entrenched in his soul. He'd thought he'd put all his doubts and fears behind him, that the brutal months he spent training to become a SEAL, otherwise known as BUD/S or Basic

Underwater Demolition/SEAL, had beaten it all out of him. Apparently not. One loss on a river in Michigan and his misgivings came back to undermine him.

"Absolutely not," insisted Graham. "Your place is here. And when you are ready to talk, your Nighthawk family will always be here to listen. I just think you need a break. Not for long though, you're too important to the team, but you should get away for a bit. Even if you stay in a hotel somewhere, you need a break to renew yourself. Fuck, that sounds new-age-y. But you get what I'm trying to say, right?" Graham smacked a hand on his shoulder and looked him straight in the eye. "That's an order, not a request. Get your head on straight. Then come back."

Logan relented. His rational side knew that he was a danger to his team if he couldn't stay focused. And he'd die before he'd want any of them hurt.

Fuck, maybe Graham was right. He needed time away. After parting from Graham with a promise to keep in touch, he headed for the dorm-style barracks on the Nighthawk property. On his way to his room on the top floor, he stopped in the dining hall and grabbed an apple. Chef Layla was there as always, preparing dinner for the guys. He bussed her cheek quickly then headed for the stairs.

In his room, he was at a loss as to what to do next. He didn't have anywhere to go. His grandmother died years ago. He had no family left that he knew of; he'd never known who his father was and had never missed that. He'd had Papa J.

Jansen Northrup had been a father to him for the first half of his life. That was all he'd needed. Everything necessary to know about being a man had come from Papa J. But after that night, he hadn't been able to face him. He couldn't face any of them. The guilt kept him away.

The ache he always felt when he thought about his adopted family hit him square in the chest. He missed them, now more than ever. Especially the twins.

Annika.

Like a coward, he'd disappeared from her life. He'd left for boot camp the following morning, unable to face their blame and his shame. After all, he'd killed their son, her brother.

Fifteen Years Ago

Logan was momentarily stunned. Unsure of how long he sat there with a trickle of blood running down the side of his face, he blinked, tried to focus, and looked around. What the fuck just happened? It came to him in a flash. The truck. The impact.

Christ! Annika!

He called her name, getting no response. He turned his head, a wave of dizziness washing over him. Willing the nausea away, he looked over at the passenger seat. Jamie was slumped beside him. His eyes were closed, and he was covered in blood. Logan reached out a trembling hand to shake his friend awake. Nothing. Slowly, his eyes moved to the rearview mirror. He spotted Annika's shoulder. She wasn't moving.

He had to get to her. He tried to open his door, but it wouldn't budge. Instead, he climbed out the window. Swallowing the nausea that rushed up his throat with every movement, he went to Annika's door.

She lay prone to the side, red discoloring her golden hair. He cried out her name, but when there was no reaction, he yanked on her door. Fuck, the damn thing wouldn't open.

He had to get to her, had to know.

Please don't be dead.

Reaching for her through the window, he pulled her closer to him. He stroked her face, pushing her hair out of the way. Pleading with her to open her gorgeous blue eyes, he ran a trembling hand down her throat, praying for a pulse. There! Was that it? Christ, he hoped so. It was faint, just a tiny beat under his fingertips, but it gave him hope and spurred him into action.

He struggled to the back of the jeep, fighting his way through the tall grasses that threatened to wrap themselves around his ankles and hampered his mobility.

Thankful he'd left the top off, he climbed up behind her and grabbed her under her arms. He pulled, but she wouldn't budge. She was trapped. Something was blocking his attempts to save her.

Frantic and near tears, he paused to study the back seat. The blood from his injury was running into his eyes, blurring his vision; with his arm he wiped some of it away. Blinking to clear his muddled mind, he studied her position again. Everything looked clear around her, so why couldn't he get her out.

Shit! The seatbelt was still holding her. Imprisoning her.

He tried the release but nothing happened. Figuring the thing must be damaged, he reached for the pocketknife Annika had given him last Christmas. Flipping open the blade, he hacked through the belt then pulled her up and out of her seat. He jumped off the back of the jeep with her in his arms, grateful to see her chest moving with her breathing. Placing her gently on the ground a safe distance away, he turned back to get Jamie. That's when he noticed the flames.

The fuel tank must have been punctured. There was gas everywhere, and something had ignited it. Before he could blink, the engine block was completely engulfed. A trail of fire followed the path of gas leading under the car. It was only a matter of time before what fuel was left in the tank exploded.

He raced to Jamie on the passenger side but couldn't reach him because of the tree. The flames were spreading quickly. Too quickly. Licking at Jamie.

He climbed up on the running board and leaned through the window beside Jamie as best he could, his knife grasped in his trembling hand. Logan sliced Jamie's seat belt, ignoring the heat from the flames burning his hands.

He had to get Jamie out; Annika needed her brother. It was a mantra set on repeat inside his mind. He didn't care what happened to him as long as Jamie was safe. Annika couldn't live without her twin.

Come on, you fucker. Cut faster!

The explosion caught him unaware, sending him flying through the air. He landed on the ground, dazed. Someone screamed his name.

Annika. She ran to him and started hitting him everywhere. He glanced down at himself in shock. He was on fire! She was trying to put the flames out with her bare hands. He quickly pushed her away and rolled back and forth on the ground smothering the flames. He crawled to her and together, they got to their feet. Her eyes wide with shock as she stared at the jeep.

Jamie! He started to go back for Jamie, but Annika grabbed him, preventing him from moving further. Her lips were moving, but he couldn't make out the words. His ears were ringing from the explosion, a tinny sound buzzing in his ears. Still, he struggled against her hold, desperate to get to Jamie.

Annika grabbed his face, forcing him to focus on her. Her blue eyes imploring him, pupils wide with trauma, nearly obliterating the color. Through the drone in his ears, her words penetrated slowly. "You can't! He's gone! Don't make me lose you too!" That last bit sunk in deep. That and her tears.

He tore his eyes from her tortured ones and looked to the jeep. It was fully engulfed. Christ! He'd failed. He'd promised to always protect the Northrups, had joined the Navy to do just that. And he'd failed to save his brother. The best man he'd ever known.

Logan sank to his knees, his grief overwhelming. Annika was right there with him, her arms wrapped tightly around him. He gathered her close, and together they sat in the weeds holding each other tight as they helplessly watched as Jamie burned.

Present Day

Logan closed his eyes and took a deep breath, trying to clear the memories that haunted him. If he had just moved faster, shaken off the shock and dizziness faster, maybe he could have gotten them all out. But he didn't, and Jamie paid dearly for his failure.

So, he'd hidden from the only family that had ever mattered to him. Filled with guilt and remorse, too ashamed to face any of them, he'd stayed away. They called, texted, and emailed constantly in those first few months but he'd ignored them all even as each message ripped his heart out. He'd been too much of a coward to reply, but he'd saved them all. The little folder on his computer still taunted him every time he turned on his computer. Eventually, the contact dwindled until finally ceasing. He'd grieved all over again.

He'd lost his best friend. Then through his shame and cowardice, he'd lost his family. He'd lost Annika. She had been the last Northrup to break off contact with him. She'd tried for over three years; her parents had stopped after one. He still had her last email to him.

Surprisingly, after he'd left the SEALs and joined Nighthawk, he'd received another email. Johanna was reaching out again. She'd berated him for being such an idiot and ordered him to come back home to them.

Logan had bitten the bullet, swallowed as much of the guilt as he could stomach, and wrote back, "I'm sorry. I don't know how."

Six little words. It was only six words, but they had taken everything in him to write. It had been fifteen years, and all he could manage was six words to the woman who'd been like a mother to him. But she hadn't given up. Those six words turned into eight more. And more still. They now emailed or texted each other a couple of times a month. They never talked about anyone else, only themselves. Logan didn't know if the others knew about their contact. She'd never told him, and he'd never asked.

Remembering something she'd told him over fifteen years ago, he reached for his phone to shoot off a text.

Logan: Need to get away. Can I stay at the lake house?

The response was almost immediate.

Mama Jo: Absolutely. You remember where the key is hidden?

He did.

Mama Jo: Is everything ok?

Was everything okay? No, not really. But he couldn't tell her that. Their relationship was still too fragile. They shared only surface things with each other, nothing too personal.

Logan: Got some time off work. Just looking for someplace to stay for a while.

Mama Jo: Ok. You let me know if you need anything.

Logan: Will do. Thanks.

Mama Jo: Anytime, Kiddo.

Logan smiled. Mama Jo always called him that. He was glad that she'd reached out to him after so long. And he was glad he'd pulled up his big boy pants and responded. It'd been easier than he thought. Even if they hadn't yet talked about that night and the days that followed, and he didn't know if he'd ever be able to talk about it with her.

Shaking off his reverie, he grabbed his duffle and started to pack, making sure to grab the picture of him with the twins that was always with him.

Chapter 3

ANNIKA SAT IN HER mother's family room, trying in vain to untangle the Christmas lights. The cursed things were so fricking frustrating, her brain immediately thought of a quote about how feeding the frustration's wants was the only way to fight it or something like that.

"What are your wants?" she asked the strand of lights angrily. She shook a strand irritably, hoping to dislodge the tangle, but that sent a twinge of pain to her still healing shoulder and made the tangle worse. She winced.

Ever vigilant, Johanna heard. "You okay, Sweetie?"

"I'm good, Mom. Just a little cramp." Johanna studied her for a moment then continued placing ornaments on the tree. Johanna loved Christmas time. Nothing gave her more joy than pulling out each ornament and remembering. She'd given her children their own ornament each year, hoping that by the time they had houses of their own, they'd take their ornaments with them and start their own traditions. Annika had once shared in her mother's joy, reminiscing about the ornaments and what year they came from. But ever since losing Jamie, she struggled to find the joy. She still loved the holiday, but some years her enthusiasm was missing.

Not Johanna. She still felt the joy as she pulled out each one of Jamie's ornaments.

"You know what, Sweetie?" Annika paused in her detangling to listen to her mother. "I think it might be a good idea for you to go stay at the lake house for a little while."

Shocked, Annika said, "What? Why? Are you trying to get rid of me?" She didn't think Johanna would ever want to let Annika out of her sight again.

"Of course not. I just think that after the last few months, you need to get away. You don't need your old mom hovering over you every second of the day anymore. Go. Let the fresh lake air rejuvenate you."

Annika thought about her mother's words. It had been a long time since she'd been to the lake house. There were too many memories, and she didn't know if she was ready to face them yet.

"I don't know, Mom."

"Do it for me. I think it would be good for you."

Annika relented, "I'll think about it."

Feeling nostalgic for the first time in fifteen years, Annika pulled out her old photo album after her parents had turned in for the night. She sat on the bed, the album still closed on her lap. *It won't bite; just open it.*

But still, she kept it closed. How could she be so scared of a few pictures? It was time. Past time. She needed to start remembering the good times and stop dwelling on all that she'd lost. Taking a deep breath, she opened the cover.

Now open your eyes, dummy. She pried her eyes open and looked at the first picture. The album was filled with pictures from when they were in high school, the first photo being of the three of them at graduation, two short months before the accident. She looked closely at the faces. Full of life. Full of potential. The rest of their lives lay before them. Those faces had no idea the tragedy that would befall them all.

Annika refused to think about it. Instead, she focused on the two men standing on either side of her, their arms around her shoulders, large grins on their faces. Jamie was on her left. His blond hair shone in the sun, hanging in his eyes as always. He was tall. Six feet compared to her five-five stature. His blue eyes, so like hers, were full of mischief. His black graduation robe hung open, revealing what he'd worn underneath. Annika remembered her mother's groan of exasperation upon seeing the outfit, cargo shorts, and a bright red Hawaiian shirt covered in colorful parrots. Jamie had a zest for life that people were drawn to. As the self-proclaimed class clown, there wasn't much that could ruin his good mood unless someone tried to mess with her. Nobody disrespected Jamie Northrup's sister.

Logan, on her right, was Jamie's polar opposite. She'd often teasingly called him dark and brooding. He was a couple of inches taller than Jamie, with dark brown hair cut short. For once, his dark eyes didn't look so serious in this picture. They'd all been so happy.

Annika had always wondered if the reason no one messed with her was because of Jamie or if it was because they were scared of how Logan would react. While Jamie was all talk, Logan was all action. She'd never thought of that before now. It described the difference between the two of them perfectly.

Annika paged through the album until she found the pictures she had originally wanted to see. Another picture of the three of them. The boys had their heads on her shoulders, grinning in that ridiculous way they had.

After graduation, the three of them had spent the summer at the Northrups' house in Lake Haven, a little town on the southeastern shores of Lake Michigan. That summer had been the best time in her life. Three teenagers with not a care in the world, using those months to still be teenagers before their future responsibilities took hold. When they were not at their summer jobs, they swam nearly every day and took the boat out to explore Lake Michigan. They walked those shorelines hoping as always to spot a Petoskey stone, never finding one. They stayed up late and made s'mores at the firepit. And they talked, sharing their fears of the future.

It was during one of the last days that Annika had broken down and begged Logan not to join the Navy. She'd been so afraid she was going to lose him. Feared he would die alone on a distant battlefield.

He'd left for the Navy soon after that day and never looked back. He never came home. She'd lost him anyway. And not to some terrorist looking to kill Americans.

Looking at that smiling face and remembering all of the broken promises, she was angry now. He'd promised her that day that he would always be there for her. That nothing was going to happen to him. He'd assured her that nothing could keep him from coming home to his adopted family. To her. But he'd lied. He had left her and never came home. He'd left her to deal with her crushing grief alone.

A tear dropped onto the picture, surprising her. She hadn't realized her little torturous trip down memory lane had stirred up so many emotions.

Annika slammed the photo album closed and grabbed her suitcase. Her mom was right; she needed to get away. She needed time to deal with ... everything. So much loss threatened to drown her. She needed to figure out how to let it go ... again. She'd go to the lake house. Tonight. Now, or as soon as she was done packing. Her parents would understand her leaving so abruptly. She'd leave them a note explaining herself and promising she'd be back in plenty of time for Christmas.

Logan unlocked the door using the key they'd always kept hidden in the gazebo at the side of the house. He was suddenly feeling apprehensive about going inside. The memories swamped him, especially the ones from that last summer. He almost headed back to the car, unsure if he could do this.

Squaring his shoulders, he took a deep breath and forced himself to cross the threshold. They were only memories, most of which were good ones. They may hurt a little, but they wouldn't kill him.

Stepping into the great room, he saw the same couch they'd spent hours on watching movies and eating popcorn. The same fireplace. The same pictures still sat on the mantel, most of them featured the three of them. It was surprising to see those photos there, as if to show him that they hadn't removed him completely from their lives.

Exhaustion flooded him. He locked the front door and headed down the hall to his usual bedroom, where not much had changed either. Maybe some new bedding, but that was about it. The dresser held more photos, including a large one in the center of him in his dress uniform.

Surprised, he wondered how they had gotten that picture; he'd never sent it to them. Knowing Johanna, she must have badgered his grandmother until she got it from her.

Logan put his bag down to unzip it. Reaching inside, he pulled out the picture he carried with him everywhere and placed it on the nightstand as the memories of the day it was taken swamped him.

Fifteen years ago

Logan lounged on a blanket under the large oak tree on the bluff that overlooked the water at the Northrups' lake house. Annika lay perpendicular to him, her head propped up against his side. Her long blonde hair was thrown across his torso, and he combed his fingers through the silky-smooth strands, fascinated by the play of colors. When the sun hit it just right, her hair shone like tinsel.

It had been the perfect summer for their last hurrah. Logan, Annika, and Jamie. The best friends Logan had ever known, they had been with him through so many personal tragedies. From his mother's incarceration to her eventual death, the twins had been a steady constant in his life. Logan didn't know how he would have got through the last ten years without them.

Being the new kid at school at age eight was not an easy thing to go through, especially when your mom was a con and your dad was unknown. But the twins didn't care about any of that. They took him into their circle from the first day he asked to sit at their lunch table. Logan would never be able to repay them for their kindness and love. Even the Northrup parents had accepted him practically as one of their own. The extra kid that made their twins triplets. He loved Mama Jo and Papa J as if they were his own parents.

Laying in the grass at their lake house, he was enjoying the company of the girl he wished could be his more than anything in the world. He longed to tell her how he really felt about her, but they had been friends for so long he didn't want his conflicted feelings getting in the way of the good thing they had going.

Plus, there was Jamie to consider. What would he think if he knew Logan had feelings for his sister? It had the potential to be a cluster fuck of massive proportions. So, he kept his thoughts to himself as he played with Annika's mesmerizing hair.

"Hey, Logan?" Annika asked him.

"Mmm?"

"What would you say if I asked you not to go?" He knew she was talking about the Navy. He was headed off to boot camp in a few short weeks. His dream was to be a Navy SEAL and head into the worst of the worst places to help people. Or, as Jamie liked to put it, kick some terrorist ass. He'd known Annika had mixed feelings about it, but this was the first time she'd ever voiced them with him.

"I'd ask why?" He absently twirled a lock of her hair around his finger.

"Because I don't want you to go."

"That's not really a reason, Sunfire," he said, calling her the nickname he'd given her years ago. She had a sunny outlook on life, and her smile could light up even the darkest heart. But she also had a stubborn fire in her as well, especially when it came to standing up for others.

She sighed. "Because I'll miss you."

"I'll miss you too. But we'll talk all the time. Write, text, video call each other. Whatever. And I'll spend any leave time I get with you guys. You may just get sick of me."

"Never."

"Don't worry, Annika. We'll never lose touch," he promised.

She sat up unexpectedly, pulling her hair out of his fingers. Suddenly, she straddled him, her hands on his shoulders as she leaned over him. "And what if I pinned you down and refused to let you get up to leave?" He'd been trying all day to control his raging hormones around her, and Annika's position on top of him just ratcheted his blood up to boiling.

The hardest thing he'd ever had to do was keep his eyes on hers and not look down at the tempting tits that were hanging exceedingly close to his face. Or let his hands slip up the tantalizing expanse of leg exposed beneath her too-short shorts. He prayed she didn't feel his sudden hard-on.

He grabbed her hips and flipped them over until she was on her back and he was on top of her. Her eyes went wide as her pupils dilated. He could see the sudden heat flare in her eyes. He wanted to kiss her. Badly.

"I'd say you lose," he teased. That must have been the wrong thing to say as Annika burst into tears. Big fat tears slipped from her eyes down her temples to disappear in her hair.

"Ahh, Annika." He rolled to her side and gathered her into his arms, squeezing tight as she sobbed.

"I'm so afraid, Logan. I'm afraid something is gonna happen to you. I don't want to lose you. I don't think I could live if I lost you," she finished quietly as more sobs overwhelmed her.

"You won't lose me," he promised, kissing the top of her head. "Nothing is going to happen to me."

"You p ... promise? Promise me you won't take any undue risks."

"I promise," he vowed as he rubbed his hand up and down her back. She wore a bikini top with shorts. Logan closed his eyes and gritted his teeth, willing himself not to enjoy the feel of her smooth skin under his fingertips too much.

"Logan?" she asked as her tears started to subside.

"Yeah?"

"Don't die." His heart squeezed painfully. It was a promise he couldn't really make. Who knew what the future would hold for them? He could die tomorrow crossing the street, after all. But he was going to make sure he trained hard so that he could avoid dying at all cost. For Annika.

"I'll never leave you, Sunfire," he promised as he lay in the summer sun with Annika in his arms.

Jamie came out of the house just then. "Shit, man. Did you break my sister?"

"She seems to be malfunctioning," Logan answered.

"Must be a type of malware."

"Or a virus."

"Did you try turning her off and back on again?" Jamie quipped.

"I would, but I can't seem to find the off button."

"All right. All right." Annika rolled away from him and sat up. "You two done?"

The men looked at each other and shrugged. Then burst into laughter. Jamie sat on the other side of Annika and took his camera out of his pocket. "Let's get a picture."

"Oh, Jamie, no. I must look like a wreck," Annika complained.

Logan scooted closer to her and wiped an errant tear from her cheek. "You look beautiful."

"As always," Jamie agreed.

The boys put their chins on Annika's shoulders with big cheesy grins. It took several tries to get the perfect shot, and their teasing and joking around was exactly what Annika needed to distract her from her worries.

"Let's go do something fun," Jamie requested.

"What did you have in mind?" Logan asked.

He thought about it for a second. "Let's find some place that has a zipline."

"What?" Annika was shocked. Logan and Jamie were adrenalin junkies, Annika, not so much, but she was a good sport and often tagged along to watch their adventures.

"I'm in!" Logan agreed.

"I'll watch," Annika moaned.

Present day

They had indeed found a place with a zipline. They'd even managed to talk Annika into trying it once. Logan could still remember the look of unexpected joy on her face as she zipped across the sky. It had been a perfect day. Lost in his memories, he fell into bed fully clothed and dropped off to sleep staring at Annika in that photo.

The nightmare came again. Logan wasn't surprised, given where he was, but he was baffled that he hadn't had the full dream as he usually did. Something had woken him.

He sat up and threw his legs over the side of the bed, running his fingers through his hair as he shook off the remnants of the nightmare. He heard another noise then, coming from the great room. He was off the bed in a flash. Someone was in the house.

His SEAL training kicked in as he crept silently to the door and opened it without a sound. Making his way quickly down the hall, he peered around the corner. Someone was in the kitchen. In the refrigerator. *What the fuck.*

He watched the intruder for a few moments, wondering what the person wanted in the Northrups' house. He wasn't about to let some vagrant steal from his family. He'd have to move quickly to take them by surprise and hope they didn't have a weapon. From the light of the fridge, Logan was shocked to see the prowler was a woman. He'd have to rethink his takedown. Not as much strength was needed to take out a woman. But then she turned, and he saw a golden head of hair. He nearly gasped.

Annika.

It had been fifteen years since he'd last seen her, and she hadn't changed much. Maybe a little taller, hair a little longer. Logan stood stock still and watched her move around the kitchen. With only the muted light over the sink illuminating the area, he couldn't make out her features, and she hadn't turned on any of the other lights yet. But he could still see she was just as beautiful, just as graceful as ever.

She winced as she reached into a high cabinet to grab a glass. His heart gave a painful lurch wondering if she was injured. Even after all this time, he still wanted to know everything about her. He still wanted to fix her hurts and protect her from harm.

Annika filled the glass with water from the sink. She turned toward him to take a sip and spotted him standing there. She screamed and dropped the glass, conveniently in the sink, where it shattered into dozens of pieces. He went to her then, hoping she hadn't hurt herself on the broken glass.

"Annika." He reached for her hands to check for cuts.

She slapped him.

Hard.

Across the face.

Chapter 4

L OGAN. HE WAS STANDING right there in front of her.

And she'd just slapped him.

She'd never slapped anyone before, and her hand stung. The ache in her shoulder had protested the sudden movement and was making its discomfort known as well. She stood frozen, eyes wide in shock, stunned that she'd hit him. The residual anger that had been stirred up when she'd looked through the photo album several hours ago had still been churning inside her. Seeing him so suddenly unleashed her anger.

"Are you hurt?" he asked. His deep guttural voice sent a ripple through her body. The tempting tones like a caress, heating her blood. She shivered.

"What?" her voice croaked. He indicated her hands with a gesture. "No. No, I'm fine." Fifteen years and here he stood as if he belonged there. As if he'd never abandoned her.

She ran her eyes over him. He'd changed quite a bit. His dark hair was no longer buzzed short. It lay across his forehead in soft waves. He was bigger too. Not taller, just ... more muscular. All that time in the Navy had given definition to his muscle mass. He wore a navy-blue t-shirt with a flying bird logo over his impressive pecs, the sleeves straining against his biceps. Dark cargo pants covered his long legs. He still towered over her.

Her scrutiny finally moved to his eyes ... They were the same. And they were gazing at her with concern and uncertainty. Deep chestnut brown irises shrouded by thick lashes. Their intensity brought back things she wasn't ready to feel.

Fifteen fricking years! "What are you doing here?"

"I ... Your mom ... I didn't know you'd be here."

"That's what you're going with? You didn't know I'd be here? Well, then, I'll just gather my stuff and get out of your hair." She was angry. Very angry. Every hurt feeling over the past fifteen fricking years surging through her.

She tried to move past him to leave, not wanting to face any of this right now, but he grabbed her arm. The warmth of his palm seeping straight through cloth, skin, and bones. Warming places deep inside she hadn't realized were chilled.

"Annika." She glared at him, tears threatening. He said only her name, yet she felt it deep inside her. The shelter she'd craved from him surfaced with just one spoken word. "Please."

She squeezed her eyes shut, willing the tears to disappear. "No, Logan," she whispered. Everything she wanted to tell him, she was unable to articulate. In that moment, she feared the sound her voice would make as it came bleeding out of her heart. "I can't. I'm tired." She extracted her arm from his grasp, immediately missing the warmth.

Grabbing her suitcase from where she'd dropped it, she retreated to her bedroom. Shutting and locking the door. Shutting Logan out and reinforcing the icy crust she'd built up over her heart.

Annika leaned against the locked door, breathing hard. The tears spilled over, and she trembled. Still angry, she pulled out her phone and sent a quick text to her mom.

Annika: You knew he'd be here, didn't you? You set me up.

She ended it with a mad face emoji.

How could Johanna have done this to her? She didn't want to see him. There was too much bitterness and anger. It was better to freeze all that out. That's why she'd stopped writing to him all those years ago. The hurt and disappointment she felt after sending each email became too much. Waiting with hope and anticipation after each message sent only to be crushed ... again ... when he didn't reply. It had nearly killed her.

Her mother knew he was here. So, apparently, he did reply to one of the Northrups. To Johanna. *Why her and not me?* She bit back the scream that fought to be released.

Why did Johanna never tell her? Did she even tell dad? Annika threw herself face down across the bed. Wanting to kick and scream and have a full-blown tantrum like a toddler, she appeased herself by releasing her tears and letting them flow.

The alert of an incoming text woke her the next morning. Groggily, Annika grabbed her phone and read the text from her mother.

Mom: You two need each other. Talk. Get to know each other as you are now. Heal the hurts.

Gee, thanks, mom. She sent the eye roll emoji back.

Annika: Don't think that I'm not still mad about this.

Mom: I know, Sweetie. But you love me, so you'll forgive me. You can do the same for him.

God mom! Can you be any more obtuse?

How was she ever going to forgive him? He'd abandoned her when she'd needed him most. She could have forgiven him for the first couple of weeks. After all, he'd been grieving too. But fifteen years! And not one word from him. Annika didn't know if she could ever forgive him for that. She forced herself out of bed before the tears swamped her again. Reaching into her suitcase, she grabbed her running gear. She'd go for a long run, try to escape her anger, and refuse to think of it as running away from her problems.

Logan sat at the kitchen table, head in his hands. The bowl from the cereal he'd eaten an hour ago sitting near his elbow. Sleep had been elusive since he'd found Annika in the kitchen, so he didn't even bother to try. His mind felt like the proverbial hamster on the wheel. Running and running. Around and around.

He'd made so many mistakes throughout his life but staying away from Annika for fifteen years had to have been the biggest and stupidest. His mind had chased its tail all night long, trying to figure out a way to make it up to her. The first step had to be to apologize.

Now, if only she'd let him.

He heard her door open; his heart thumping loudly in his ears. Shit, he was nervous. How could he possibly be so scared to face her? It was just Annika. They'd been close once.

She was fitting earbuds into her ears and thumbing through her phone as she entered the great room. She wore tight spandex over toned legs. The zipper of her black hoodie was partially down, revealing the creamy skin of her chest above a purple sports bra. Logan blinked. She looked hot as hell, and his dick took notice.

She looked up then, and her steps faltered as she spotted him sitting there. Her eyes narrowed warily. "I'm going for a run." Annika worked out? That was new.

He stood up so quickly he nearly knocked over the chair. "Want some company?"

"No," she said simply, then was out the door.

Christ. She wasn't going to make this easy on him. How could he apologize to her if she wouldn't give him the time of day? He walked slowly to the door she disappeared through and stepped out onto the porch. She was halfway down the street already. Running as if her demons chased her. He fought the desire to go after her, instead watched the way the spandex pants hugged ... everything.

Shit. He could *not* go there. But damn, she looked good. She'd always been pretty but in a sweet innocent sort of way.

Now, she'd grown into a stunningly sexy woman. They were definitely no longer eighteen. He could appreciate the way his old friend had matured.

Not *if you want her to forgive you.* Well, that was it then. It was hopeless. She'd always been a stubborn little thing growing up; that's why he'd always called her Sunfire. It didn't look like that had changed much.

Logan sighed and went back inside, searching for something to do. He *needed* something to do. He went to the fireplace to make a fire. It was cold outside, and Annika might like to warm herself when she returned. But that took less time than he thought it would. At a loss as to what to do next, he sat on the couch and stared into the flames, wondering how he could have made such a mess of things.

Annika ran. One mile turned into two. Then three. The sound of her steps like a mantra in her head: *jerk, jerk, jerk, ass, ass, ass, stu-pid, stu-pid.*

She wasn't sure who she was calling stupid. Him for what he'd done, or herself for running away from the confrontation. Yes, she was running away from her problems, but it was cathartic for her. Running was a way for her to compartmentalize her jumbled thoughts and feelings.

Her therapist had suggested she find an outlet. Since she couldn't draw or paint worth a damn, and crafting was beyond her, she'd tried running. She took to it instantly because it allowed her the quiet time she needed to think, to reason through her problems and feelings. She'd been running ever since.

Realizing how far away from the house she'd gone, Annika paused to take a breather, regretting being too focused on escaping to grab a bottle of water on her way out.

Logan's abandonment all those years ago was still too raw. But when she saw him sitting at the table this morning, he'd looked so miserable. She immediately felt the need to go to him, to comfort him, just as she used to. She had to escape before she gave in to those old feelings for him. And then when he'd offered to go with her, his dark eyes pleading, she needed to shut that down.

She could tell he needed to talk to her, but she wasn't ready. It had been such a shock to see him yesterday that her mind and heart hadn't had time to process and recover from the jolt.

Despite the fact that he'd looked so wretched sitting there, he also looked really good. He looked as if she could sink into his embrace and lose herself for days, as if in his arms, she could forget all the horrors that haunted her. Annika knew deep down that he *would* just hold her. He would take on her demons and banish them if she let him. The temptation to let it all go was so great.

She started running again back toward the house. She couldn't let it go. Not yet. She had to understand why first.

Chapter 5

Fifteen years ago

Annika lay on her bed, Johanna's arms wrapped tightly around her as she cried. It was the night before the funeral. Annika thought she'd cried so much that surely there weren't any tears left inside her. But she'd been wrong. The tears never stopped.

"Where is he, Mom?" she wailed.

"I don't know, Sweetie. His grandmother says he's at boot camp."

"But why hasn't he called? Surely the Navy allows phone calls."

Johanna smoothed Annika's hair back from her forehead. "Maybe when you are new there, you aren't allowed much personal time."

Annika picked at the bandages on her hand that covered the burns she'd suffered while trying to smother the flames that had attacked Logan. "He had to have told them about the funeral, though, right? They have to let him come home for the death of a family member."

"But we are not officially his family. Maybe there are rules against that."

"Why don't they understand a stupid piece of paper doesn't make a family? He is family!" she insisted. "And he's needed. God, Mom! I want Jamie! I want Logan! How could *they have both left me?" She wept, overcome by her tears again. Johanna squeezed her tighter. Her father must have heard her sobs. He came and sat at her other side, gathering both women in his arms. The three of them stayed like that all night. Another trio. But not the trio Annika wanted with all her heart.*

Present Day

Annika didn't know why that memory had popped into her head. The grief had nearly destroyed her. To lose both of them at once, it had taken her a long time to accept that they were gone. And even longer to forgive them. After about three years or so, and numerous therapy sessions, she'd learned to forgive Jamie. He hadn't left her by choice. And she knew that someday she'd see him again. He was her brother. Her *twin*. A part of him would always be with her. She could feel him even now.

But Logan, he'd left her by choice. He chose to abandon her and cut off all contact. How could she ever forgive that? She would never have done that to him. She would have fought anyone who stood in her way if he'd just lost his twin. She would have been there for him.

He chose not to fight. She could understand if the Navy wouldn't let him off for the funeral. She understood how that would have been difficult. But why did he not call? Why had he cut them out completely? Surely, he had been grieving just as much as they had. They could have helped him through it. *She* could have helped him through it. They could have helped each other. Why did he throw them away? Had they ... had *she* meant so little to him? Once Jamie was gone, why bother with the rest of them? Was that it? She thought they had meant more to each other. That he loved her just as much as he loved Jamie. It didn't make any sense. It never did, and it never would.

Having returned to the house, she passed through the great room and went right to the shower. She'd seen him sitting on the couch. He'd made a fire, and he sat staring into the flames, as lost in his thoughts as she had been. Annika almost went to him but couldn't force her feet to change direction. It was too soon.

After her shower, she sat on the edge of her bed, trying to talk herself into leaving her room. Her stomach was protesting the delay. But she was too chicken. Her stomach growled again. *Okay, I get it. You're hungry. Sorry I thought about chicken.* Why was she such a coward? Compared to what she'd faced in the last month, this was a piece of cake.

Just get up, go out to the kitchen, make yourself something to eat. Simple. One step at a time.

Mind made up—not like her stomach was giving her much choice—she got up and went to the door. Hand on the knob, she paused and took a deep breath. *You can do this.* She forced her hand to turn the knob and open the door. Then she forced her feet to walk down the hall.

See, one step at a time. Easy. She stopped when she reached the great room. Logan was no longer on the couch. Instead, he was in the kitchen, cooking.

"I hope you still like eggs?" he said when he noticed her standing there. "I'm afraid the repertoire of meals I'm capable of making hasn't improved much over the years."

"Eggs are fine," she managed to squeeze out.

"Good. Have a seat." She sat, and he brought her a plate filled with eggs, bacon, and toast. Her stomach was doing a happy dance.

"Thanks." She picked up her fork and dug in as he sat with his own plate across from her. *Ugh, what now?* She didn't want to look at him, but she couldn't *not* look at him. She felt like she was on some sort of awkward first date, at a loss as to what to say and not knowing what to do with her hands. So, she did the only thing she could. She ate while staring at her plate.

Coward. Darn tootin' she was a coward. This was so scary with so much potential to be hurt all over again.

Logan watched her as she ate. She looked nervous, and she shouldn't be. She hadn't abandoned him, she hadn't hurt him; that was all on him. If anyone should be nervous, it was him.

Her silence was unnerving. She hadn't necessarily been a chatty kid, but she had always been able to talk to him, including sharing her love of literary quotes that she enjoyed imparting. Even if it was silly or stupid, she told him everything. They'd had an easy camaraderie. A deep friendship. They could tell each other anything. He'd told her things he'd never told Jamie. Clearly, his actions had blown that all to hell.

He took advantage of her distraction with her food to study her more closely. She was flushed from her shower, a healthy glow to her cheeks. She wore no makeup; she didn't need it. With her eyes cast down, her delicate, long eyelashes hid her blue eyes from him.

How he wished he could look into her gorgeous blue eyes and see the joy and love she once shared so freely.

She had tiny gold leaves at her ears, and a gold chain disappeared under her pale pink sweater that perfectly matched the color glowing on her cheeks.

Annika was heart-achingly stunning, as she'd always been. And if he could get her to smile, she would light up the room. Her smile had a special magic. Nobody could resist her smile; especially not him.

"How was your run," he tried.

"Good."

"You were gone a long time."

She shrugged her shoulders, still looking down at her eggs. "Yeah, lost track of how far I'd gone."

"When did you start running?" She glanced up at him as if to say, 'why do you care?'

"It's been a while now," she answered, returning to her eggs.

"I like running." She didn't reply. *No wonder, you sound like a fucking idiot.* They both continued to eat their meal in silence. Neither willing to break the tentative silence. This wouldn't do, Logan thought. Here he had a chance to fix the mistakes of the past. But it wouldn't happen if he didn't open his mouth and say something to her.

He sighed. "I noticed the woodpile was getting low. I think I'm going to go chop some more."

Fucking chicken!

Nah, not chicken. Just choosing his words carefully. It had been a shock to see her again. He needed time to compose the right thing to say to her in his head. He was being smart, he thought, as he rinsed his plate and put it in the dishwasher. Not chicken. He couldn't screw up ... again. He could feel her eyes on him as he went out the back door to the woodpile. He wasn't sure, but he thought he could feel the daggers she was shooting at him hitting his back. He resisted the urge to shudder.

The two of them spent the rest of the day trying to avoid each other, and that was fine with Annika since she wasn't ready to talk. She wasn't sure if she'd ever be ready to talk to him. So, she sat in the armchair by the window that overlooked the lake, hiding behind a book.

Logan spent hours outside cutting the wood. She couldn't help but steal several peeks at him. The power he used in wielding the axe, splitting the wood in one easy blow. And who could blame her for peeking again when he came back inside with his shirt in his hand, wiping the sweat off his forehead. He was tanned, probably from all the outdoor work he was sure to have done with the SEALs.

But it was the muscles that had her mouth going dry. He was all hard, smooth muscle, not a hair in sight. She had been right; he had bulked up, but not enough to be obscene. It was just the right amount. Perfect for a woman to run her hands over.

Wait ... what? Where had that thought come from? And ... Oh my God, does he have a woman?

So what if he does? How is that any business of yours? Fifteen years was a long time. He probably hadn't been celibate all those years. He could have even been married. Could still be married.

Annika realized how woefully ignorant she was about his life.

While he was in the shower, Annika heated up some soup and threw a few sandwiches together for them to have for dinner. When had it become easier just to cook for both of them? He thanked her for the food as they ate in silence together.

"It's probably going to start snowing soon," he remarked. So, they didn't stay completely silent. They had each tried to start up an inane conversation here and there.

Annika took a sip of her water. "Really? I didn't know it was supposed to snow."

"I could feel it coming when I was out there."

"How can you feel it coming?" She'd never heard that one before.

"I've lived here by the lake long enough now to know the signs."

"You live here? In Lake Haven? Wait ... did Mom give you this house?" How close had he and Johanna become since they'd started their little secret relationship?

He chuckled. "No, of course not. I live just outside of Lake Haven. Have for about three years now. In the Nighthawk barracks."

"What is Nighthawk ... wait. Are you telling me you're part of that group? The ones that do all those rescues? Are you one of the guys who rescued Marcus Rayne?" If he was a Nighthawk ... well, that was just amazing. Those guys were heroes. Most of Michigan and the surrounding states knew of the Nighthawks. Annika certainly did. She'd even watched the interview the owner did for 20/20 a while back. Now there was an interesting story. She'd heard rumors that Marcus Rayne wanted to make a movie about the Nighthawks. She and Johanna had often said they'd be first in line for tickets to see that movie. And now to find out he'd been one of them all this time. Would Logan be in the movie too?

He was laughing. "Yes, I'm a Nighthawk. And, yes, I helped on the Marcus Rayne thing. But don't let my boss hear you gushing over it. He hates the notoriety."

"Oh my God! I can hardly believe this." And she couldn't believe it. What happened to his dream? He'd always wanted to be a SEAL. Why did that change? "But what about the SEALs? Did you make the teams?"

"I did. I was on the teams for twelve years."

"You did it then," she said, happy and sad at the same time. She was happy he'd achieved his dream but sad she hadn't been there to celebrate his accomplishment. She felt the tears threaten again and squeezed her eyes shut against them.

Logan reached across the table and placed his hand over hers, his heat enveloping her hand. "Hey," he coaxed. "Why so sad all of a sudden?" She looked at him and saw the worry in his eyes and felt a sudden and quick spark of anger. Why, after all this time, should he be worried about her?

She pulled her hand out from under his. "It's nothing. I still get overly tired sometimes."

"Are you okay?"

She stood and took her plates to the sink. "God, Logan! I can't do this," she hissed. "I can't pretend everything is okay."

"I know," he said, walking his own plates into the kitchen. "But I'm trying here. Tell me how to fix this."

She shook her head sadly. "I don't know if it can be fixed."

He stepped toward her, and she backed away. "You left me, Logan. You disappeared. I had to bury my brother, and my best friend had cut me out of his life. Can you understand how that feels? I lost both of you. I had to mourn you both!"

"Annika, I'm sorry," he said, holding out a hand to her.

"You're sorry," she scoffed. "Like that makes up for all the tears. I couldn't live ... couldn't go on ..." she paced, unconsciously rubbing her left wrist. "I couldn't go on the way things were. You don't know what it was like for me."

"Then tell me," he begged.

"I could understand you not being able to come to the funeral. You'd just started boot camp. The Navy wouldn't let you off. Jamie wasn't a blood relative. Whatever. But you cut me off completely. Wouldn't answer my calls, my texts, or my emails. Hell, I even tried snail mail. Nothing. You left the hospital that night without a backward glance. No goodbye. Nothing! You were just gone."

She was crying now. Great gulping sobs escaping uncontrollably. Taking a deep breath to get her emotions under control, she swiped angrily at her tears. "Did I really mean so little to you?"

He tried once more to reach for her, and she backed away again. If he touched her now, she'd break. "Fuck, Annika, no! It wasn't like that. I loved you. I loved Jamie. All of you. I just ... didn't handle his death well."

She made a sound of scorn in her throat. "*You* didn't handle his death well," she mocked, rubbing her wrist again. "Imagine how it was for *me*! It was like you both died. Only your death was much slower. Much more painful. Each time I tried to contact you, it was with a little bit of hope that you would finally answer. For *years* I tried! The disappointment after each time was too much. It was like mourning your death again every time. I couldn't deal ... I had to stop for my own sake. The grief was ... monumental, all-consuming."

She caught herself rubbing her wrist and forced herself to stop as she pulled her sleeve down to cover it; he didn't get to know everything. She wouldn't let him know how broken she'd been. How far she went to ease the pain.

"I know. It was like that for me too. I grieved alone for Jamie. For you," he admitted.

"The difference is that you chose to grieve alone. I did not. You chose to cut me out of your life. We could have helped each other through our grief. I needed you. You promised you would always be there for me. Remember? That day at the lake, you promised! You promised you'd never leave me. You broke that promise." Annika wished she could control her tears. Her emotions. Everything she had felt for the last fifteen years was spewing out of her.

"One of the worst parts was never knowing if you were alive or dead. You went to war. If you had died there, we would have never known. Even though you cut me out of your life, I never stopped loving you. Never stopped worrying for you. Every day of my life!"

"Annika," his voice cracked with emotion. She let him reach for her then. He placed a hand on her upper arm and stepped closer. Then she was in his arms. Oh God, it felt like home. He was so strong it felt like he could chase all her demons away. All her fears. All her anger. All her worries. It could all just evaporate in his arms. "I'm so sorry, Annika," he crooned. "If I could change my actions, I would. Can you ... will you ever be able to forgive me?"

Annika forced herself to push him away. She turned her back on him, whispering sadly, "I don't know if I ever can."

"Annika," he murmured. The anguish she heard in his voice was nearly her undoing. She had to get away from him. She needed time. It was all so overwhelming.

"I'm tired," she said before he could say anything else. "I think I'll go lay down."

"Annika?" She heard him call her name, but she was already in her room, closing the door. Hoping to shut the emotions out as easily as she could shut him out with the door.

Chapter 6

LOGAN SPENT ANOTHER RESTLESS night staring at the picture on the nightstand that used to bring him such comfort. Now, it only caused heartache. For the past week, when he'd slept, the nightmares had come. Jamie, the woman from the river, Annika. They were all interchangeable. And he'd lost them all.

But none hurt as much as the thought that he'd lost Annika forever. At dinner that first night she had briefly seemed like her old self, like his Annika. She'd been happy to hear of his career choices. Proud even. But then the sadness had returned. And so suddenly.

Hearing how hard it had been for her had ripped his heart to shreds. Each word she spoke tore away at the scar tissue surrounding his heart. He had spent years building hardened callouses to protect himself from feelings, from caring too deeply, and they had worked well to keep people out ... until Annika.

Her pain slashed at him, and he'd done that to her. He'd caused that pain. She had been everything to him. He'd loved her, and he'd broken her. His guilt again was overwhelming. He knew her grief would have been as profound as his, and he'd left her alone to deal with it. He didn't know how she could ever forgive him when he certainly couldn't forgive himself.

He owed her an explanation. He'd fucked things up. He did her wrong. But he was trying to fix things. It was time.

If only he could keep her from running away from him. It had been nearly a week since their surprise reunion, and he still owed her the apology of a lifetime, but she kept shutting him out, avoiding him like the plague. How could he get down on his knees and beg her forgiveness if she continued to turn away from him?

Giving up on sleep, he wandered out to the great room. It had started snowing sometime during his tossing and turning. He watched it fall in big fluffy flakes for a while, then wandered over to the family pictures on the mantel. He knew most of the photos, had been a participant in the events pictured in them. Birthdays, soccer games, lazy summer days at the lake. He'd been part of them all. A member of the family.

But there were also the new photos. Those he'd been absent from. Annika's college graduation was in a large frame at the corner of the mantel. He wondered if she became a teacher as she'd always wanted.

Logan took the frame off the mantel and ran his fingers over her image. She stood in the sun, her hair glowing like tinsel. In her hands was a booklet that held her diploma from Purdue. A grin was on her lips but not in her eyes. Those blue eyes, so like the lake on certain days, were despondent. He could imagine that must have been a difficult day for her. She and Jamie were supposed to have done it together. The courage it must have taken her to go on without him and to succeed took a strength more powerful than anything he'd ever had to do with the SEALs.

And he'd missed it. He'd missed it all. A tear dripped onto the glass, surprising him. He'd only cried one other time in his life, and that was the night he'd lost every-thing.

He crumpled to the couch, wiping the wetness from the glass.

Christ, what have I done! How could he have run away from the only people who'd ever loved him?

He squeezed his eyes shut. He could imagine himself in that graduation photo standing next to Annika, his arm thrown around her shoulders and his pride for her shining in his eyes. And she'd smile at him, so happy to have him there beside her to share in her accomplishment.

They'd share a quiet moment to mourn their missing brother, but they'd bring each other out of their moroseness to celebrate. There'd be cake. There was always cake when Mama Jo was celebrating something. Logan would dig a finger into the icing before she could cut the cake and get a slap on the back of the hand for it. And he would have loved it because she'd cared enough to admonish him. He'd kiss her cheek as an apology, and she'd smile, never able to stay mad at him for long. Jansen would be there with his camera, recording every joyful moment as they celebrated Annika.

And Annika. She would look splendid in whatever dress she'd worn under her black gown. She would grab a taste of the icing for herself as Johanna was busy reprimanding Logan. They'd share a laugh, and he'd hug her because he could. And she would have hugged him back.

But none of that had happened; he'd thrown all that away. His guilt had overcome his better judgment. He couldn't see past the fact that he'd killed their son and brother. He hadn't been able to see how they could have forgiven him for that. He was a poor substitute for Jamie, and he'd felt deep down they would resent him because of it.

Eventually, his tears dried up, and he drifted off to sleep, the picture of Annika still clenched in his hand.

Annika found Logan asleep on the couch the following morning as she got ready for her run. He looked like he'd had another rough night. She could relate. She was hoping the run would rejuvenate her. But as she turned away to leave, something on the floor next to him caught her eye. Praying he'd stay asleep, she inched nearer for a closer look. It was the picture of her at her college graduation. She'd just received her master's in education. That had been a day full of joy and sadness. She'd done it. She'd graduated with honors. Even though she'd delayed starting school until the spring semester after Jamie, she'd still managed to graduate. She'd worked hard, taking as many classes as possible, some of which hadn't even been in her field. But she'd stayed busy, and that kept her mind off her grief. Fall, Spring, even Summer semesters, she'd filled them all. And after she'd had her degree in her hand, she had celebrated with her parents, waiting until she was alone to let her grief crash over her. She'd missed her boys so much. Both of them.

She wondered about the significance of that picture near him. They had settled into a kind of silent truce over the last week, managing to avoid each other as much as possible. Annika lost herself in her books while he spent hours chopping wood or exercising. They came together for the occasional awkward meal, full of clipped commentary.

Logan had never been much of a talker, but this was taking that to the extreme. He was entirely too stoic when she was near, even as she could tell he wanted to talk. But she remained just as stubborn, just as committed to avoiding the elephant in the room. She was not ready to let go of her anger yet. But her ice walls were melting quickly the more time she spent around him. Every glance into his dark brown eyes put another chip in that wall. The anguish and pain she saw there she craved to soothe. She knew that soon she'd have to let go of her hurt and pain to begin the conversation they both desperately needed.

Her thoughts were a jumbled mess as she closed the front door behind her, ready for a good run. There were a good three inches on the ground, and it was still snowing. Big, fat flakes. The world was a winter wonderland.

Annika paused for a moment and raised her face to the sky, enjoying the feeling of the snowflakes melting on her skin. She loved running in the snow. It was so quiet and peaceful. And yet it was her favorite sound in the world, that soft whoosh as the snow fell. She left her earbuds out so she could listen to the music the snow made. The crunch of her sneakers thrilled her even as they filled with snow. No matter, she'd make it a quick run.

She followed the road as it curved closer to the bluff that overlooked the lake. Hearing a pitiful sound coming from the edge of the bluff, she stepped off the road and moved closer to the edge looking for the source.

Aware that erosion had done a number on the bluff in recent years and more earth could collapse into the lake at any time, she carefully inched closer until she found it. A dog was trapped in the underbrush with his leash and collar tangled up in the branches. The poor thing was soaked to the skin and had several scratches, a few deep enough to draw blood. If it kept trying to fight, it might get even more hurt. Annika got to her hands and knees and crawled closer, regretting the lightweight spandex she'd chosen to wear as the cold and wet seeped through.

"Hey, boy." She spoke calmly, hoping her voice would soothe the dog. "How'd you get so stuck in there? Did you chase a squirrel? Bet you regret that decision now, don't you?"

She found the end of the leash and started to untangle it. Unfortunately, the worst of the tangles were deeper in and closer to the edge. She crawled cautiously nearer, untangling as she went. "Okay, buddy, nearly there." The dog, seeming to sense she was there to help, sat quietly and let her work. Even licking her hands every now and then.

Finally, she'd freed the dog. She grabbed it up under one arm and backed out of the brush. As soon as she stood, it struggled to get down. Annika put it down, but before she could look at the tag to see who he belonged to, he took off.

"You're welcome!" she called after it. "Don't go chasing any more squirrels!" She smiled as she watched it race away. The smile turned into a squeal as the ground gave way beneath her, and she tumbled down the bluff.

The closing of the door woke Logan from where he'd fallen asleep on the couch. He jumped up and looked out the window in time to see Annika turn her face to the sky. His heart clenched as a small smile turned the corners of her lips up while she let the snow melt on her face. Could anything be any more beautiful?

Heart thudding hard as she ran off down the road, he turned away from the window and went into the kitchen to start a pot of coffee, wondering what he should make them for breakfast. Most likely, it would be the same as yesterday since that was all he knew how to make. As he fixed his coffee, he decided to wait to make breakfast until he could see her making her way back up the road. No sense in it going cold while she ran.

He took his coffee back to the couch, surprised he'd actually fallen asleep on it again. And the nightmare hadn't come back either. Peeking out from under the couch, the picture frame he'd been holding lay on the floor. He'd forgotten it had fallen there when he fell asleep. Thinking it would be awkward if Annika spotted it, he quickly picked it up and put it back on the mantel, not wanting to have to explain why he'd been sleeping with her picture. The last week had been awkward enough. He wanted more than anything to have the conversation they needed, but he'd never been very good with words. He spent most of his time planning the right words to say, but each time he tried, his mind went blank, the words sticking in his throat.

It became easier and less painful to avoid each other, which did neither one of them any good. He needed to man up and wrest the words out. And soon. Even if she did turn her back on him every time he tried to speak.

He sat to wait for Annika. Maybe today she'd let him talk to her. They couldn't keep tiptoeing around each other, or they'd both go crazy. He'd apologize, and she'd forgive him ... eventually. She had to. He couldn't live without her in his life any longer.

Curious, though, why it was suddenly so important to him after fifteen years to have her love and friendship back. It had been a lonely fifteen years. Sure, there had been other women; he hadn't been a monk. But none of them had ever filled him with joy the way a simple smile from Annika could.

He'd once thought she was like a sister to him. Although, in those last few months before everything went to hell, he'd started to feel differently around her. Every time she'd reached for his hand, every hug she gave him, his response to her grew more intense. He'd found himself becoming aroused around her more often. Even the smell of her shampoo made him hard. And oranges. Christ. He couldn't eat an orange without thinking of her and how her scent had surrounded him that last day they were together.

He'd started to crave her touch in their senior year. And that last day when he'd pulled her down on top of him, he'd wanted so badly to kiss her. He thought she wanted to as well if the look in her eyes was any indication. Logan still remembered how her pupils had dilated, and her tongue had darted out to lick her lips. Tempting him.

But as soon as the desire flared, they both quickly suppressed it, each of them knowing they had a good thing, a rare friendship. They didn't want to muss everything up with sex. And he was very aware that Jamie was his best friend and Annika's brother. The unspoken bro code was always hanging in front of him.

Logan glanced out the window ... again, beyond worried as the time closed in on two hours. It was snowing harder, and the wind was picking up. It must be bitingly cold out there, and her spandex didn't offer much protection from the windchill. Something must have happened to her.

Making a decision, he went to the closet, grabbed his parka, and started for the front door. But before he could reach it, he changed direction and headed to his room, grabbing his rescue pack that the Nighthawks took with them everywhere. In it, he had everything he'd need on a rescue, including a coil of climbing rope, a harness, and a med pack. He raced out the door.

Fighting the wind that threatened to topple him, he did his best to follow Annika's footprints, which were quickly being covered by the blowing snow. Reaching the bend in the road near the bluff, he knew. His heart squeezed painfully as he followed her path to the edge. Something had obviously drawn her here. He could see handprints in the snow. She must have crawled under the overgrowth. He carefully inched closer to the edge spotting the area where a recent collapse had been. He peered over the edge.

Fuck.

She lay at the bottom, twenty feet below, on her side facing away from the lake. Unmoving. The water lapped at her back, and her blonde ponytail floated while the waves undulated beneath it.

No!

She couldn't be dead. *Shit. Please don't be dead.* Moving quickly, he tore his rope out of his pack and tied one end off on a tree far enough back that he wouldn't have to worry about erosion claiming it. Not bothering with his harness, he climbed down to her, the rope burns on his hands going unnoticed.

"Annika!" He'd called to her the whole way down with no response. The wind was intense, repeatedly banging him into the cliff. He ignored that pain too.

He jumped the last few feet and ran to her side, sliding to his knees beside her. He touched her cheek; it was ice cold. Feeling for a pulse, he called to her again. Still nothing but he felt the steady beat under his fingertips.

Steadying her neck as best he could in case she had a neck injury, he rolled her to her back. That placed her more in the water, but it couldn't be helped until he ascertained her injuries. His paramedic training kicked in and took over. He felt her limbs for broken bones, and finding none, he moved to her head to see why she was unconscious.

There it was. A large goose egg on her temple, sticky with blood. A concussion but no broken bones. But she was cold. Too cold.

Hypothermic.

He had to get her out of here and get her warm. Figuring it was safe enough to risk moving her, he picked her up and moved her out of the water. Once on drier land, he put her down and tore his coat off. He put it on her, one arm at a time. Even zipping it and putting the hood up.

He tried to block the worst of the wind with his body. It was essential to get her out of the wet clothes, but he needed to get her inside first. He reached in his pack and pulled out the emergency blanket pack. Ripping open the packaging, he unfolded it and wrapped it tightly around her.

Now to figure out how to get her up out of here. He thought about carrying her up the beach toward the house. There was a path that wound its way up the bluff—if it was even still there. But the water was right up against the bluff most of the way. It would be too dangerous. One slip on the rocks, and they'd both be in trouble. He couldn't afford to get hypothermic too. So, the only solution was to get her up right here.

He grabbed his knife—the same one Annika had given him so many years ago—and cut off the excess rope. He fashioned a harness for her so that he could tie her to himself. Needing his hands free to climb, the rudimentary harness would have to do.

"Okay, Sunfire. Let's get you out of here." He stepped into his own harness and hooked himself up to the rope. Squatting in front of Annika with his back to her, he grabbed the ropes he'd rigged up, lifted her, and tied her to his back. Once he was done, he bounced up and down a few times, testing his handiwork until satisfied she'd stay in place in the makeshift sling. Having trained so often during his SEAL days carrying either his heavy pack or a fellow teammate, Annika's weight on his back was comparatively slight. He'd never imagined he'd be thankful for that part of his SEAL training in his civilian life. Still, he would have liked to have his teammates as backup, but he couldn't wait the amount of time it would take them to arrive.

Tamping down the nerves that hit him as he let go of her, he grabbed the rope he'd used to climb down, choosing to trust in his skills. After a deep breath, he began to make the slow arduous journey back up the bluff, hoping she didn't wake up mid-climb and panic.

Once he'd pulled himself high enough, he braced his feet against the cliff, using hands and feet to climb. The wind tried it's hardest to hamper his movements, buffeting against him. Rocks crumbled under his feet, causing him to slip several times, but he kept climbing. He ignored the strain in his muscles, focusing entirely on his task. At one point he feared Annika was slipping, but he pressed on, forcing his muscles to work harder and faster.

Back up top on solid ground after taking a battering from the snow and wind, he untied her from his back and lay in the snow willing his muscles to relax. Once the shaking had subsided, he stood and reached for Annika. With one arm under her knees and the other behind her back, he left the ropes and ran, carrying her back to the house.

His relief at reaching the house was short-lived. The wind had knocked the power out, and the house was cold. Logan knew time was of the essence to get her warmed up and couldn't wait for the paramedics. He doubted they could get to him quickly through this mess anyway.

The best way he knew how to warm a person up quickly was with body heat. She was going to hate this, but it was the only way. He took her to her room and laid her on the little couch there so he wouldn't get her bed wet. Logan took a deep breath. "Sorry about this," he said as he commenced stripping her.

He began to push up her shirt and found a long scar on her side. It looked similar to a graze from a bullet. Brow furrowed, he pulled her shirt off completely, shock driving him back on his heels.

Fuck. Were those ... gunshot wounds?

Two of them. The abrasion on her side and both an entry and exit wound on her right shoulder.

And they were recent.

Annika had been shot! Shock rolled through him, making it difficult to breathe. He drew in deep, gasping breaths. How could he not have known? Why hadn't Johanna ever told him? This had to have happened a month ago, maybe two. And she'd never said a word. Why?

Because you acted like you wanted nothing to do with her. She was protecting her daughter from more hurt. He couldn't blame her. He'd never asked about Annika, and she'd never volunteered any information about her.

"Christ, Annika. You've been through far too much pain," he whispered, reaching out to stroke her cheek with a trembling hand. Her skin was ice cold.

Snapping out of his shock, he finished stripping her then placed her under the covers on her bed. Quickly tearing his own clothes off down to his boxers, he climbed in next to her, covering them both with the blankets. He gathered her into his arms, turning her into him. Tucking her head in under his chin, he breathed in her citrus scent, closing his eyes.

They lay with torsos touching, one of his legs thrown over her. He tried to get as much of his skin touching hers as he could; she was so cold it made *him* shiver. He rubbed her back, her arms, anything he could reach. Willing her to warm quickly.

She felt good in his arms. He tried not to look, but he couldn't pull his eyes away. It was impossible not to look and appreciate her beauty. Her breasts which were pressed to his chest, were perfect with firm with pink-tipped nipples. Her body was slender with captivating curves that were both devastating and delectable. She was stunning.

His eye was drawn to the wound on her shoulder. He'd been lucky during his time with the SEALs, never having been shot. He couldn't imagine the amount of pain she'd been in. Scenarios of what might have happened rolled around in his head, from plausible to fantastic. He shuddered, his body unwilling to accept what his eyes were telling him. She was a teacher, for Christ's sake, not a dangerous profession. So how, then, did she get shot?

He remembered a news story he'd recently seen about a teacher who saved a classroom full of kids from an armed gunman. Natalie had called the woman a hero. The brief glimpse he'd caught of a blonde woman from that story had snagged his attention, reminding him of Annika. But they had moved on to the next story before he could get a second look. Could that have been her?

He squeezed his eyes shut, attempting to block out his racing thoughts and instead focusing on Annika. Willing himself to ignore the way she felt in his arms and his reaction, he kissed the top of her head. "Come on, Sunfire. Wake up."

He kissed her temple. "Please wake up. I need you to wake up so that I can apologize to you." He continued to talk to her, hoping the sound of his voice would penetrate her mind and wake her.

"Annika? Can you hear me? Follow my voice back and wake up. Open your eyes. Give me one of your magnificent smiles. You have no idea what one of your smiles does to me. I miss your smile. Open your eyes, Annika. Please." He placed his forehead to hers, staring at the wisps of her lashes against her cheek.

"I'm so sorry I left, Annika. Please wake up so I can tell you how incredibly sorry I am. I should never have left you alone. It was a mistake I will regret for the rest of my life. And if you let me, I'll spend the rest of my life trying to make it up to you."

He tried a different tactic. "You're mad at me, right? Wake up and yell at me. Hit me. Anything. Get mad and wake up!"

He ran out of things to say as he held her tight. Her skin slowly warmed. He must have dozed off because when he opened his eyes again, the room was dark. Annika was still in his arms and much warmer. He felt a flutter of movement against him. He kissed her forehead. "Annika? Can you wake up now?"

She stirred more, trying to open her eyes. They opened slowly, striving to focus on him. "Jamie?" she whispered.

His heart broke for her upon hearing the hopefulness in her voice. What he wouldn't do to give her brother back to her. "No, Sunfire." Only the pathetic replacement for Jamie.

"Logan?" She tilted her head back farther to look at him and winced.

"Don't move too fast. You have a head injury," he informed her.

"Wha ... what happened?"

"You fell off the bluff."

Her brows furrowing in concentration, she gingerly touched her temple. "There was a dog. Tangled in the bushes. I freed him." That explained why she'd crawled under the bushes. She could never stand to see an animal suffer. "Then ... then ... I can't remember."

"I'm guessing the ground gave way under you. Erosion has been bad around here lately."

"You saved me." He nodded, feeling an uncustomary blush creep up his face. "Thank you."

"You're welcome."

She lay quietly for a few minutes, and he watched as reality sank in. "Logan?"

"Yeah, Sunfire?"

"Are we naked?"

Chapter 7

Annika struggled to understand what had happened, but her aching brain could only concentrate on the feeling of Logan's skin against hers. It was luxurious. He was so warm it was like she was enveloped in a cocoon of heat. Her nipples rubbed against his firm chest, coming to hard peaks. The feeling was scintillating. She loved it, but for the life of her, she couldn't understand why they were naked in bed together.

"Umm ... yeah. Sorry about that. The fastest way to warm you up was with body heat. You were severely hypothermic." Well, that made sense. "Now that you're awake, I'll go ..." He started to move away from her.

"No! Not yet." She snuggled deeper into his arms. "You're so warm." So deliciously warm.

"As far as I could tell, you don't have any broken bones. Does anything besides your head hurt?"

She concentrated on her aches and pains for a moment. Nothing felt too different. The twinge in her shoulder was a little more pronounced, but that was probably normal after falling off a cliff. She shook her head, which she regretted when a flash of pain knifed through her.

"I would have given you warm fluids intravenously, but my med bag was sorely lacking in supplies."

Intravenously? Did he mean an IV? "Are you a doctor?" she asked, shocked to think that he had gone to medical school too.

She felt him smile into her hair. "No, Paramedic. The SEALs taught me most of what I needed as a field medic. But when I joined the Nighthawks, Graham, my boss, wanted someone else to become a paramedic. I volunteered. Guess I'm not a very good one since I let the supplies in my kit get so low."

She mulled that over. "There's so much I don't know about you."

"I know. And I'm sorry about that. You have no idea how sorry. There's so much I don't know about you too." He touched the scar on her shoulder, and she flinched. "I don't know how this happened to you and I'm so sorry it happened at all. Will you tell me about it ... when you're ready?" She nodded. Her eyes were getting heavy; she was so tired.

"Go to sleep, Sunfire. Get some rest."

"You ... you won't leave, will you?" Sudden tears filled her eyes. The thought of waking up alone again was terrifying.

"I'm not going anywhere. I'll be here when you wake up." She drifted off to sleep with his lips at her temple.

She knew even before she opened her eyes that Logan still lay beside her as his sandalwood scent wrapped around her. Opening her eyes slowly, she saw a now fully clothed Logan facing her. A flash of disappointment swept through her; she'd liked feeling his skin against hers entirely too much.

She took the opportunity to study his features while he slept. Mostly, he resembled the same boy she used to know with only a few minor differences. Same rugged jawline but sprinkled with beard stubble, unlike the clean-shaven look he had in high school. Same nose, although it seemed like at some point it had been broken. There was a tiny scar near his right eye. And another across his right cheekbone. His brow line was the same if a little more disheartened. His forehead had worry lines etched in deep.

What had his life been like these last fifteen years? If the scars were any indication, it must have been pretty rough. Her life hadn't been a picnic either, but at least she'd had her parents to help her heal. He'd been alone.

This was Logan. Her best friend. A stoic man accustomed to doing things on his own. If she'd learned anything, it was how to let go of past hurts and live life. The ice walls she'd built up against Logan over the years were melting fast.

She itched to place her lips on his scars, to heal them from the outside in.

Aw, to hell with it. She leaned closer and placed her lips over the scar on his cheekbone. He woke instantly with a sharp inhale. She moved her lips higher and kissed the one near his eye as well. She threw caution to the wind and placed her lips just at the corner of his mouth on the left. Then at the other corner.

She drew back to look into his eyes. Eyes that were so dark and mesmerizing under thick brows, made of chestnuts so dark she couldn't tell the iris from the pupil. And they were captivating her with an assessing emotion she couldn't name hiding in their depths.

She stared, entranced, then, taking the biggest risk of her life, she brushed her lips across his in a barely-there kiss.

"Fuck, Annika," he hissed. Threading his fingers into her hair, he stared down into her own eyes, her scalp tingled at his touch. His other hand settled on her cheek, his thumb gently stroking her jaw. He must have seen what he wanted in her expression because his pupils flared before his mouth came crashing down on hers, his tongue curled around hers.

Heaven. It felt like heaven. He kissed her with desperation, as if he were afraid he'd wake up and she'd be gone. Her heart twisted with an ache for the loneliness she could feel from his kiss. She poured in her own loneliness and pain.

He broke off and backed away a bit to look down at her, his hand still tangled in her hair.

It was then she noticed the wetness on his cheeks. She reached up and wiped his tears away with her thumb. He grabbed her hand and placed his lips against her palm, then kissed the tears from her thumb.

"I'm so sorry, Annika." He held her hand to his heart. "I've missed you so much," he said quietly, his voice breaking with emotion.

Annika felt her own tears spill over. "I've missed you too." His mouth was on hers again. Devouring her. He slid his arms around her and pulled her closer, her breasts flattening against his chest. She felt possessed by his kiss, and her worries were lifted and shoved away. She knew it was crazy, but at that moment, with his sandalwood scent filling her senses, she felt safe.

She was suddenly very aware of her nakedness, but she didn't care. Logan was home. She was safe in his arms. That was all that mattered.

He ended the kiss again but still held her close. "Can you ever forgive me, Annika? I am so sorry. I should never have left. Please forgive me." His begging demolished the last of her ice walls.

Wanting to see his eyes, Annika tilted her head back. Vulnerability burned in the dark chestnut color there. Reading the anxiety in his features, she placed a hand to his cheek, forcing him to maintain eye contact with her. "I was mad at you for a very long time. I once read somewhere that the hardest goodbyes are the unexplained ones. The ones that are left unsaid. It was exactly that. The unexplained goodbye. An ache that never went away. I still am a little mad at you, but none of that matters now. You are home. You came back to us. To me. That's all I've ever wanted."

She sighed and continued before he could say anything. "I don't understand why you left. I can't begin to comprehend what it had been like for you. The pain you must have been feeling. And to face it alone ... I can't imagine that. I prayed every night that you would reach out to us. Every night for fifteen years."

"Fuck, Annika! I've failed you in so many ways. First with Jamie. Then—"

"Wait. What do you mean with Jamie?"

He drew in a deep, shaky breath, his eyes lowering as if unable to look at her. "I killed him, Annika. It's my fault he's dead."

She shook her head emphatically. What the hell? How could he have ever thought it was his fault? "Logan, no. You didn't kill ..."

"Yes, I did," he interrupted. "I was driving. I can see it so clearly. I was distracted. By you and that little kiss you gave me in the parking lot. Even just looking at you in the rearview mirror distracted me. If I'd been paying more attention to the road, I might have been able to react more quickly to avoid that truck."

"Oh, Logan."

He tore himself away from her and threw his legs over the edge of the bed. He sat shoulders slumped with his head in his hands, breathing heavily. Tears trickled down his face.

"After we were hit, if I had moved faster, got you out faster, maybe ..." He grasped his hair tightly, agony pouring off of him. "I nearly had him, Annika. He was right there. I nearly had him free of the seatbelt."

He stood up suddenly and began to pace. His hands tore into his hair again before coming to rest linked at the back of his neck, elbows jutted out in front of him. "If I had been able to move faster ... It's my fault he's dead. I failed. I wasn't fast enough. I wasn't good enough. I'm so sorry, Annika. It's my fault he's gone. If I could trade my life for his, I would gladly die for him."

Annika gingerly got out of her side of the bed, a wave of dizziness slowing her down. She reached for her pajamas, putting them on. Flannel pants and a Foreigner t-shirt. His Foreigner t-shirt. It was a little worse for wear, the image faded, but she could never part with it, it was all she had of him.

Walking over to him, she stood directly in front of him to stop his pacing. She grabbed his elbows and pushed down, making him lower his arms. Then with a hand on either side of his face, she drew his head up, forcing him to meet her gaze. His eyes were so tortured, dark and brooding as always, filled with agony and desperation. "Listen to me, Logan. Nothing that happened to Jamie was your fault. Do you hear me?" She shook his head slightly. "Not your fault. You didn't fail me. You saved me. If you hadn't pulled me out, I'd be dead too. You are a hero. And you always will be to me."

"But your parents must blame me ..."

"No, Logan. We never blamed you. Never. Not once did any of us think it was your fault. I've spent years in therapy trying to come to grips with what happened. The only conclusion I've been able to come to is that it was just his time. I've comforted myself by imagining that God had something important for him to do in heaven. And that makes me happy. You know why? Because it means that someday, I will see him again. We all will. Even you, Logan."

He tried to shake his head, to deny what she was saying, but she wouldn't let him. "Yes, even you. Jamie is still with us. He's here right now. He's always been with us. In here." She pointed to his heart. "Jamie opened your heart and brought you back to us. He knew that you needed us as much as we needed you."

He released a lungful of air as he mulled over her words. "I think Mama Jo had something to do with that the day she sent me a new email."

"Maybe. Or maybe Jamie told her it was time to reach out to you again. That you were ready to come home."

"I don't know, Annika ..."

"But I do," she said emphatically. "Is that why you stayed away for so long? You felt guilty?"

"Yes. Of the two of us, Jamie was the better man. It should have been me. You lost your twin. Your other half. And it should have been me."

She dropped her hands from his face, grabbed his hands, and held them tightly. Pulling herself straight up to her full height, she peered directly into his eyes. "I'm only going to say this one more time, and I hope I never have to say it again. It was not your fault."

"How can you be so sure?"

She shrugged. "I just am. I know you, Logan. Or at least I used to." He winced. "What I mean is, you are a good man. You would never wish ill on anyone. So, tell me, can someone who's so kind and giving ever willingly kill someone? No," she answered for him. "No, they wouldn't. You are a hero. You wanted to be a hero long before the accident. Remember? You always wanted to be a SEAL. You were a hero that night too. You saved me. And you risked your life trying to save Jamie."

She paused to take a breath. "And look what you've done with your life since. I've done some research on what it takes to become a SEAL. I know what they put you through. You overcame impossible conditions and succeeded. And I'm willing to bet you played the hero on numerous missions. Even now. Logan, you're a Nighthawk. If those men are not the true definition of a hero, then I don't know what is. You risk your life every time you go out to save someone else, to help a total stranger. I watched you do it that night when you risked your life for Jamie. And you probably risked an awful lot to get to me at the bottom of the bluff. You are the bravest man I know."

She kissed his hands that were still clenched in hers. "Besides, did it ever occur to you that Jamie might *not* have been my other half. That maybe *you* are my other half?"

His eyes widened with shock. "Sure, Jamie was my twin. We shared a special connection, and I loved him. But you were always the one I wanted to be near the most."

"Fuck, Annika. The things you say. I don't know how you can be so forgiving after everything I've put you through for all these years."

"Because Jamie told me it was time." And she believed that with all her heart. Then she gave a sly smile. "'When you forgive, you love,'" she quoted. "That's from Krakauer's *Into the Wild*. It's beautiful, isn't it? Now, if you could only forgive yourself."

Yes, if only he could forgive himself. He didn't know if what she believed about Jamie was true or not, but it sounded awfully nice. Maybe he should start listening for Jamie's voice. He studied her face closely. A face that had haunted his dreams for the last fifteen years. She was so pure, so beautiful. He could lose himself for days in her bright blue eyes. He squeezed her hands. "Having your forgiveness goes a long way toward me forgiving myself."

She smiled as she glanced behind him, causing his heart to clench. "Look. The sun is rising. It's a brand-new day. A fresh new day with no mistakes. The faults of yesterday are in the past. Each day is a clean slate. A chance to start over and try to do good again." She stood and went to the window. The sun shining off the snow highlighted her silhouette with light, and he'd never seen anything more beautiful. She turned to face him with her arms outstretched in joy. "Isn't it beautiful?"

Logan went to her and placed a gentle hand on her cheek. "My Sunfire. It certainly *is* beautiful." She wrapped her arms around him, her ear against his heart. Definitely beautiful.

"Welcome home, Logan," she whispered. He felt the burn of tears again. She was pure sunshine. Her rays of goodness surrounded him as he held her. He could feel her light and warmth reaching the darkest places of his heart. But a tiny part of him wondered if he was worthy of her light. The things he'd done over the years had marked him. Sure, he'd been in service to his country, but he sometimes felt his blackened soul was tainted and undeserving.

She looked up at him, her chin on his pec, and smiled. His heart melted, and his dark thoughts fled. He touched the corner of that smile with his finger. "Christ, that smile. You have no idea what that smile has always done for me. I've dreamed of that smile every day for the last fifteen years. I never thought I'd see it again."

"Well, anytime you want one from me, you only have to ask," she teased, her smile deepening.

"I'll remember that."

Her stomach growled, making him laugh. "What? It's been over twenty-four hours since I've eaten. So sue me for being hungry."

"Right. Well then, let's get that monster in your tummy fed." He stepped back and looked down at her. Suddenly it registered in his brain what she was wearing. "Is that my shirt?"

She smiled shyly, and a slight blush tinted her cheeks. "Yes."

"Why do you have my shirt?"

The blush deepened. *Fuck, that was adorable.* "You left it here, at the lake house. I knew I should have found a way to get it back to you, but after you went away ... It was all I had left."

"And you're still wearing it all these years later?" His heart felt lighter knowing she'd kept something of his so close to her. Not to mention, she looked sexy as fuck wearing his clothes. Especially with her hair disheveled as if she'd just enjoyed a night of hot, sweaty ...

Fuck, not going there. He'd already had a hard enough time controlling his baser instincts while lying in bed with her, her beautiful, naked body in his arms. And when she'd kissed him ... It had taken everything in him not to ravage her then and there. He'd never been turned on so fast before. He wanted to fuse her body to his and never release her. He could spend eternity in the sweet taste of her kiss and never be completely satisfied. He would always need more, thirst for more of her, crave her taste as if starved for her.

"I know it seems silly, but your shirt has always comforted me. And since I couldn't have you near me, it was the next best thing." She lifted the neckline up to her nose. "I used to imagine I could still smell you on it. It acted as a solace ... a hug ... from you. I know ... silly."

"No. Not silly. Come with me." He took her hand and led her into his bedroom. Picking up the picture of the three of them, the one from that day at the lake house, he handed it to her. He watched closely as she looked down at it, studying her expression. Her eyes widened briefly in surprise before settling into wonder.

The picture had been taken after she had broken down and asked Logan not to leave. Annika, as always, was in the middle. They were both hugging her from either side. Their chins on her shoulders and their customary big silly grins on their faces. The boys were tanned and healthy-looking, Logan wearing the shirt she now wore. Annika, of course, was as beautiful as ever, even with the slight redness in her eyes from the tears she had cried that day. Looking at her now, he could see a sheen of tears begin to build again as she gazed at those smiling faces.

"That picture never leaves my side. I've taken it with me everywhere. You can see the crease lines," he pointed to two lines in the picture where he'd folded and unfolded it over the years. "It's been in my pocket on every mission. I was never without it. At night, I would fall asleep staring at that lovely smile of yours. My comfort."

Annika stared up at him in amazement as a tear slipped down her cheek. He reached up and wiped it away. He studied the face that was more familiar to him than his own, reveling in the fact that he was looking at the real Annika and not a photographic representation of her.

"Thank you for showing me this," she told him, an emotion he couldn't quite name filling her eyes. "It ... I always wondered ... oh, never mind." She shook her head and looked down at the picture in her hand, her lashes cloaking her eyes so he couldn't read her expression.

He tilted his head to the side and bent his knees to be closer to eye level with her. Swirling emotions filled her eyes with a raw vulnerability that captured his heart. "What? What did you wonder?"

She sighed. "For a long time, I thought that you left because, without Jamie, there was no one left that you cared about. That all those special times we shared were just you being nice to your best friend's sister. I didn't think I meant as much to you as Jamie did."

Chapter 8

LOGAN FELT LIKE HIS heart had just splintered; the ache he felt for the pain he'd caused her was that intense. He ran the backs of his fingers across her cheek, wiping another tear away. "I left *because* I cared. It would have killed me to see you look at me with hate for what I'd done. I was convinced I was responsible for Jamie's death. And like a coward, I ran from the blame I was sure you'd all feel was mine. It had been easier to leave with all the good memories before they turned sour with your anger and hate."

She shook her head sadly. "Nobody ever blamed you, Logan. I never hated you. I hated that you disappeared and left me all alone. But I never hated you." She dropped the photograph on the bed and leaned into him. Resting her forehead on his chest, her tiny hands grasped the belt loops at his hips. She took a deep breath and sighed. "God, what a mess we've both made of all this."

He wrapped his arms around her, hugging her to him tightly, his lips resting in the hair at the top of her head. He breathed her in, the orange fragrance calming his churning emotions. "This was all on me. I was the coward who ran. You did nothing." He had a lot to make up for when it came to her. He should have known his actions would hurt her. *He was an ass.*

She looked up at him and his breath caught in amazement. Her luminous blue eyes were filled with forgiveness and understanding. He did not deserve her. "Oh

Logan, stop trying to carry the weight of the world by yourself."

He smiled; she had such a unique way with words. He'd always loved that about her. "That's going to take time to fix since I've been doing it most of my life."

She laid her cheek against his chest again, and they held each other quietly until her stomach reminded them she was still hungry. He laughed. "All right already. Stop badgering me." He poked her in the stomach, making her giggle.

On the way out of the room, the picture of him in his dress uniform caught his attention. "How did Mama Jo get that?"

"What?" she asked, poking her head back through the threshold.

"That picture of me in the middle."

"Oh. Your grandmother. Mom spotted it one night when we were making dinner for her. She asked if she could take it to make a copy." She turned and started walking down the hall again. He followed in disbelief.

"You made dinner for my grandmother?"

"Yeah. All the time."

Suddenly stopping as he entered the room, he asked, "What?"

"What what?" She reached into the fridge for the eggs.

"You spent time with my grandma?"

"Why is that so hard to believe?"

"Because you never did before."

"She was never alone before. She always had you around to take care of things. Mom figured you were family, so that made Grandma Jean family. And family takes care of one another."

His heart squeezed painfully again. Not only did he have guilt for abandoning the Northrups, but now he felt shame for not looking after his grandmother more often. She never told him the Northrups were helping her out. *Christ, he really was a fucking ass.*

"But she hated you."

Annika laughed as she placed a pat of butter in the saucepan. It sizzled as it melted. "She'd mellowed a lot after the funeral." She stopped fussing with the food for a moment. "Did she ever tell you she came?" He shook his head. "She came to the funeral and afterward she gave me the biggest hug. God Logan, she'd squeezed me so tight. From that moment on, she became my grandmother as much as she was yours."

"She never said a word to me."

"I guess she figured you needed time to grieve and bringing up the family you were trying to distance yourself from would have been too painful for you." She went back to cooking, cracking eggs into the melted butter.

Logan joined her in the kitchen and grabbed the coffee carafe. He took a few minutes while he made the coffee to let this new information sink in.

"She really did care about me," he mused.

"She loved you. She just didn't always know the best way of showing you." She placed a few slices of bread into the toaster and pressed the lever down. "I was with her when she died."

He was in the process of taking the mugs down and that revelation startled him so much that he knocked one of the mugs against the edge of the shelf. "What?"

Annika dumped the eggs onto two plates and put bacon in the pan to cook. "Those last few weeks, we knew it was only a matter of time. One of us was with Grandma Jean at all times. We took shifts. It just happened to have been my time. I sat with her and held her hand. She spoke of you," she finished quietly.

"What ... what did she say?" He was so stunned he could hardly think of the words.

Flipping the bacon, she replied. "Well, she regretted how strict she'd always been with you. I told her that you knew she was just trying to protect you, that she didn't want you to turn out like your mother. She started talking about the day you left and that she'd never seen you like that before. How did she put it?" she mused as she put the bacon on the plates with the eggs. "So lost. Haunted was the word I think she used. She told me she never understood why you cut yourself off from all of us."

She picked up the plates and put them on the table. As she went back for the toast, he saw her wipe yet another tear away. "Just before ... just before she passed, she patted my hand, telling me to be patient. That you would come home and would need me and made me promise that I would stay strong for you. And she asked me to forgive you. I told her there was nothing to forgive. She smiled and closed her eyes. Then she was gone," Annika finished as she sniffed back more tears.

His shock so profound, he was unable to do or say anything as he watched Annika put the toast on a plate and grab the butter and jelly. She gestured for him to join her as she sat. He forced his legs to obey and went to sit at the table with her. He picked up his fork but still couldn't get his brain to function.

Finally finding his voice, he spoke ... bumbling through his words. "I ... But ... none of you were at the funeral."

"Oh, umm, we figured you had a reason for cutting us off. We didn't want to create a scene as you buried Grandma Jean. We had a private moment, just the three of us, at her grave after everyone had left."

Still too stunned to think of anything to say, he stared at her with his fork hovering over his plate. "I saw you that day," she continued, surprising him even more. "My parents and I were sitting in the car waiting for everyone to leave. You were standing next to her all alone. So handsome in your uniform. But you looked ... I wanted to run to you. Wrap my arms around you." She sniffed again, looking like she was desperately trying to control her emotions. "My hand was on the door handle. I'd nearly had it open when Dad reminded me that I needed to let you go. It nearly killed me to stay in my seat. I couldn't stop crying."

She stopped and took a deep breath. "When you'd finally left, we got out of the car. It was then I noticed the tears on Mom's face. I never asked her if they were for me or for you."

Logan couldn't stop himself. He dropped his fork and was on his knees beside her in an instant. He wrapped his arms around her waist and laid his head in her lap. "Fuck, Annika. I don't understand how you can possibly forgive me. I do not deserve you." He felt her fingers in his hair, stroking in comfort.

"That's not true," she argued gently. "You deserve to be happy just as much as anyone else in this world. You, my lonely warrior, are deserving of so much."

He looked up at her, and she smiled serenely down at him. "Your words. You have such a beautiful way with words."

"I'm an English teacher. It's my job to have a firm grasp of the English language."

He laughed. Then raised himself until he could fit his lips to hers. "Thank you. For everything. For Grandma Jean. Everything. Thank your parents for me too."

"Uh-uh. You are going to do that yourself the next time you see them."

He sat back on his heels and ran a hand through his hair. "I don't know, Annika. I don't know if I'm ready to face them."

"Yes, you are," she assured, smiling down at him. "Because there is nothing to face. They love you. They never stopped loving you. They will be overjoyed just to have you home again."

She gave him a little push. "Now, go eat your cold eggs."

He kissed her as he stood to do her bidding. "Yes, ma'am."

When he started eating his, yes, very cold eggs, she asked something of him that shocked him all over again. "After we get dressed, let's go get a Christmas tree and all the trimmings."

"Did you forget about all the snow out there?" he said, pointing to the windows.

She made a sound as if to say pish posh. "Are you a true Michigander or not? That little bit out there wouldn't stop a true Michigander. Besides, the town is probably clear by now."

Soon he sat behind the wheel of his truck, willing the thing not to get stuck in the snow. "So where should we go?" he asked the little snow bunny sitting beside him. She was all bundled up, hat, gloves, scarf, and overlarge parka with furry trim around the edge of the hood. She looked adorable.

"I think there's a tree farm on Stafford."

"Think it will be open?"

"I hope so."

"Well, if it's not, maybe with your eloquent words, you can sweet talk the owner into opening up for us," he said with a wink.

"Very funny." But she didn't need to use her expertise with words since the lot was indeed open. Trudging through the snow while looking for the perfect tree, she stopped at a Fraser fir and circled it. "This one," she stated with certainty.

Well, that was quicker than he'd expected. He bent over with the saw to cut it down, then the owner helped them bundle it up and put it in the back of the truck.

"Okay, now the trimmings," she said, climbing into the cab.

They'd stopped at a big box store for everything they would need, and on returning to the house, Logan worked on straightening the tree in the stand as Annika directed, telling him which way to move it. "Perfect!" she said, ripping lights out of the boxes.

"You know, this would have been a whole lot easier if we had just bought one of those pre-lit fake trees," he mused as he made a pass around the tree with the strand of lights.

"Maybe, but there is nothing like the smell of a live tree," she said while inhaling. "That smell says Christmas. And we have the added benefit of seeing the perfume, the tree with all its baubles, instead of just being able to smell it. It's a magic that works its way into people's hearts, making everything soft and lovely. It reminds us of childhoods long left behind and fills our imaginations. It's like you can inhale the aroma of the pine and fill your soul with wonder and dreams. I'd forgotten all that for a long time."

Logan paused in his trip around the tree and smiled at the beautiful words spoken by the exquisite blonde on the couch. He had every intention of filling his soul with the wonder of her and dreams of them together forever. "Can't argue with that."

The smile she sent his way distracted him so that he tripped over the strands of lights he was working with, causing a mess of tangles. The lights somehow managed to get twisted around his feet, and he shook his left leg to free himself. Growling his frustration as he attempted to untangle the lights, Annika's laugh drew his attention.

"'I've learnt you can tell a lot about a person by how he handles these three things: a rainy day, lost luggage, and tangled Christmas tree lights.' Maya Angelou was spot on." She laughed even harder when Logan glared her way, but he couldn't stay mad for long. Her laugh did more to fill his soul than the magic of a twinkling Christmas tree ever could.

She captivated him. Watching her laughter was like watching the sun finally break through the clouds in spectacular bursts after a week of rain. He'd spent so much time crawling through the shadows that her light was blinding. He couldn't look away. And he didn't want to.

He responded to her light, wanting to scoop it up and drink a cup every morning to irradiate himself. He would fill his darkest recesses with her light until all the shadows of his past were banished. She had always been able to do that for him; he'd forgotten that for far too long.

"Oh Logan, look," she cried excitedly, pointing to the floor. There, on the carpet, were a multitude of miniature rainbows. The sun shining through the windows had caught the glass ornaments at just the right angle while they waited to be placed on the tree, creating the effect. Tiny spectrums of light dancing across the floor. As he watched, Annika stepped into the light's path, allowing the rainbows to cover her. She twirled around with a bright giggle, and his heart skipped. He stood still as she danced with the light, too enthralled to do anything more than breathe.

"Remember that glass prism ruler you had in the fifth grade?" she asked as she spun, watching the colors dance around her. "You used to try to catch the sun with it to make rainbows on my desk. It always made me smile. Your little rainbows would never fail to brighten my day."

She stopped dancing and bestowed her brightest smile on him. He felt like he'd taken a hit, the projectile being myriad colorful energies that eradicated the dark specters in his soul, breaking his heart open to allow her light to pour in.

Her power was phenomenal. To have experienced so much pain and not let it defeat her was remarkable. She was still as bright as she had been as the young girl he'd once loved. Her scars, both inside and out, were a representation of her walk through the shadows. But even if the darkness threatened to swallow her, her light pushed through, burning those shadows into oblivion.

He felt the same thing happening to him. Her joy in something as simple as rainbows did more to restore his heart than anything he'd ever experienced.

His childhood memories were filled with rainbows, laughter, literary quotes, holding hands, smiles, and his love for a girl. Now, there were still all of those things, only his love for the girl was changing. A breathtaking woman full of warmth and light stood before him, and he wanted her.

He wanted her laughter, to listen to her quote from great literary works. He wanted to watch her dance with rainbows, and to hold her hand through life's twists and turns. But most of all, he wanted her as a man desires a woman.

Her smile slipped slightly as he stood entranced. "Is everything okay?"

Pulling himself out of his reveries, he crossed through the rainbows to her. Cupping her face with both hands, he leaned down until his lips were a whisper away from hers. "Everything is perfect, Sunfire. You are perfect. And I would love to give you rainbows every day."

While standing surrounded by diminutive rainbows and the vivid joy of his Sunfire, he kissed her. And there was nothing more that he wanted or needed at that moment. Her kiss filled him with color, just like the rainbows she'd danced in. He broke the kiss and rested his forehead against hers, needing a moment to absorb the rush of feelings as the color overwhelmed him after so long in the shadows.

Fifteen years ago

Logan found Annika reading as usual in the big armchair by the windows that overlooked the lake. He plopped down beside her and put his arm around her shoulder. She settled back against his chest and continued to read.

"Whatcha readin'?"

"A book," she replied with a smirk.

"What's it about?"

"People. Places. Things," she replied sarcastically. "Oh, and there's a cat too."

"Of course, there is." He sighed and let his head rest against the back of the chair, content to sit with her quietly as she read. He would miss moments like this when he was gone. His chest ached; he would miss her. It hurt to think of a time when he wouldn't be near her. Wouldn't be able to smell that intoxicating aroma of oranges in her hair. Wouldn't be able to see one of her golden smiles that warmed the deepest darkest places of his heart. It was times like this that he seriously contemplated throwing all his dreams away just so he could stay near her.

"Logan?"

"Mmm?"

"What's it like to kiss somebody?" Of all the things she could have asked him, that was the last thing he expected. Sure, they talked about most everything, but that seemed like a question to ask a girlfriend. But, of course, Annika didn't have many close girlfriends, choosing to spend all of her time with him and Jamie instead. Less drama, she often said.

"What?"

"I want to know what it's like to kiss someone. What does it feel like?"

"It's ... nice."

"Just nice?" She shifted until she was facing him. His arm still wrapped around her, his hand just under her breast. If he moved his thumb just a tiny bit, he could feel the underside.

"Well ... if it's with the right person, it can be really nice." His eyes fell to her lips. How he'd love to find out what kissing her would be like. He had a feeling that if he went there, he'd never be able to stop.

"Show me?" she asked quietly.

"What?" He was stunned. He couldn't kiss her ... could he?

"I want you to show me," she asked again.

"Annika, I can't do that."

"Why not? What's the worst that could happen?"

Everything! If he kissed her, he had a feeling he'd lose his heart forever. "Annika, we can't. I can't," he insisted.

"Please, Logan, I would really like to know what it's like from someone I trust."

Logan groaned inwardly. How could he argue against that? He drew in a deep breath and let it out slowly. "Fine," he said before leaning toward her and placing a quick kiss on her lips.

"Not like that. I want a real kiss. I need to know." He looked from her eyes to her lips and back to her eyes, unsure how to proceed. But it was Annika who leaned toward him. She pressed her lips against his, her tongue darting out for a taste. He gasped at the sensation, and her tongue slipped inside. He met it with his own. Suddenly, he couldn't get enough of the taste of her. He pressed her to him and took control of the kiss. His tongue sliding into her mouth, exploring, tasting, devouring. He was on fire for her taste.

The sound of a door slamming broke them apart. They sat there for a moment, staring at each other, breathing heavily. Annika was the first to move away. She grabbed her book and opened it, acting as if nothing had happened as Jamie entered the great room. Logan casually grabbed the throw pillow and placed it on his lap, hiding the bulge in his shorts.

"Shit, guys. Can't you do anything more exciting than reading a book? Boring!" he teased, feigning a yawn.

"Hey, she's the one reading. Not me." Logan hoped to God Jamie hadn't noticed what they'd been doing just a few seconds ago.

"Yeah, whatever. I'm starved. Let's go into town to eat."

Annika closed her book and stood. "Good idea. Give me a minute to change."

"What you have on is fine!" She rolled her eyes at him. "Women!" Jamie threw his hands up and walked into the kitchen in search of a pre-dinner snack.

Present Day

Annika lay with Logan in that same armchair enjoying the glow of the Christmas tree lights on a quiet afternoon as a little lake effect snow fell outside the windows. It was no wonder that memory had popped into her head. It was so similar to the present day. Just like then, Annika was sitting in the chair reading a book. And just like then, Logan had plopped down next to her. She even snuggled back against him just like she had fifteen years ago. And he was just as content to hold her as she read.

"You seem lost in thought," Logan remarked. "Care to share?"

"I was remembering something from that summer here with you and Jamie." She smiled as the memory struck her again.

"That kiss."

She shifted to face him, just as she had then. "How did you know I was thinking about that?"

He grinned down at her. "I couldn't help but notice the similarities. It's one of my favorite memories," he confessed, sliding a finger down her cheek and across her lips.

"Mine too. I'd never been kissed like that. It was ... hot!"

"Yeah, it was. I'd never been kissed like that before either."

"Seriously?" she squeaked.

"Seriously. That kiss was ... intense." Annika blushed, pleased that he'd enjoyed it just as much as she had.

"I thought for sure Jamie had seen us."

"Yeah, me too. It was a little while before I could stand without revealing the hard-on I had. I definitely didn't want Jamie to see that."

Annika giggled. "No, I guess that wouldn't have been good."

"I noticed you ran away pretty quickly," he teased.

Annika remembered why she had escaped to her room so fast, thankful for the excuse to change her clothes. "I had to. I had to escape before the tears fell. I didn't want you to see me cry ... again."

"Fuck, Annika." He hugged her tighter.

"So, yeah, I ran to my room. My feelings were overwhelming. I wanted you. And I really wanted more kisses like that one. I wanted you to stay. I wanted to have more time with you, to possibly explore where a kiss like that could take us. But I knew I couldn't have any of that. And I didn't want my tears to ruin what time we had left." Annika remembered closing the door and leaning back against it, then sinking to the floor. She had placed her head on her knees and hugged them to her chest. Her anguish over her burgeoning feelings for Logan beyond her ability to cope. She was going to have to say goodbye to him. That kiss had been the most erotic thing to ever happen to her. She'd never been kissed before, and it had been marvelous. Heavenly. She hadn't wanted it to end. But it had to. And if she were ever going to say goodbye to him and keep her sanity, she knew it could never happen again. So, she'd dried her tears, changed her clothes, and joined her boys for dinner. And never broached the subject of that kiss with Logan until this very moment, fifteen years later.

"I'm sorry Annika. If I could go back ..."

She placed a finger to his lips to stop him. "I know."

"For what it's worth, I carried the memory of that kiss with me everywhere." She smiled and kissed him as tears floated just at the surface. "No tears. These are happy memories."

"What if they are happy tears?"

"Well, those are okay, I guess."

"I wonder what Jamie would have done if he'd caught us that day?"

Logan didn't share in her laughter. He looked pensive instead. "I can't believe I forgot. About a week after that time at the lake, he asked me if there was something going on between you and me. I assured him there wasn't. He muttered something, and I swear he said, 'Too bad .'" They shared a sad smile as their thoughts turned to Jamie. She had wondered what Jamie would have thought of her and Logan as a couple. It eased her mind to hear that he may have wanted it for them.

They grew quiet then, Annika resting her head on his chest. After a few minutes of watching the snow burst outside, Annika asked, "Hey, Logan?"

"Mmm?"

"Wanna make out like teenagers?" She tilted her head back to look at him.

"Absolutely," he answered before claiming her lips in a hot and passionate kiss.

Lost in his desire for the woman in his arms, it took Logan a minute to realize the buzzing from his pocket was a text alert. Breaking the kiss, he apologized to Annika and pulled out his phone to read the group text. The Nighthawks and assorted family were meeting at Jolene's for dinner that evening. He thought of introducing Annika to his friends, but he wasn't sure she would be willing to go with him.

Remembering his sorely empty supply packs, he texted Graham separately from the group text.

Logan: Hoping to come tonight. May be bringing a friend. Need a few supplies. Hoping you can help.

Since the explosion that had destroyed the Nighthawk warehouse and nearly killed Graham, he knew that most of the supplies were low and felt a pang of guilt for having had to cut up his rope to save Annika.

The woman who'd tried to kill Natalie had cornered them inside the warehouse, firing a gun at them. Her shots had punctured the gas line. All it took was one spark, and the whole place went *kaboom*. Logan had thought for sure Graham and Natalie were dead. The entire team ran to them and found Natalie trying to lift a two-thousand-pound beam off Graham, though she had a broken wrist. They got both of them out, alive and whole. But the same was not true of the woman they all used to work closely with. They still grieved for her and the madness that had taken her over in the end.

Graham's text came back almost immediately.

Graham: Good to hear you made a friend. What do you need?

Logan texted him the list, and Graham replied, as perceptive as usual.

Graham: What happened?

Logan: Friend fell from bluff. Had to cut up my rope to get her out.

Graham: She ok?

Logan: Slight concussion but otherwise good.

Graham: Good. See you tonight.

Talking Annika into going out with him was the next issue. Nervously, he wiped his hands down his pant legs before he took her hand and brought it to his lips, "A bunch of my teammates, my friends, are meeting for dinner tonight in town. I was hoping ..." he trailed off, not quite knowing how to ask her.

"You want me to meet your friends?" He nodded. "I'd really like that."

"Great!" It was hard to hide his pleasure. "We're meeting at Jolene's around six."

"Jolene's? I love that place."

"You've been to Jolene's?"

"It's been a few years, but I remember they have the best burgers there."

Shortly before six, Annika joined him in the great room, his jaw dropping as he took her in. It wasn't so much what she wore — after all, it was just jeans and a sweater — but it was how she wore it. And how she looked when she smiled at him. Her sweater was that otherworldly green color that he'd only ever seen in the Aurora Borealis and made her blue eyes stand out. Her jeans hugged her curves in just the right way sending the blood rushing to certain parts of his body. His heart thudded. She was so beautiful she took his breath away.

He wondered if there would ever be a moment when this woman wouldn't steal his breath. But then again, he didn't mind if she stole his air for the rest of his life. He could live with a few missed breaths now and then, but he couldn't live without her any longer.

When he didn't say anything right away, her brow furrowed. "What? Am I not dressed right?"

"No, Sunfire, you're perfect." She smiled and went into his arms for a hug. He loved that she did that so freely. Having her in his arms, her curves pressed against him felt ... perfect. He kissed the top of her head. "Ready to go?" She nodded.

Chapter 9

As Logan ushered her through the door of Jolene's, a fit of nerves struck Annika. What if his friends didn't like her? What if she didn't get along with them? And what if she didn't like who he was around his friends? She'd once dated someone who, though sweet when they were alone, berated and belittled her when he was with his friends.

She'd walked away from that relationship without a backward glance. But if Logan treated her like that, it would be devastating.

"Don't worry, they'll love you." He brought her hand to his lips, then nodded his head toward a large group. "There they are in the usual spot."

The usual spot was in the middle of the restaurant. A bunch of tables had been pushed together to accommodate them all. The sheer number of them surprised Annika. She hadn't had much time over the years to make many friends. She'd gone out a few times with some of her coworkers, but she couldn't call any of them close.

Now she was even more nervous since she didn't make friends easily. Jamie had been the social one, she'd been the tag along. But Jamie had never treated her like a third wheel, so she never realized how much she depended on him for friends until he was gone.

"Logan!" A gorgeous woman with dark hair and striking green eyes called out to him. She stood and crossed over to him, giving him a big hug. "It's so good to see you!"

"You too. How's school?" Annika felt a surge of jealousy at the easy rapport between the two of them. She knew the feeling was misplaced but seeing him smile at the beautiful woman sent an ugly emotion into the pit of her stomach. She had no claim on Logan; she couldn't fault him for having a past without her.

"Chaotic. The little ones are entirely too hyped up for Christmas. It's a herculean task to keep them focused."

"And she loves every minute of it," said a tall man who came and put his arm around the tiny woman. He held his hand out to Logan. "Glad you could make it."

"Me too." He turned to Annika and placed a hand on her back, the heat of which infused her skin, easing some of her anxiety. "This is my boss, Graham Whitaker, and his better half, Natalie Ghannon." The knot of jealousy in her belly loosened with those words.

"Nice to meet you," she told them politely.

Logan turned to the rest of the group. "Everyone, meet Annika Northrup." There were hellos and waves as Logan went around the table and introduced everyone. It would be a feat to remember all those names.

Natalie linked her arm through Annika's and led her to one end of the line of tables. "Don't worry; you'll learn who everybody is eventually. Come chat with us girls a moment."

"All right." She followed Natalie's lead.

"Okay, so, I'm Natalie. I work at Lake Haven Elementary as the art teacher." She pointed to a blonde woman across from her. "My sister Maddie. She's a freelance bookkeeper. That's Emma," she continued, indicating the woman with the short haircut. "She's the newest member of Nighthawk and former Coast Guard."

"And so many other things that we won't go into right now," said a redhead that had just joined them. "Hi. I'm Jolene."

"Annika." She shook her outstretched hand. Jolene's hair was pulled into a ponytail that swung over her shoulder. Even dressed simply in a long-sleeved t-shirt and dark jeans, her beauty was remarkable. "Wait ... Jolene? *The* Jolene?"

"Hear that, girls! I'm *The* Jolene."

"Your burgers are to die for," Annika told her.

"Bless your heart," Jolene answered in a deep southern drawl. "You've had my burgers?"

"I'm from near Grand Rapids, but my parents have a house on the lake. We always make sure to come here anytime we're in town."

"It's a wonder I've never seen you here before because you are just stunning!"

Annika blushed. "It's been a few years since I've visited."

"So, which of my burgers is your favorite?" Jolene asked.

"The one with the bacon, of course."

"Coming right up." She ran off to what could only be the kitchen.

"She'll have the kitchen put a rush on it, and you'll have your burger in no time," Emma informed her, swiping a strand of her short brown hair behind her ear. Annika clenched her hands in her lap as Emma's intelligent brown eyes studied her. Logan's teammate was another striking woman who looked every inch a badass even while appearing lithe and graceful.

"That's very sweet of her."

"That's Jolene."

After the boisterous bar owner rejoined the women, they asked her how she knew Logan. "We grew up together."

"Aww, that's just like you and Graham, Natalie," Jolene mused. "Let me guess, you've just been reunited after many years apart, and now you're together."

"Not exactly. It's more complicated than that."

"Isn't it always, Honey," Jolene muttered.

"That's always been my experience," joined Natalie. "Are you the one who fell off the bluff?"

"How did you know about that?"

"Logan texted Graham earlier asking for help in replacing his supplies. He mentioned helping a friend who'd fallen. Are you okay? He said you had a concussion."

"I'm fine. It's down to a dull throb now. And I don't get dizzy anymore when I stand, so I'm grateful for that."

"Yeah, concussions are a bitch."

"What were you doing out there in that weather anyway?" Emma wondered.

"I went for a run. The snow wasn't too bad when I started."

"You run?" Emma's eyes lit up, and Annika nodded. "Goody! Maybe we can go together sometime. The rest of these lazy girls don't do the running thing."

"Why run unless something is chasing you," Jolene teased.

"But how do you know you could outrun whatever is chasing you unless you practice?" Annika wondered.

Jolene's eyes widened as she gasped, and they all laughed. "I never thought of it like that. Okay, Emma, train me."

Emma rolled her eyes. "Right now?"

"Well, no. After Christmas. We'll call it a New Year's Resolution."

"You never stick to your New Year's Resolutions," Emma quipped.

"Details." Jolene waved Emma off. "So, Annika, you were running, but why so close to the edge?"

"A dog was tangled up in the bushes. I freed it. Then the ground gave way."

"And Logan saved you?" Jolene sighed, looking like she thought the whole incident was a lovely dream.

"I guess."

"You guess?"

"Well, I was unconscious. I woke up hours later in my bed."

"Oh my God! That is so romantic." Jolene clasped her hands together under her chin, eyes shining with hearts.

The women groaned. "Jolene," Natalie admonished. "Falling off a cliff is not romantic."

Natalie's sister, Maddie, put her two cents in, ignoring the swooning woman. "I wonder how Logan got you up by himself. And why he didn't call the team." Maddie was striking in a different way from the other women. While the others were dressed casually, Maddie looked like she'd just arrived from work. Sharply pressed dark slacks and silk blouse gave her an elegantly polished appearance.

"I think I must have been partially in the water. He said something about me being hypothermic."

"He must have thought time was of the essence and couldn't wait for the team to get there," Emma stated. "And the weather was really bad. He probably figured the trucks or even an ambulance couldn't get through."

"When Graham found me in that well, I was hypothermic too. He used his body heat to warm me. It was delicious to feel some warmth finally," Natalie declared.

"A well?"

"Shortened version," Jolene started, leaning closer to Annika as if to impart an important secret even though she did nothing to soften her voice. The whole bar could hear her sweet southern drawl. "Crazy lady tried to kill Natalie because she wanted Graham. She was trapped at the bottom of a well for three days before we knew she was missing."

"God, that's awful!"

"You can watch the rest of the story when the movie comes out," quipped Maddie.

"Are you really going to put all of that in the movie?" Emma wondered.

Maddie explained for Annika's benefit. "Marcus Rayne wants to make a movie about Graham and the Nighthawks."

"That's right. I remember hearing something about that."

"Who hasn't," Natalie stated.

"Hasn't what?" asked Graham as the men joined the ladies. Logan pulled up a chair next to Annika. She reached for his hand, in need of that little boost of support. He linked their fingers and squeezed.

"Marcus Rayne," answered Maddie with a smile.

Graham rolled his eyes and moaned. "That man is going to haunt me forever."

"That *man*," Natalie reminded him, "is giving you millions to rebuild the warehouse."

"Again, Annika," Jolene whispered loudly to her. "You'll have to watch the movie to see what happened there."

Everyone laughed except for Graham, who groaned.

Maddie was staring at her, causing Annika to shift uncomfortably in her chair. "Why does your name sound so familiar?"

Annika shrugged. "I don't know?"

"It's such a pretty name. Unusual," Jolene said just as the waiters brought out all the food. The burgers looked as good as Annika remembered. And the taste ... She nearly moaned out loud after taking her first bite.

"Oh my God, Jolene," moaned Emma after taking a bite of her burger. "Will you marry me?"

"Hey," called the red-haired man from across the table. Annika thought his name was Finch. "I called dibs on her months ago!"

"Bless your hearts," Jolene teased. "Both of you."

An older woman wandered over to their tables, and Finch stood as she approached, she waved him back into his seat. Logan leaned close to her. "Finch has some very old-fashioned manners," he whispered. "He's always doing stuff like that."

Natalie greeted the woman warmly. "Hi Letty, won't you join us?"

Graham got up and pulled another chair over. "Miss Letty, this is Annika, an old friend of mine," Logan introduced her. Letty was plump, a cardigan pulled taut around her girth, and wore canvas sneakers. Annika had never seen someone her age wear sneakers like that, except for Mr. Rogers. "Letty is the principal at Lake Haven Elementary."

"My fearless leader," Natalie called.

"Nice to meet you," Annika said, shaking the woman's hand.

"How are you doing, Miss Letty?" Graham asked.

"I'm fine now that Fred is home," she said, relief evident in her voice.

"Who's Fred?"

"My dog. He went missing for most of yesterday. When he finally came back, he was covered in scratches, cold and wet but otherwise unharmed."

Annika gasped. "Is your dog a small white fluffy thing?"

"Yes, that's Fred. You've seen my Fred before?"

"Yesterday when I freed him from the bushes by the bluff. He ran off without saying goodbye. I'm glad he made it home."

"It was Letty's dog you freed before you fell from the bluff?" Jolene asked. "Imagine that."

Miss Letty gasped. "You fell off the bluff?"

"More like the bluff fell out from under me," she joked.

"Oh, how horrifying for you. And after you saved my Fred. You're my hero. I don't know what I would have done without my Fred." She reached over and gave her a big hug. "I'm sorry for what happened to you, though. I hope you weren't hurt."

"No, not really. Logan got me out."

"Of course, he did. Another hero."

"Miss Letty, you don't know how true that is." Annika reached over and squeezed Logan's hand.

"Okay," called Jolene. "In honor of Logan introducing us to his lovely Annika, who has a good story to share about the man?"

Annika watched as the team of men looked at each other, sly smiles on their faces. After some mysterious telepathic communication, they all nodded then concluded together, "The Germans."

Logan groaned and dropped his head into his hand.

"The Germans?" Annika asked, curious about Logan's reaction.

Finch started the story. "We got a call about a couple of climbers who were experiencing some trouble in the Upper Peninsula. So, we pile into the helicopter and head out. It was decided that Logan would go down to help the climbers."

"Tin Man was there too," Logan complained. "It wasn't just me."

"But they only had eyes for you," a man with the cutest dimple she had ever seen replied. Annika assumed he was Tin Man.

"Especially after that protective move you pulled on them," teased Finch.

"What happened?" Jolene asked, fully involved in the story.

Tin Man smiled at Logan, obviously ready to throw him under the bus. "Logan and I rappelled down to them. Turns out they were German and spoke very little English."

"You're forgetting that they were also drop-dead gorgeous," Finch announced.

"And very um … shapely," a brown-haired teammate with gorgeous blue eyes intoned with a dry wit. Annika recalled his name was Evan.

"Dude, they were stacked," extolled Finch. He held up both hands suggestively in front of himself to illustrate just how well-endowed the Germans were. Logan groaned, shaking his head at Finch's antics.

"Fuck, Finch. With the refined manners you like to shame us all with, you'd think you'd show a little more respect," criticized Graham's brother, David.

"Oh, I have plenty of respect for the female form," Finch replied, sending a wink at the women.

"So, anyway," continued Tin Man. "Our path to them was hampered by a lot of loose rock from recent heavy rains. Logan reached them first, and I, unfortunately, knocked more rocks loose on my way to them. One particularly large rock was falling directly for them. Logan threw himself over them, taking the brunt of the hit."

"Hurt like hell, and I had a giant bruise on my back for weeks," grumbled Logan. Annika squeezed his hand in sympathy.

"Oh, poor baby," Finch goaded. "Those two ladies were only too happy to ease your pain despite the language barrier."

"They were so grateful to Logan they fawned all over him, flaunting their ... assets."

"They were very enthusiastic," Evan said dryly.

Finch laughed. "That's an understatement. They were ready for some freaky-deaky stuff." Never one to compare herself to others, Annika was surprised to feel insecure about her own attributes. As the men described the German women's figures, she wondered if that was the type of women Logan usually went for. In high school, he'd dated the girls that had developed a lot sooner than she had. Did he still prefer a well-endowed woman as an adult? And would her average C cup size be enough.

Shaking herself out of her musings, she realized how ridiculous her thoughts were. Every woman felt unattractive and insecure at some point in their lives, and after everything she'd gone through since losing Jamie, she was finally confident in her own worth. But that tiny niggle of doubt still reared it's ugly head at times, and this moment was no different.

"Did you take them up on their offer?" wondered Jolene, bringing Annika out of her thoughts.

"Fuck, no." The men laughed at Logan's assertion.

"Like Logan, the monk, would ever do something so depraved," Finch complained.

"The monk?" ventured Annika, observing Logan's wince of embarrassment.

"Yeah, we never see Logan going home with any hottie. Guess now we know why," Finch teased with a wink for Annika, causing a blush to heat her cheeks. She didn't know why, but she felt entirely too pleased to learn Logan didn't succumb to the German's seduction.

"Christ, can we stop with the teasing now?" Logan requested. She looked around at the men in the group. Each and every one of them had that warrior physique that made women's mouths water. They were all handsome in their own way, but what they all had in common, besides their muscle definition, was their mutual love and respect for each other. Annika could see that even though they teased mercilessly, they were staunch friends who would do anything for each other. She was glad Logan had found this Nighthawk family.

"You better be careful, Finch; turnabout is fair play. Just wait for the day you bring a girl to meet us," cautioned Graham. Annika watched, stunned, as a blush colored the big man's cheeks and his gaze momentarily rested on Jolene before quickly darting away. Guess the jokester was smitten with the southern belle.

"So, what do you do, Annika?" Natalie asked, changing the subject before more ribbing could start.

"I'm a teacher."

"College?"

"No. High school English."

"Oh, I just assumed college because you are here instead of up in Grand Rapids; that's where you're from, right? I thought maybe you were done for the semester," figured Natalie.

"I had to take some time off."

"Wait ... I know now," Maddie started. "I know why your name is familiar. You're that teacher, aren't you?" Annika blanched, shifting in her seat again. She hadn't talked in public about what had happened to her and was uncomfortable someone had recognized her. She hadn't even told Logan the story yet and didn't want to do it publicly in front of all his friends.

"What are you talking about, Maddie?" Logan asked.

"About a month or so ago, there was a story that made all the news outlets about another school shooting and a hero teacher. That was you!" Annika wanted to deny it. Wanted to hide from the reality of it. Her parents told her it had been all over the news, so she should have expected this.

"I heard about that too," Emma chimed in. "She saved all her students from a gunman."

"Not all of them," she whispered, looking at her hands clenched in her lap.

Logan reached over and placed his hand over her clamped ones. "Annika?"

"Yes, that was me." Crap. The cat was out of the bag now. There was no way she could shove it back in.

"Jeez, Annika. You were shot too, weren't you?" Maddie asked.

"Yes."

"And you still managed to talk the gunman into giving himself up? Amazing!" Maddie exclaimed.

"A true hero!" Emma announced, raising her glass to toast Annika.

"I'm not a hero. I just did what I had to do," she remarked uncomfortably.

"That, my dear, is the true definition of hero," informed Jolene.

Graham leaned over to her. "Welcome to notoriety. It sucks." Everyone laughed, which lightened Annika's mood.

"'Notoriety is not real glory.' Louisa May Alcott," Annika quoted. Logan squeezed her hand again.

"Well, isn't that just a humdinger of a quote," Jolene stated. Everyone laughed again.

"Humdinger? Your southern is showing again, Jolene," Emma teased.

Then amazingly, the conversation moved on to other topics, and they had an enjoyable evening. The friendship they shared was beyond compare. They teased and praised each other, just like family.

The night would have been absolutely perfect if she hadn't felt Logan pull away from her after learning about the school shooting. He didn't pull away physically; he still held her hand throughout the night. And even occasionally put his arm across the back of her chair and lightly brushed his fingers against her shoulder.

He was just quiet and not truly engaged in the conversations around him. He looked lost in thought and somewhat angry. She worried he might be peeved at her for not telling him about the shooting. It was a nightmare she was trying desperately to put behind her. Knowing she had to tell him everything, she suddenly felt very tired and not at all ready to divulge all her secrets.

The night wound down, and everyone was getting ready to go. Logan had his hand on Annika's back to usher her to the door. Before they could reach it, a man grabbed Annika and spun her to him, holding her firmly at his side.

Confused at first, she watched as Logan made a move to pull her back but he paused when the man wrapped an arm around her throat, a prickle of fear then rose in her. He held Annika firmly in a chokehold, and she could feel something hard digging into her back from his side under his coat. She froze and felt her limbs tremble when she realized the item could very well be a gun. Had the man not been holding her so tightly, she feared her legs would have given out on her.

"Mr. Petersen?" Logan asked angrily.

The man pointed a trembling finger at Logan. "You. Look at you. Not a care in the world. Having a laugh with your friends." She could sense the remaining Nighthawk men circle around her and saw the man sneer at them out of the corner of her eye. "You make me sick. You're nothing but a murderer. You killed my Carlie!" He was shouting, the words overly loud in her ear. Obviously drunk, spittle flew over her as he yelled.

"No, Mr. Petersen. I didn't kill your wife," Logan replied calmly. "Please let her go."

"Yes, you did! You were there, and you let her die!" Annika watched Logan's eyes flare. There was anger there but also guilt. Her heart broke for him. The last thing he needed was more guilt for another death.

Graham stepped up beside Logan. "Mr. Petersen. Your wife succumbed to her injuries before we could reach her. There was nothing anyone could have done," Graham said, attempting to defuse both men. "Mr. Petersen. You have a daughter, don't you? She needs you."

"She needs her mother!" he yelled, his arm tightening around her throat. She reached up and grabbed his arm, attempting to pry it from her neck.

"Go home to your daughter," Graham directed quietly.

Annika could feel the tense anger surging through Mr. Petersen's body as he shouted, "My Carlie is dead because of you!"

"No, sir." Logan tried to take a step closer to them but paused when Annika gasped. The arm around her throat had tightened even more as he raged.

"Liar!" Petersen yelled before Logan could say more. "You took her away from me. Now you'll go home and fuck this bitch." Annika could feel his derision as an audible gasp from the patrons of the restaurant reached her ears. "How would you feel if I took *her* away from you?"

Annika saw Logan stiffen. A tic went through his jaw, and his hands were clenched into fists so tight his knuckles were white. She knew instinctively he would risk everything to protect her. She had to do something to defuse the situation before it erupted into violence.

"Mr. Petersen!" His arm loosened at her sudden shout, and she twisted around to face him. "Mr. Petersen, look at me." She looked into his red-rimmed eyes and endeavored to control the tremor of fear she felt in her body. He was so shocked at her actions that he could do nothing *but* look at her. "Mr. Petersen, what would your wife think if she heard you use such language!"

In complete astonishment that she would speak to him like that, he dropped his hand from her shoulder where it had come to rest after she'd spun around. Annika took a slight step back away from him. "I ... uh," he stuttered.

"She'd be ashamed, wouldn't she?" Annika insisted.

He looked down at the floor for an instant, shame in his posture. Then he looked back up and over her shoulder. His body stiffened, and his eyes turned angry as he spotted Logan and the others.

"Eyes on me, Mr. Petersen!" Annika shouted, using her best teacher voice. She'd shocked him again. He stared at her, his glassy eyes wide open.

"Here is what is going to happen," she began sternly. "We are going to call you a cab. You are going to go home and find a picture of your wife. You will then apologize to her for the way you acted tonight," she ordered, leaving no room for argument.

"Tomorrow, you will allow your daughter to play hooky from school, and you will spend the day with her. A daddy-daughter date. Go ride a carousel. Eat junk food. Walk on the beach. Play in the snow. Go see a movie. Whatever. Just give her the special day she deserves!" She paused, letting her words sink in. "Do you understand?"

He nodded, his greasy hair flopping over his forehead.

"Good. Now go home and take care of the daughter your wife loved more than life itself."

He nodded again. Graham stepped closer and placed a hand on the grieving man's shoulder. "There's an Uber waiting for you outside. Let's get you home," he said quietly, walking Petersen out the front door. The rest of the Nighthawks followed in a united front.

When the men all exited the bar, Annika let go of the breath she'd been holding and slumped into the nearest chair. Her new friends crowded around her. The glass of water Jolene handed her trembled with the remnants of adrenaline flowing through her.

"Are you okay?" Natalie asked, her eyes full of concern. Annika nodded.

"Damn, Annika," Jolene exclaimed. "I've never seen anyone talk to a grown man like that before. You must be a *very* good teacher."

"Sorry about that, Annika," Natalie said, giving her a hug. "He's just a grieving widower."

"Yes, I understood that. He blames Logan."

"Well," Natalie started. "Carlie, his wife, was in a really bad accident. Her car went into the river. Logan was inches away from reaching her when she slipped below the surface and disappeared, succumbing to her extensive injuries. They searched for her for hours."

"Does Logan blame himself?" she wondered.

"Graham seems to think he does. That's why he gave him some time off."

"Not again," Annika breathed. Just like with Jamie, he was placing the blame for another accidental death squarely on his own shoulders.

"What?" The men returned, saving Annika from having to reply.

Logan kneeled down in front of her. "Are you okay?"

"I'm fine."

He hugged her tight to him, then sat back on his heels. "What the *hell* were you thinking, Annika?" She stared at him in disbelief that he would speak to her so harshly but could see the underlying fear in his expression. "That was a risky move. He could have had a gun or something."

"He did. I felt it."

Logan blanched and grabbed her to him again in a fierce hug. "Fuck, Sunfire. That was just about the craziest thing I've ever seen."

"Go easy on her, Logan," Miss Letty said. "She did exactly the right thing by defusing the situation."

"He's just grieving and looking for somewhere to place that grief," Annika said after Logan released her again. "I just gave him something to focus on. Gave him a purpose. At least for the next day or so."

"I, for one, hope he does exactly as you ordered," Emma said.

"Only time will tell," Miss Letty responded sadly. She patted Annika on her hand. "You are a wonder, my girl.

Simply amazing," she mused, then said her goodbyes to the group.

Logan reached for her hand to help Annika stand. "Let's go home." She nodded.

They all said their goodbyes, and Annika promised she'd see them all again. She and Logan spent a quiet ride home. There was a tension radiating from his body, and his knuckles were white as he squeezed the life out of the steering wheel. Annika wished these new trucks still had those bench seats so that she could slide closer to Logan and put her head on his shoulder, offering him as much comfort as she could with her body.

As soon as they were in the house, she was in his arms, and he was kissing her like a starved man. "Annika," he moaned against her lips.

<h1 style="text-align:center">Chapter 10</h1>

B REAKING THE KISS, HE stared at her, rage still coursing through him. "That was a fucking reckless thing to do, Annika."

She stiffened and dropped her arms from around his neck. "I only did what I thought was right."

"You should have let me handle it. The guy was unhinged. There's no telling what could have happened. Christ, Annika. He had a gun." He paced away from her, running his fingers aggressively through his hair.

"I know that—"

"Then what were you thinking confronting him like that?"

"Logan," she started softly. She was trying to calm his rage, but he was resisting. He wasn't ready to let it go yet.

"Fuck, how could you act so stupidly?" He regretted the words before they were even out of his mouth.

He watched as Annika shrank before his eyes, her arms wrapping around her stomach before her face flushed with anger. She dropped her arms and stiffened her spine. She jutted her chin out, finding her fierce inner Sunfire; he was in for it now.

"As I said, I did what I thought was right. I know how situations like that can get out of hand quickly. And I knew that you would risk violence to protect me. Making him focus on me, I made him see me as a person, not his victim. I drew his attention away from what was causing his anger. And it worked. I calmed him down without the violence I know you would have resorted to."

Logan winced, her jibe landing dead center. Seeing the hurt and fire in her eyes, knowing he'd put it there, dampened his own anger.

She made to storm past him, but he grabbed her arm, pulling her into him. "I was so scared he was going to hurt you," he breathed, placing his forehead against hers. He'd never survive it if he lost her, having just got her back. "I can't lose you."

She sighed and placed her hands against his cheeks, forcing him to look at her. "You won't. I'm here, Logan. I'm fine. And I'm not going anywhere."

She crushed her mouth to his, her hot tongue pushing past the barrier of his lips. He moaned, grasped her hips, and pulled her closer, taking control of the kiss. His tongue tasted her sweet mouth greedily. He needed more of her. More kisses. More skin beneath his hands.

With that thought in his mind, he slid his hands behind her, one slipping under her sweater, his fingertips skimming the soft skin of her back. It was her turn to moan as she pressed herself against him, a sound that shot straight to his cock.

He caressed her cheek with his other hand as he kissed her. Feather-light fingers drifted down her neck until he was cupping her breast through her sweater. She whimpered and pressed herself more fully into his hand. He ran his thumb over her pebble-hard nipple, and she trembled in his arms.

He had to see her. Had to touch her. He grabbed the hem of her sweater and pulled it up and over her head. The puckered scar on her shoulder drew his attention momentarily, causing his gut to roll. He ignored the turmoil flowing inside him at the thought of her pain and focused on her pleasure instead. His hand went to her breast again, the lace of her bra doing nothing to protect it from his greedy touch. He kissed his way from her lips to her neck, reaching his tongue out to taste her pulse point.

He growled when he saw the red marks on her neck where Petersen had held her. Then his tongue slipped out to soothe the marks on her perfect skin, intending to erase those blemishes with his passion.

He moved his mouth steadily lower until he reached the swell of her breasts. He lifted his head away from her skin for a moment to look at her as he released the clasp of her bra, the lace fluttered to their feet.

In awe, he raised a hand and caressed her, the rosy bud tightening as he drew his thumb across it.

"Fuck, Sunfire, you're perfect." He lowered his head, taking it into his mouth. Annika gasped and arched her back, pressing more of herself into him. He sucked, licked, and teased until she was squirming in his arms. Then he moved to the other breast, affording it equal attention.

Sliding his hands around her, he grabbed her ass and lifted until the heat between her legs was against him. She groaned and swiveled her hips, grinding herself against him. He nearly came out of his skin at the sensation, his cock stiffening unbearably hard.

He lifted her higher, and she wrapped her legs around his waist. Supporting her against the wall, with his hands under her ass, his mouth swathed her breast again as she arched her back. She rocked herself against him, and he cursed the invention of clothes.

The sound of her gasps awakened something feral inside him, and he couldn't help but wonder what sounds she would make when he was deep inside her. He wanted to be inside her more than he wanted his next breath. He needed to feel her heat encase him. Needed to feel her pulsing around his cock. He had to know if she felt the same way.

"Annika," he breathed, his lips brushing the soft skin of her neck. "I want you. I need you." He held his breath, waiting for her response as his dick throbbed uncomfortably against his zipper.

"Please," she whimpered and rocked herself against him again. That was all it took. He turned them and walked down the hall to her room, Annika still wrapped around him. He didn't bother with lights as he placed her on the bed and followed her down, her arms and legs wrapping around him again.

He kissed her as she struggled to get his shirt off. Taking pity on her, he moved to help. He tore his shirt off over his head then watched as she wiggled out of her pants, her tits bouncing with the movements. Every cell in his body was on fire as he watched her sexy wiggle. *Fuck, that was hot.* He could hardly breathe; he'd never seen anything as sexy as that.

Logan rushed to remove his shoes and pants and rejoined her on the bed. "That was the sexiest thing I've ever had the pleasure to watch." She shivered when he murmured into her ear, and a blush traveled up her neck to her cheeks. He pressed his body against hers. Skin to skin. He was free to enjoy the sensations this time as he ran his hands down to cup her ass. Grabbing her under one thigh, he hitched her leg up over his hip, opening her up for him as he settled between her thighs. He kissed and licked his way to her breast. He couldn't get enough of feasting on her perfect tits.

Trailing a hand down her side, he released her breast and watched her bite her lip when he followed the seam of her thigh until he found her core. She was slick with her desire, hot and wet. He parted her with his fingers and found her hot little clit. She cried out his name as he flicked his thumb across it. Arching her back, she squirmed against his hand, wanting more. He obliged, sliding a finger then two inside her. He moaned. She was wet and oh so tight. He toyed with her, bringing her just to the brink.

"Please, Logan. Please. I need you," she moaned.

He stopped suddenly. "Shit, I don't have a condom."

"I'm on the pill."

"Are you sure? I'm clean, we get annual checks at Nighthawk. But are you sure?"

"God, Logan, I'm clean too, but if you are not inside me in the next two seconds, I may just scream."

He chuckled as he moved over her and cupped her head with both his hands. "Let's see if I can make you scream *while* I'm inside of you," he teased, the tip of his cock just breaching her core. Her heat encased him as he slowly entered her. She was so tight he was afraid he would hurt her. She raised her knees, and he slipped deeper. They both groaned. Suddenly, he was in her to the hilt.

She was made for him; they fit so perfectly. He rotated his hips and withdrew, then plunged in again. A wave of awe rushed over him. He was inside Annika, and she felt like heaven. Nothing had ever felt so right during the last fifteen years as being buried deep inside of this gorgeous woman who was moaning beneath him.

"Fuck, Annika. You feel so perfect. I'll never get enough of you."

"Oh God, Logan," she sighed. "It feels better than I ever dreamed it would."

He took a moment to enjoy the sensation of her moist heat wrapped around him as he tenderly kissed her lips. Then he moved again, rocking his hips. Gliding out and back in, her inner muscles clamping onto him with each thrust. He wasn't sure how long he was going to last, but he wanted to make this good for her. He reached between their bodies and found her clit, pinching it as he moved within her. She screamed, shattering in his arms, her orgasm shuddering through her so suddenly. Her tight walls pulsed around him, strangling his cock. He smiled and helped her ride it out. Making it last.

But he wasn't done with her yet. Gritting his teeth to delay his own impending orgasm, he placed a hand under her ass, changing the angle to thrust harder and faster. He brought her desire back up to the peak again.

Flicking her clit with his fingers, he plied her nipple with his tongue, working interchangeably between the two. Flick, lick. Flick, lick. She trembled and wrapped her legs around his hips, her heels digging into his back.

Lifting his head, he watched her as he rocked into her harder. Her tits jiggled, and she threw her head back. Her entire body tensed, her thighs squeezing his hips as she came for the second time. He forced his eyes to stay on her as he tumbled over the peak with her, the tight clamp of her pussy milking him dry.

There had been many moments since the day he'd met Annika that her beauty stunned him. But none more than this moment, watching her come apart in his arms. It was a memory, an image, that would be imprinted on his brain forever.

Slowly, they both returned to solid ground. Logan rolled off to her right side. He could see the puckered redness of the bullet wound scar on her shoulder that was not quite fully healed. He leaned closer and placed his lips gently over the scar, his heart clenching at the thought of her being hurt. "Want to talk about that yet?"

"No. Want to talk about that man yet?" she countered.

Touché, Sunfire. There was no way he wanted to admit to another failure at this moment. "No."

"Let's just enjoy being with each other like this and not let reality intrude too soon."

"Deal."

She rolled to her side, lying face to face with him. He ran his hand from her shoulder, down her side, and over her hip, watching as his fingers traced over her curves. She was more beautiful than any image his imagination could conjure. He used the calloused tips to tease the skin above her hip. Silky smooth skin slid softly under his hands. He was enjoying touching her so much he didn't notice she had fallen asleep. He kissed her forehead and reached for the covers. Wrapping his arms around Annika, he pulled her close to him, covered them with the sheets, and drifted off to sleep, content for the first time in fifteen years.

"Good morning, Caleb." As he entered her classroom, Annika greeted the boy, but he didn't answer as he usually did. "Are you okay?" Worried about him, she knew he was having a rough time lately with the pressure of getting into the right college. His parents were pushing him hard which only added to his anxiety. Most of her older students were at their breaking points at this time of year. Annika did her best to guide them through the uncertainties of their futures.

Annika studied Caleb closely, sensing something wasn't quite right. He was fidgeting and not making eye contact with her as she conversed with him. And he was sweating ... a lot. Since the school building always felt cold to her, she was curious as to why he felt so hot.

She was about to ask Caleb if he was feeling all right when he bent and reached into his backpack. Standing upright, something metallic was grasped in his hand. Annika had a moment to register the object was a handgun before all hell broke loose.

The sound of the gun firing was deafening. The acrid odor invaded her senses. She felt something hit her right side, then her right shoulder, knocking her to the ground. Her brain felt sluggish as she tried to decipher what was happening, taking entirely too long before the pain registered. Hot, searing pain. Unlike anything she'd ever felt.

Her mind instantly went to a dark place as a bizarre thought popped into her head. I'll finally see Jamie again.

No. She would not let that thought take hold. She was a survivor, and this situation would be no different. Besides, her kids needed her.

Her students were screaming all around her. Some hiding under desks. Some fleeing through the door seconds before Caleb closed and locked it, trapping them all inside with him.

Looking around her, Annika tried to concentrate, but the pain was overpowering. She could see a few students huddled in a group sitting on the floor in the corner, and others crouched under the desks. Some of them were bleeding. Suzanna lay close to her in a puddle of blood that was steadily growing larger. Annika tried to sit up, pain erupting through her. Struggling, she managed to prop herself up against the front of her desk.

Caleb was by the door, pacing, gun clasped in his hand. He was muttering to himself. "Caleb." Was that her voice? It sounded like it came from a thousand miles away. "What are you doing? Why are you doing this?"

"I ... I can't anymore, Miss Northrup."

"Caleb," she tried again as she glanced at Suzanna, who was far too still. "Put the gun down, Caleb."

"I can't."

"Caleb, your friends need help. Can we get them some help?"

"What? No. No. No."

"But we need to stop the bleeding. Will you let me try to stop the bleeding?"

"I ... I guess." She crawled closer to Suzanna, placing her good hand over the oozing wound in her chest. "Caleb, I need help. Will you let Sam and Liam help me?"

"Okay."

"You promise not to hurt them?"

"Yeah." He resumed his pacing and muttering. Annika waved the boys over. "We need to find something to stop this bleeding."

Liam took his sweatshirt off and handed it to her. "I ... I can't put enough pressure on it. Put the sweatshirt over the wound and push down as hard as you can. Sam, can you find something to hold it in place. Some tape or something." Before moving to search the drawers of her desk, he shot a look at Caleb, who seemed to be too distracted with his thoughts

He came back quickly with a roll of duct tape. "How's this?

"Perfect. Tear off a piece big enough to cover the wound. It might take several p ... pieces." He did that, then, as if by instinct, he rolled the sweatshirt up again, placing it over the wound. As he wrapped the roll of tape around her body, Liam helped to lift her.

"Thas good." Her words were starting to slur as a blackness hovered at the periphery of her vision. She knew she was losing too much blood, the loss making her actions and thoughts sluggish. She needed ... needed to think! She had to get the kids out. She couldn't let the darkness take over. Keep your eyes open!

"Now you, Miss Northrup," she heard Sam as he kneeled in front of her. She could feel him placing the tape over her wounds, and she clenched her jaw in an effort not to cry out at the pain. He wrapped the tape around her middle as he had done for Suzanna, after he covered the wound in her side. Then he moved to her back and wrapped more tape around both sides of her shoulder. Had she been shot three times? She only remembered two.

Caleb was growing more agitated. He waved the gun at the boys. "That's enough. Go in the corner." The two looked at her, and she whispered for them to go.

Once the boys had moved, Caleb walked closer to Annika. He brought the gun up and pointed it directly at her forehead. "I can't anymore, Miss Northrup."

"Caleb! No!" she screamed as she sat bolt upright. Warm arms embraced her from behind. Gasping, she struggled to steady her breaths before she hyperventilated.

"Breathe with me," Logan said softly. He leaned her back against his chest and she tried to match her breathing to his exaggerated inhalations. It was working, but then the trembling started. Logan quietly held her until she defeated the worst of the fear. When she was calm enough, he wrapped the blanket around her and lifted her into his lap as he leaned back against the headboard. She laid her head against his shoulder.

"Tell me ... please," Logan begged quietly. "It was a school shooting, right?"

Annika nodded. "Caleb. He was one of my best students," she started. "He'd been having a hard time, college pressures. He lost a scholarship to another one of my students. I didn't know it at the time, but he blamed me. When he lost the scholarship and Yale all in one day, he snapped."

"He came into my classroom at his normal class time, pulled a handgun out of his bag, and started shooting." She hesitated, and Logan prompted her to take a deep breath. "I was hit first. Twice. It knocked me to the floor. I was stunned, but I could hear the screams from all around me. He blocked kids from escaping through the door, locking it, trapping us in with him. Kids were huddled in groups, trying to make themselves as small as possible. The fear in their eyes ..." She broke off shuddering. She'd always heard the stories about other school shootings. Kids texting their last words to their parents while they hid. These kids were too afraid to move. They were frozen in fear.

"Suzanna was lying beside me. There was so much blood. I knew she needed help quickly. I tried to sit up, eventually making it upright enough to lean back against my desk. Caleb was pacing and muttering to himself. I have no idea what he was saying. I asked him if we could get help for the injured kids. He wouldn't allow that, but he did let me go to Suzanna. I crawled to her and placed my hand over the hole in her body. But I was too weak to do any good. I couldn't stop the blood. I begged Caleb again for help. He let two boys help me. They found some duct tape and covered Suzanna with it. Then they covered my wounds. I didn't know it at the time, but the one in my shoulder went straight through. I wondered why the boys were taping up my back at the time."

"How did you stay conscious? You must have lost a lot of blood too?"

"I have no idea. I could feel the blackness hovering nearby. I knew that I couldn't give in to it. My kids needed me. I had to save my kids."

"That's a lot of responsibility."

She snorted. "Tell me about it." She didn't want that type of responsibility. Not ever again. "For some reason, I knew that I could talk Caleb down if I could just get him to listen to me. He shooed the boys back to the corner of the room and came toward me. His gun was pointed at my head."

"Fuck."

"I screamed his name."

"Is that when the nightmare woke you?"

"Yes. It usually ends there."

"But it didn't end there. What happened next? How did you escape?"

"When I screamed at him, it shocked him. It was like he'd suddenly woken up. He looked at the gun like he didn't know how it had gotten in his hand. I started talking to him. Gently. He'd listen sometimes. Then go back to pacing and muttering other times. Suzanna was still bleeding. She was so pale. I knew she didn't have much time left, but I couldn't get Caleb to put the gun down. I could hear people in the hall, a hostage negotiation team or something like that. There was no way Caleb was going to listen to a stranger. It was up to me."

"Those guys go through extensive training. And they're pretty good at it. They might have been able to do it."

"They couldn't see him. Every time they spoke to him, he became more agitated and waved the gun around. I was afraid it would go off and kill somebody. I had to get his attention back on me. He was calmer when I talked to him. I think the negotiator realized that, too, after a while. He backed off."

"That's good. But you know they were probably watching everything with a camera pointed through the window. They *could* see him. And you." He had her hand in his and was absently playing with her fingers, the movements calming her.

"Maybe. I don't know." She played with his fingers, loving the feeling of his big warm hands on her.

"So, how did you finally talk him down?"

"I was still with Suzanna, holding her hand while blood still seeped past the tape. I was losing her; I needed this to end. She needed it to end. Quickly. I had a little couch in my classroom. Kids liked to sit on it to read or work on projects together. I got him to sit down on it, and we began to talk."

"Christ! How did you do that? How did you stay conscious for so long? You must have been very weak. How much time had passed since he entered the classroom?"

"I don't know, maybe thirty minutes to an hour. I'm not sure. I guess the adrenaline was flooding my system. I sat on the floor across from him, and we talked. I got him to tell me everything he was feeling. The pressure his parents were putting on him to get into Yale. They were basing his entire future on Yale; no other college would do. And when he didn't get in, he snapped. Since he couldn't take it out on his parents, he turned his anger on me. There had been an essay contest for a scholarship. It was between him and another student. I wasn't a judge, but I'd helped both of them write their essays. He thought I'd helped her to win it, thought I'd told her exactly what to write to win. It wasn't true. I told him I thought he was a shoo-in to win and was surprised when he didn't. And that was the truth. He was the better writer. But hers tugged at the heartstrings."

"It was Suzanna, wasn't it?" She was surprised he'd figured that out, but she shouldn't have been. He had always been very perceptive.

"Yes. It was."

"Do you think he was aiming for her?"

"It seemed like he was firing wildly when he started, except for me. He'd aimed for me first. The investigators told me later they thought that Suzanna had crossed in front of me when Caleb started firing. The bullet went in through her chest, causing extensive damage before it exited. That's when it went into my side, though it had lost a lot of its momentum. It didn't do as much damage as it would have had it been the full force. I'm not sure if he even knew he'd shot her."

"Maybe not if he was as crazed as you say he was. I'd be surprised he saw anything clearly enough to aim."

"He certainly saw clearly enough to hit me the second time," she mused.

"Unfortunately," he uttered, kissing her temple.

"He kept looking over at the other kids huddled in groups. I was so afraid he was going to start shooting again. I didn't know how many shots he'd already fired, so I didn't know how many bullets were left in the gun. I kept saying to him '*eyes on me*,' or '*look at me*' to get his attention off the students. I had to keep his attention on me. If he was focused solely on me, he wouldn't notice the others in the room. It was the only way I could think of to protect them."

"That was awfully brave of you. Sounds like it worked too. Just like it worked tonight with Petersen." She hadn't realized at the time she'd used the same tactic from that awful day with Mr. Petersen. She had just acted on instinct.

"It did," she acknowledged. Then after a deep breath, she said, "He gave me the gun, Logan."

"How did you manage that?"

"I fell back on my books. He shared the same love. We talked about pressure, mistakes, and forgiveness. I wracked my brain to think of what the big literary geniuses say about those topics. Sophocles, Frost, Fitzgerald.

Even my favorite *Anne of Green Gables* author." Some of the best life advice came from Lucy Maude Montgomery.

"At one point, he wanted to end it all by putting a bullet in his brain. He had the gun to his head. He knew he'd screwed up royally. He thought there'd be no hope for his future now. I reminded him about something we'd just read from Ibsen. 'Many a man can save himself if he admits he's done wrong and takes his punishment.' I told him that if he gave himself up, let everyone go, he'd save himself. He could make amends and eventually be forgiven."

"Holy fuck," Logan declared. "You must be an amazing teacher." She smiled sadly. It certainly didn't feel like that at the time. She felt like she'd failed Caleb. She knew he was struggling. If only she'd taken the time to talk to him sooner, Suzanna would still be alive.

"After what seemed like hours, he gave me the gun. I reached up and took it from him. I didn't want to leave Suzanna." That was all she could think about from that point on. "I held her. Felt for her pulse. But it was another fifteen minutes before Caleb unlocked the door. She ... she died as I held her." She stopped talking then, her sudden tears overwhelming her. Her grief for Suzanna had been devastating. She'd grieved hard for Jamie. But this had been different, senseless, and the guilt had been debilitating. She knew exactly how Logan had felt after Jamie died. The *what ifs* were all she could think about. If she'd gotten Caleb to calm down sooner. If she'd gotten the gun away from him sooner. So many *ifs*.

"That's what you meant earlier when you said you didn't save them all. You were thinking of Suzanna." She sniffed and nodded.

Logan held her quietly as she cried out more of her grief. She'd thought she was done with the tears for Suzanna. She'd cried for weeks. He held her tightly in his lap. Her face pressed into his chest. His lips resting in her hair. He rocked with her. A gentle motion that had a calming effect. Eventually, her tears dried up.

"It wasn't your fault."

"I know."

"Do you?"

"No," she admitted. "It's all the *what ifs* I can't get past. The guilt."

"You focus on all that you did right. How many other kids were trapped in that room with you?"

"Fifteen."

"Any of them hurt?"

"A few had grazes."

"You saved sixteen lives."

"No. Fifteen."

"Sixteen. You saved Caleb too. If you hadn't been there … If it had been some other teacher … we might be talking about more deaths. And possibly Caleb's death too. Either by his hand or the authorities. I'm sure the hostage team was positioned to take Caleb down if they had to. But because of the connection you had with him, he listened to you. And after some intense therapy and most definitely some jail time, he may have a future. And so will those other fifteen students." She had never thought of it that way. She'd always been focused on her failure, her inability to save Suzanna. She couldn't see past Suzanna to the other students she *had* saved.

"Christ, Annika. I've known men with injuries like yours who could never have done what you accomplished. In fact, it's a miracle you are alive."

"I give credit to the two boys who taped me up. The duct tape slowed the blood loss. The doctors told me that if they hadn't done that, I probably would have died."

"Well, then I owe those two boys a beer."

"They're seventeen."

"Coca-Cola. I meant to say Coca-Cola."

She snorted, then sobered, still thinking about Suzanna. "I couldn't go to her funeral. That killed me. I wanted to be there for her. For her friends, my students. But I was still in the hospital. My parents went in my place. It hurts that I couldn't go." It had been devastating to her not to be able to say goodbye. Suzanna had been a jewel of a student. Creative and fun. Her loss was deeply profound for the entire community.

"I know. It still hurts me sometimes too. I should have gone to Jamie's. I will regret that forever."

"Logan—"

"But you know what helped me?" he asked, interrupting her thought. "I went to his grave once. And I talked to him."

"I didn't know that."

"It helped. How about sometime soon we take a drive to visit Suzanna's grave."

That sounded like a nice idea. She'd like the opportunity to tell her how sorry she was and to say goodbye. "I'd like that."

"Think you can go back to sleep now?"

She nodded so he gathered her into his arms. Annika snuggled deeper into his embrace, filling her lungs with his sandalwood scent. It calmed her, letting her drift off to sleep.

The next morning Annika woke up surrounded by Logan. His hot hand stroked her stomach before moving up to cover her breast, her nipples hardened instantly against his palm. A moan escaped her lips while his mouth discovered the sensitive spot just below her ear. Then he kissed her with desperation as if after their conversation the previous night, he realized how close he had been to losing her, and he needed to reassure himself she was whole.

They went slower this time, each of them enjoyed finding what made the other quiver. Annika took the time to explore his body more thoroughly. And what a body it was. All hard muscle. All male. She lightly ran her nails down his abs, and he trembled. She loved that she could elicit that type of response from him just from her touch. But she wanted to do more than touch. She wanted to taste. She pushed him to his back and straddled him just as she had all those years ago by the lake. But this time, she took full advantage of the position.

Feeling his hardness at her core, she ground herself against him, forcing a moan from him as she kissed, nibbled, and tasted her way across his throat to his chest, thrilling at the hard smoothness of those magnificent muscles. She slid her hands over, around, and down his toned body until she grasped his erection.

That was it for him. It was all he could take of her torture. He growled low in his throat and flipped her over, coming to rest on top of her. She opened her mouth to protest the change in position, but he silenced her as he took her mouth with an unrivaled passion, leaving her to luxuriate in the sensations.

Logan pulled his mouth from hers to drag his lips down her neck to her breasts, where he spent significant time lavishing attention on them. But then he went lower. Her stomach muscles quivered as he kissed his way down her body. She protested again when he skipped the area of her body that most wanted his attention. But then his lips pressed kisses up her inner thighs. The kisses moved steadily higher, and the closer he got, the more her pussy ached in anticipation.

He stopped torturing her with kisses, and she could feel his breath on her most intimate of places. Not feeling anything else from him but the soft puffs of air, she opened her eyes and looked down her body at him hovering between her legs. He was looking at her core as she fought the urge to close her legs to hide from his intense observation. But then his eyes slowly moved up her body until they met hers. There was unbridled lust in his eyes but also something else. Something deeper. He was looking at her as if she was the most beautiful thing in the world. Like a treasure he had hunted his entire life to find.

"I want to spend an eternity right here," he said reverently. "Right here between these perfect thighs." He kissed one leg just close enough to her core, the scruff from his beard tickling the sensitive skin. Then he moved his lips to the other thigh, placing a gentle kiss there, before sliding his lips higher until he found the throbbing center of her. He parted her with his fingers, revealing her core to his hungry gaze, pausing again.

"So beautiful," he murmured before his lips covered her clit and sucked. Annika jolted, her hips shot up, and he placed an arm across her belly to hold her still. He didn't go easy on her. Once his lips latched onto her clit, he devoured her like a starving man. She grasped the sheets in her fists on either side of her and arched her back. He licked at her, slurping up her juices as he feasted on her with his tongue. He'd bring her to the precipice before backing off and changing his angle of attack.

Logan consumed her until she was a needy whimpering mess. Just when she thought she couldn't take anymore, he slipped a finger inside her. Annika cried out as a second finger joined the first, reaching exquisite places inside her that had never been reached before. Annika couldn't have stopped herself from grinding herself on his face if she tried.

With her eyes squeezed tight, she came with a sudden burst of colors erupting behind her eyelids that would put the Aurora Borealis to shame.

Before she could take her next breath, he moved up and entered her in one quick motion, not giving her a chance to come down from her orgasm. Annika wrapped her arms and legs around him, loving the feel of his weight on her. The fullness ignited those colorful sparks behind her eyelids again, and she held on for dear life as he thrust into her harder and faster, every muscle in her body tightening until she burst all over again. She cried out his name as together they went over the edge. Collapsing on top of her, his body crushed her into the mattress. She held him in her arms as they both struggled to control their breathing, his face pressed in her neck. He gave her little kisses there, soothing the still sore areas from her encounter with Mr. Petersen.

Logan had made love to her with such passionate tenderness she was nearly brought to tears, her nightmares were a distant memory. After fifteen years of just existing day to day, she suddenly couldn't wait to see what the future held for them.

Chapter 11

THE SOUND OF HER ringtone woke her later that morning. Surprised they'd both fallen back asleep, she rolled over to grab her phone as Logan got out of bed. "I'll make breakfast," he said as he grabbed his pants and left the room but not before giving her a splendid view of his ass. Her mouth suddenly went dry.

"Hi," she croaked, answering the call. She cleared her throat and tried speaking again. "Hi, Mom."

"Hi, Sweetie. I've let you be for — what is it, nearly a week? How are things going?"

Annika laughed. "Fine, Mom."

"Fine? That's it? Just fine?"

"No. Things are good. Great, actually."

She could hear a sigh of relief through her phone. "I'm so happy to hear that."

"Mom," she started, wondering how much to tell her about what happened after Jamie.

"What is it, Sweetie?"

"Did you know?"

"Know what?"

"Did you know why he went away?" How much had they really talked during their secret email relationship? Did he tell her ... anything?

"No," her voice sounded sad. "I never knew."

Annika debated for a moment whether or not she should tell her mother of Logan's confession. But she knew that just like her, the Northrups did not hold him responsible for the accident. "He blamed himself."

"What?" Johanna cried, shocked.

"He blamed himself for Jamie and couldn't face us. He thought we'd hate him because he hadn't been able to save Jamie. He thought the whole accident was his fault."

"We never blamed him," she replied softly.

"I know that. The guilt he felt was all-consuming. Like my guilt with Suzanna."

"We'll be there in two hours."

"What? No. Mom?" But she'd already hung up. Alrighty then. Her parents were coming. Should she tell him? Warn him? It might be fun to let them surprise him. Maybe.

After breakfast, Annika went to shower and get dressed. Logan joined her as she was rinsing the shampoo out of her hair. He inhaled deeply. "God, that smell. Oranges. I've never been able to eat an orange without thinking of you, and well ..." he looked down, indicating his erection. Annika giggled.

But her giggles soon turned to moans of pleasure when he grabbed her loofa, soaped it up, and caressed her entire body with it. His hand followed the path of the loofa through the soap, luxuriating in her skin that was as smooth as silk. What had he called it in high school? Alabaster. She was as perfect as a Grecian marble statue. He teased every sensitive nerve ending she had as he explored her body. His mouth devouring hers as he lifted one of her legs and propped it on his hip, opening her up for him. He reached down to tease her sensitive bud before slipping two fingers inside her moist heat. Curling his fingers inside her to find that elusive spot, Annika threw her head back and groaned. He placed his lips on her throat, slowly working his way down until he reached her breast.

She moaned again and writhed against his hand, holding on to his shoulders. She was so responsive to his touch. Keeping his fingers inside of her, he went to his knees and found her sweet clit with his tongue.

"Logan!" she gasped, and her hand smacked against the shower wall as he fucked her with his fingers and mouth. The fingers of her other hand tunneled through his hair, holding him to her.

"I can't get enough of the taste of you," he moaned as he teased and played with her until she shuddered and came apart screaming his name.

Before she could come down from her orgasm, he stood and lifted her. Immediately, her legs were wrapped around his hips, and he plunged into her. With her back against the shower wall, he plundered her mouth as he thrust. Her hands squeezed his shoulders, her legs squeezed his hips, and her inner muscles squeezed his dick. Gritting his teeth to stave off his impending orgasm, Logan brought her to the peak again. The pulsing of her eruption caused him to follow her headlong over the edge toward ecstasy, crying out her name.

Breathing heavily, Logan let her legs drop to the floor as he sought to slow his pounding heart. He held her tightly to him, not wanting to let her go. She was his everything. His light. His life. And he'd been a dumbass, missing fifteen years with her. He was determined not to miss a moment more.

Later, after their hearts had slowed to a normal rhythm, they got dressed and sat down to watch a movie together. When the doorbell rang, Logan got up to answer it.

"You stubborn son of a basket weaving jackal, what do you mean by blaming yourself?" Johanna stamped over him as soon as he opened the door, her finger poking him in the chest with each word as he stumbled backward. Logan was so shocked he didn't know what to do as the little irate hummingbird backed him up as she charged. He'd never feared something so little in all his life. Even that time he and Jamie had collided while riding their bikes. They had been playing chicken, and neither one of them moved out of the way. Neither flinched, and they had each declared the other the winner and had the battle scars to prove it. But facing the wrath of Mama Jo put a damper on their victories. She chewed them out with her creative cussing even while tending their wounds. He'd felt loved and chastised all at the same time.

But now, the fierceness in Mama Jo's eyes was terrifying. And her finger stabbing into his chest was damn sharp. He'd spent years dreading this confrontation and now that it was here, he didn't know how to react. He could hear Annika giggling, but he feared taking his eyes off the little battering ram in front of him.

"Well?" she prodded, placing both hands on her hips to glare at him. Logan rubbed the spot on his chest where he was sure her fingernail was embedded. "How could you blame yourself? God, Logan, you ninnyhammer, it wasn't your fault!"

"I—"

"I'm not done." Her razor-sharp fingernail poked him once more. He suddenly wished he were wearing his body armor from his SEAL days. A strong chest plate could surely stop her talons from skinning him alive.

"Yes, ma'am," he replied, snapping his mouth closed, afraid to open it again. Annika giggled some more. Did she just snort giggle? He wanted to glare at her, let her know that he was not happy she was so amused at his expense but couldn't look away from the angry bee poking him in the chest with a stinger that resembled a finger. Fear unlike anything he'd felt before, washed over him as he braced himself for Johanna's censure, convinced she would blame him for the death of her son, despite what Annika had assured him.

"How could you ever believe that I ... that we would hate you, blame you? Jumpin' frog turds, we loved you! We still love you! So, you get that codswallop idea right out of your head." She grabbed his face between her hands and made him bend forward until he was at eye level with her. And since she was only five-two, he had to bend pretty far. Annika, he could hear, had stopped stifling her laughter.

"You listen to me, Logan Cain, you loggerheaded snow urchin, never once did any one of us ever consider that it was your fault. Never. You saved Annika. And you risked your life to try to save Jamie. That makes you a hero in my book. Got it?"

"Yesh, ma'am." He tried to answer clearly, but she was squeezing his cheeks so tightly between her hands his lips puckered.

"Good." She smiled at him then, his face still between her hands. "Spanking good to see you, kiddo!" she said before giving him a smacking kiss. She let go of his face, and he stumbled back, shocked at her words. Hope was starting to flourish in his heart, and he felt like he was waking up from an extensive nightmare. He blinked a few times, letting her words settle inside him, wondering if it was actually possible to have the family of his heart back in his life. Johanna turned towards Annika. "Hello, Sweetie," she beamed, giving her a hug. Annika looked at him over her mother's shoulder and burst into laughter again.

"You should see your face," she gasped between laughs. "You look like you think she's going to turn back and sting you at any moment. That was the funniest thing I've ever seen." Her laughter was infectious. He smiled, loving that his scolding had brought her delight.

"Logan," Jansen said, holding out his hand, sobering him instantly.

"Sir," Logan answered, shaking his hand. Then he was swept up in one of Jansen's trademark bear hugs.

"You are a sight for sore eyes. Welcome home, son."

"Thank you." Logan felt the burn of unshed tears. He would not embarrass himself in front of the Northrups, but he was incredibly grateful to see them again. And to know that they still thought of him as family was a gift he would cherish, even as a tiny niggle of trepidation tugged at the back of his mind.

Jansen turned to his wife. "Excellent use of imaginative curse words, love." This set Annika off into another laughing fit which warmed the coldest places inside him more than any fire could.

"Thank you, dear." Johanna always had a special way of using the English language. Perhaps that's where her daughter got her love of the written word. "What happened to your head, Sweetie?" Johanna asked, brushing Annika's hair away from her temple to see more of the ugly bruise that had turned a multitude of colors.

"Umm," she stammered, wincing when Johanna probed it with her fingers.

"She fell off the bluff." Logan shot her a look with an arched eyebrow trying to stifle his own amusement. It was her turn to be in the hot seat. Annika glared back.

"What?"

"The ground gave way under me. It's not like I did it on purpose," she reasoned.

"But you know enough not to go too close to the edge," Jansen scolded. "What were you doing there?"

"Apparently, there was a dog," Logan informed them as he watched Annika's ire flare in her eyes.

Johanna threw up her hands. "Of course, there was."

"He was tangled in the bushes. What was I supposed to do? Let him die? It was snowing," she argued.

"Are you okay?" Johanna asked with concern.

"Don't I look okay?"

"She was hypothermic and has a concussion. But otherwise, she's fine," Logan told them.

"How did you get back up?" Jansen wondered. "The path up to the house collapsed last year."

"I don't know." Of course, that confused them even more, so Jansen asked for clarification.

"She was unconscious," Logan supplied.

"Seriously?" Johanna wailed.

"I had to climb down to her."

"You saved my girl again?" Jansen asked. That stopped Logan in his tracks, his amusement at Annika's turn being reprimanded fading.

Johanna gave a cry and threw her arms around Logan. She kissed him on both cheeks before letting him go. "You are a blessing, kiddo." His face suddenly felt heated. He didn't think there had ever been a time when he'd ever blushed.

Annika took his hand, leaned against his shoulder, and looked up at him with doe eyes. "My hero," she quipped, with exaggerated, fluttering eyelashes.

His heart constricted, and his throat closed up. He'd never considered himself very heroic, despite the countless successful SEAL missions he'd completed. It was his job. He was not trying for heroism. Because of his failure to save his friend, he had never accepted his actions as anything other than a job. But now, the Northrups were all looking at him as if he hung the stars. He didn't know how to deal with that and had to fight against the sting of tears that threatened.

"Johanna?" Jansen asked. They all turned to see her crying.

She waved them off. "Pay no mind to me. It just does my heart good to see you two together again."

"Mom," Annika started.

"Just ignore me, Sweetie." She sniffed. Then, "Oh look, Jansen. They got a tree!"

Annika and Logan laughed at her sudden change in mood. Never a dull moment when Johanna was around.

Later while the girls made dinner, Jansen pulled Logan aside. "How is she really? Was she badly hurt?"

"I ... she snuck out when I was asleep. We hadn't really talked yet, so she was avoiding me. I watched for her to return, but it was taking so long. When the snow picked up, I just knew something must have happened."

"But you found her. You saved her."

"She was half in the water when I found her. If I'd waited any longer to look for her, she might have drowned."

"But she didn't."

"I know, but she could have."

"But she didn't!" Jansen insisted. "Because of you."

"She was so cold. Even after I got her up, she was still in danger."

"Did she go to the hospital?"

Logan looked down. He probably should have taken her to the hospital. He hoped Jansen would understand. "No."

"Good. She's had enough of hospitals."

"I figured the ambulances wouldn't have been able to get to us with all the snow. I've had experience with hypothermic victims. I knew the best way to warm her."

"Body heat."

Logan blushed again. What was wrong with him? "Yes."

"Good. Learn all that in the SEALs?"

"Some of it. Some with the organization I'm working for now. They trained me to be a paramedic."

"What organization is that?"

Annika walked over to them then. "He's a Nighthawk, Daddy."

"Really?" Annika nodded. "Well, once a hero, always a hero. Damn proud of you, son." He slapped Logan on the back, which surprisingly almost sent him to the floor. Annika giggled at him again.

He glared at her. "Would you stop giggling at me!" That made her laugh harder. He lunged for her and dug his fingers into her sides, where he knew she was most ticklish. She laughed until she couldn't breathe.

"All right. All right! Uncle!" she wheezed. "I'll stop laughing at you!"

"Good." They lost themselves in each other's eyes, forgetting they had an audience. Annika was still in his arms when they heard a throat clearing.

"Come on, you two," Johanna said with happy tears in her eyes. "Dinner's ready." She turned away but not before he saw her wipe a tear away.

"Mom," Annika crooned, going to her mother.

Johanna waved her away again. "Just sit. Eat." Jansen went to her instead and put an arm around her shoulders. He squeezed her and gave her a quick kiss on the head before taking his seat.

"Smells good, ladies." Jansen dug into the first dish. They'd made a chicken and broccoli dish with plenty of cheese, just the way Logan liked. The first bite was like coming home. He hadn't realized how much he'd missed Mama Jo's cooking, how much he'd missed this. Sitting around a dinner table talking about the day. With family.

When they finished eating, Johanna raised her glass. The rest of them followed suit. "To my warrior children. Together again at last!"

"To family," Logan added.

"Hear! Hear!" Jansen shouted as they clinked glasses. They spent another hour at the table talking. Catching up. Reminiscing. Then a flicker of light caught Logan's eye outside. He bolted to the front door before the rest of the family knew what he was doing. Ripping open the door, he found his truck on fire.

"Shit! Call nine-one-one!" He called to no one in particular, then dashed to the pantry to grab the fire extinguisher. He sprayed his truck until the damn thing ran out. Then he grabbed the shovel he'd left on the porch yesterday and started shoveling snow on top of it.

"Shit," he swore again, remembering he'd left the supplies Graham had just given him in the back. He started to climb into the bed of the truck, but Annika grabbed him.

"Logan! No!"

"It's fine. I've got to grab my pack!"

"Logan!" It was the panic he heard in her voice that stopped him. "Please," she begged. He looked into her eyes and saw her fear. He hadn't thought. He'd only reacted. Car fire. Of course, Annika would be scared for him.

He hopped down and gathered her into his arms, backing them both a safe distance away as the sirens grew closer. He held her as the fire engine arrived, and they got to work dousing the flames. He held her until Deputy Ian McClintock walked over to get their statement.

"Ian," Logan shook the deputy's hand. They'd worked a few jobs together, so they knew each other pretty well.

"Sorry about this, Logan. She looked like a damn fine truck."

"It's just stuff," he said, reaching for Annika's hand. He introduced Annika and her parents to Ian and told him everything he knew.

"Heard you had an issue with Petersen last night. Think he's capable of something like this?" Ian asked.

"Christ, I hope not. Maybe if he was drunk enough, but I'm not pointing fingers. The guy has been through enough. So has his daughter. The last thing she needs right now is to watch her daddy be thrown in jail."

"All right. I'll discretely look into him and find out his whereabouts for tonight."

"Thanks, man," Logan said, shaking his hand again. When the deputy left, Logan called Graham.

"Got a problem," he began.

"What's up," Graham asked.

"Someone torched my truck tonight."

"You call Ian?"

"Yeah, he just left."

"Think it's Petersen?"

Logan sighed. "I don't know what to think. Ian is going to poke around a bit."

"Good. I'll step up the security around here. You take care of yourself and that girl of yours. Natalie really liked her. She even Googled her. I'm sorry for what she went through."

"Thanks."

"What," he said to someone Logan couldn't hear. "Natalie wants to have you two over for dinner. Let her know when you're available."

"Will do. Tell her thanks."

"Sure thing. And Logan ... watch your six."

"Copy that." Logan hung up with Graham and went to join the Northrups at the table again. They had taken a tub of ice cream out of the freezer and were eating it directly from the carton. Annika handed him a spoon, and he dug in, feeling overwhelmed with memories of the three of them doing this exact thing in this exact spot that last summer before the accident.

"I know what you're thinking," Annika said to him. "But remember ... It's a happy memory."

He reached over and squeezed her hand. "You're right. It is."

"What is?" Johanna asked.

"The three of us did this all the time that summer we spent here. Logan always took the biggest spoonfuls," she teased.

"Nuh-uh. That was Jamie!" he insisted.

"Sure, it was," she replied, her voice dripping with sarcasm.

"I swear! Cross my heart." He drew an x across his heart, and Annika giggled.

"Look!" she accused. "Look right there. Look at the size of that spoonful! Save some for the rest of us!"

"You're right, Sunfire. I should share." He took a finger full of ice cream and bopped her on the nose with it, leaving a dollop to drip off the tip of her nose. He laughed at the shocked expression on her face.

"Ooh. I'll get you for that."

"Sure, you will," he taunted.

"When you least expect it!" she promised.

"You forget. I was a SEAL. You'll never be able to sneak up on me."

"We shall see," she quipped as she wiped the ice cream off her nose. He couldn't resist that pout. He leaned over and kissed her solidly on the lips. They both froze, then looked across the table at her parents.

"I told you so," Johanna said to Jansen, who pulled out his wallet and handed his wife a twenty.

"Mom!" Annika cried in shock.

"What, Sweetie?" she replied, all innocence as she tucked the twenty inside her shirt.

"Jeez!" moaned Annika mortified. Jansen and Logan burst into laughter.

Chapter 12

THE FOLLOWING DAY, AFTER a late brunch, the girls decided to go Christmas shopping, leaving the men to fend for themselves. They all agreed to meet up at Jolene's for dinner. Johanna and Annika were in downtown Lake Haven searching all the cute mom-and-pop shops and boutiques for the perfect gifts. Each shop was an homage to the word haven, and Annika loved the uniqueness of it. There was Hydration Haven, a juice bar, and a stationary store called Haven Notation.

In the summer, when Lake Haven became a tourist hot spot, more shops opened up. Incantation Haven, the local psychic, set up a tent on one corner. Ovation Haven, the local theater, put on shows to entertain both children and adults. Annika had always loved visiting while growing up. She and Johanna couldn't wait to hit the shops each summer to see what new things the residents of Lake Haven had come up with.

Finished with the shops on one side of the cobblestone street, mother and daughter enjoyed a cup of winter blend coffee at the corner café, Brew-tiful Haven. The subject, of course, turned to the budding relationship between Annika and Logan. Annika was surprised her mother waited as long as she did to drill her daughter.

"Are you happy, Sweetie?" Johanna asked.

"Yes, Mom. You know I've wanted this for a long time."

"I know. You've had this image of the two of you in your mind for so long. Just be careful not to let the reality of a relationship become a disappointment compared to the dream."

"Don't worry, Mom."

"I'm your mother. I will always worry about you," she teased. Taking a sip of her coffee, she was pensive. "Have you told him everything?"

Annika stared into her coffee; it was easier than seeing the judgmental look in her mother's eyes. "Not every-thing. No"

"Annika."

"He'll just blame himself the way he has for every-thing else," she reasoned. Johanna reached across the little table and grabbed her daughter's wrist, running her thumb along the scar there.

"What if he sees these? Won't that just make things worse? You can't build a solid foundation with him unless you are honest with each other. Don't keep secrets. He needs to know everything that happened." Annika knew her mother was right but had no idea how to start that conversation with him.

Annika looked out of the window at a little family that was making their way down the sidewalk. The dad had one child on his shoulders while the mom was holding the other child's hand. They were laughing. It was such an idyllic scene. One that Annika had always imagined she'd have. She was thirty-three years old. She should have been married and had two point four kids by now. At least that had been the plan when she'd imagined her future as a teenager. Of course, Logan was always at the center of that plan. She never imagined how off-kilter it would get.

She was so close to getting all that she'd dreamed of having. If she confessed to Logan how bad things had been for her after he left, would it ruin the delicate trust they were trying to build with each other? But if she didn't tell him and he found out anyway, what then? Would he hate her for not telling him herself? How does one even begin a conversation like that? 'Hey, remember after my twin died and you disappeared on me? Well, I couldn't live with the pain anymore, so ...'

Annika knew deep down in her heart that Logan would blame himself. He always carried everything on his shoulders, even as a young boy. He blamed himself for every bad thing that ever happened, including his mother's drug addiction. And especially her overdose. He always thought that if he had gone directly home after school instead of fooling around with Annika and Jamie, maybe he could have gotten her help more quickly. It didn't matter that the coroner had put her time of death during the morning hours when they were in school.

"I don't know how to tell him," Annika finally confessed. "It's still too painful to talk about."

Johanna squeezed her hand. "I know it is, Sweetie. But it might be cathartic for you ... for both of you if everything was out in the open."

"Maybe."

"Just promise me you'll think about it."

"I will," Annika vowed. The two women finished their coffee and resumed their shopping. They were done in time to meet the men for dinner. As they made their way down the block to Jolene's, Annika spotted the little family again and felt a pang for what could have been had things not fallen apart after Jamie's death.

Jolene's was busy, but the Nighthawk crew had still managed to get their usual tables pushed together. Natalie introduced them to her father and Graham's parents. Natalie's father was moving back to the area after having lived in Florida for many years. Annika saw her father was getting along very well with the two older men, and Johanna was deep in conversation with Graham's mom, Mary. It was such a warm scene, a group of new and old friends treasuring the joy of the season together.

But Annika couldn't get her conversation with her mother out of her head. It was having a dampening effect on sharing in the boisterous mood of the group. Logan, who was sitting beside her, sensed her melancholy. He placed his arm around her shoulders and leaned in close to whisper in her ear. "You okay?"

"Of course," she lied. "Just a little tired, I guess. Shopping sure took it out of me. I'll feel much better after one of Jolene's burgers."

"I've been looking forward to one all day."

"Logan, you never did tell us the other night." Finch unknowingly gave Annika a reprieve from having to explain her depressed mood. "How *did* you get Annika back up the bluff by yourself?"

"I tied her to my back." He answered simply as if the feat was a normal everyday occurrence.

"Fuck, man. Are you even human?"

"I assure you, Finch, I am just a regular human."

"No, you're not!" insisted their teammate, Jude, who sat across from them. "You are a SEAL, a frogman, not even remotely human. But frankly, I'm surprised your skinny little frog's legs could make that climb." Logan threw a bread roll at Jude, which he caught easily, laughing.

"Shit, man," Finch said. "Can we let go of the Army versus Navy battle for one fucking night?"

"Not likely," Tin Man answered. "Go Army."

"You're delusional. Everyone knows the Navy is far superior," Logan threw back.

"You're both wrong. The Air Force puts both your measly military branches to shame." At that comment, Finch found himself dodging several items that went flying his way.

Everyone was distracted for a moment by the delivery of their food. Annika didn't waste any time and dug right in. Jolene's burger always did wonders to lift her mood.

"You'll have to show all of us the contraption you rigged up," David said, bringing the conversation back to her rescue. "That might be a useful skill to have someday."

"Oh my God, the whole story sounds so romantic," Jolene swooned.

"You think everything is romantic, Jolene," Emma quipped.

"Now you know why the guy who plays superheroes on the big screen wants to make a movie about our superhuman guys," Natalie remarked. There was another audible groan from Graham at the mention of the movie, resulting in the entire table erupting into laughter.

But then Finch and Jude stood so suddenly, the rest of the table stared at them in shock until a voice came from behind Annika. "How can you all sit here and celebrate while my wife lays cold in her grave?"

Logan stood to face Mr. Petersen. "Again, sir. We are sorry for your loss. But I think it would be best if you went home. You've obviously had too much to drink."

"Why, so you can go home and fuck, not giving a thought to your guilt?" he spewed at them with such hatred, it stunned Annika just as much as it had the last time he'd confronted them. It was then she noticed the wide-eyed little girl standing behind him. The child looked about seven years old, her long blonde hair in desperate need of brushing.

Annika stood and brushed past Mr. Petersen to get to the little girl, her goal to get her out of earshot. She didn't need to hear her father like that. "Hi, Sweetie," she said, crouching down till she was eye level with her. "My name's Annika. What's yours?"

"Rachel," she said shyly.

"That's a pretty name."

"Yours is too."

"That's nice of you to say." Annika took the little girl's hand. "How 'bout we go find something to play on the jukebox while your daddy talks to my friends. I bet we can even talk Miss Jolene into giving us a few coins to feed the machine."

"Absolutely!" Jolene affirmed, taking the girl's other hand. Natalie also joined them.

"What kind of music do you like?" Annika asked the girl when they reached the jukebox. "This has a lot of

Christmas songs in it right now. Do you have a favorite?" From the corner of her eye, she could see Mr. Petersen gesticulating angrily and she worried he could possibly pull his gun on them. With her heart in her throat, she watched as Logan stood with his hands up in front of him in an attempt to defuse the out-of-control man. "My favorite when I was your age was Rudolph," she remarked, trying put her worries for Logan aside and focus on the girl.

"I like 'The First Noel,'" she answered.

"Oh, that's such a pretty one. Shall we see if we can find it in here?" Natalie pulled over an empty chair and had Rachel climb up so she could better see the labels while Jolene took a handful of coins out of the cash register behind the bar. She handed the coins to Annika while she took her phone out of her pocket.

"I'm calling her grandparents," she explained. "They'll come for her."

"Good idea," Natalie replied.

Annika turned her attention back to Rachel. "Do you know how to spell Noel?"

"N-O-E-L."

"Perfect! So, let's see if we can see that word anywhere in here." She leaned closer to the machine but could still see the men arguing. She felt some relief seeing Graham and some of the other Nighthawks were now standing beside Logan, forming a united front.

Rachel hopped up excitedly and pointed to a label, her finger pressed to the glass. "There!"

Annika looked in the direction her finger was pointing. "Yay! There it is. Want to play it?"

She nodded. Annika handed her the coins to put into the slot then showed her how to punch the correct buttons for the song. "We get to pick out two more songs. What should we choose?" Annika asked just as Mr. Petersen took a swipe at Logan, who dodged the blow with ease. There was an audible gasp from the entire bar while her heart lodged itself in her throat. Rachel was about to look over her shoulder when Annika cried, "Ooh, how about this one?" she croaked, pointing to a random song to distract Rachel. She didn't need to see her father being restrained by Finch and Jude.

"That one is nice. But let's do Rudolph since that was your favorite," Rachel told her.

"Aren't you sweet," Annika said, running a shaky hand down the back of her hair. She couldn't help but notice how unkempt the girl looked and felt a pang of sympathy for her.

They chose their third song just as the men escorted Rachel's father out the front door allowing Annika to release the breath she didn't realize she'd been holding. "I need help eating the rest of my fries, Rachel. Wanna come to our table and help me?" Rachel nodded. Annika had Rachel sit next to her after they returned to the tables, and together, they nibbled on her fries.

"Where did my daddy go?" she asked, looking around for him.

"He had to go do something. But don't worry, your grandparents are coming to pick you up," Jolene reassured the little girl. "You can hang with us until they get here."

Annika dug in her purse for her brush and some hair ties. "I love your hair, Rachel. I used to play with my friend's hair all the time when I was growing up. My favorite thing to do was braids. I had this one friend who had hair as long as yours. She always let me put it in braids for her. Can I do yours?"

Rachel's face lit up. "Okay!" Annika's heart contracted for the girl. She must miss her mother very much. Starting at the bottom, where the worst of the knots were located, Annika ran the brush through the long blonde strands, managing to brush it to a gleam. It needed a good wash, but the braids would have to do for now.

"What did you do today," Annika asked as she divided the hair in half and started to do a French braid on one side of her head.

"Daddy took me to the beach!" she answered excitedly. "He let me play hoopy from school."

"Hooky," Annika corrected.

"That's right. Hooky. That's when you miss school for a day even though you're not sick."

"Yup. You're lucky. I never got the chance to do that when I was your age," Annika told her, starting the braid on the other side. "Was it a fun day with your daddy?" she asked, hoping it was everything the girl needed.

"It was awesome!" Then her shoulders dropped as sadness weighed her down. "It's been a while since Daddy and I had any fun together."

"How lucky you are that you had today then. I bet you'll remember this day for a long time." When she had finished, Jolene produced a mirror so the girl could see her handiwork.

"It's so pretty!" she squealed, turning her head from side to side to see it better.

"I'm so glad you like it." Annika watched the smile fade to sadness as she gazed at her image. "Can I tell you a story?" Annika asked, desperate to cheer her up.

"Okay." Her tiny voice made Annika's heart squeeze in sympathy.

"I read about these guys in a book once. There were three of them. Their names were Ickle-me, Pickle-me, and Tickle-me-too. Aren't those silly names?"

"Those were their names?" she asked in disbelief.

Annika nodded. "Wanna know what they did together?" Rachel nodded, and Annika recited the Shel Silverstein poem.

"They went for a ride in a flying shoe?" Rachel laughed. "I wish I had one of those."

"Me too. It would be fun to fly in a shoe, don't you think?"

Rachel wrinkled up her nose. "Unless it was a stinky shoe."

Annika laughed, wrinkling up her own nose. "You're right. I hadn't thought of that. We'll just have to find a brand-new shoe to fly off in. One that hasn't had feet in it to stink it up," she reasoned, tweaking the girl's nose. She giggled, and Annika's heart felt lighter.

Jolene pointed behind Rachel. "Look, Rachel. Your grandparents are here." An older couple was walking toward them, obvious worry etched into their faces.

Rachel jumped up and ran to them. "Look, Nona. Look what Annika did with my hair! Isn't it pretty?"

"It's lovely," the grandmother replied.

Rachel's grandfather scooped her up into his arms. "Who is this pretty young lady? Can this possibly be my little Rachel-bean?" Rachel giggled and squeezed her grandfather around the neck. The trio walked over to Jolene. "Thank you for calling us."

"Of course," Jolene replied, as Rachel squirmed to be let down.

She grabbed her Nona's hand, dragging her to the jukebox while talking excitedly about the songs they chose.

The grandfather sighed sadly. "We've tried everything we can think of to get Rob to stop drinking. Carlie's death hit him pretty hard. But he can't continue to neglect his daughter. I filed papers yesterday to get temporary custody of Rachel."

"That's probably for the best," said Jolene in sympathy.

"She doesn't need to watch her father implode," Natalie remarked. "That's something no child would ever be able to recover from."

"Thanks for distracting her from Rob. You're right; she doesn't need to see him implode."

Jolene pulled Annika to her side. "That was all Annika's doing. She shoved right past Rob before any of us even noticed Rachel standing there."

He held out his hand to Annika, who took it in hers. "Thank you."

"She's a very sweet girl. I'm very sorry for your loss." He nodded.

"Ready to go, Poppa?" Rachel ran to Annika and threw herself into her arms. "Thank you, Annika. I love my hair!

I hope I can see you again sometime," she said hopefully. "And maybe you could tell me more stories like Ickle-me, Pickle-me, and … I've forgotten the last one."

"Tickle-me-too," Annika said, tickling the girl under her chin, eliciting those sweet giggles only children are capable of. "Next time I see you, I'll bring the book. We can read it together."

"Yay!"

"Merry Christmas!" she called after handing the girl off to her grandfather with sudden tears in her eyes. Johanna came to stand beside her and linked her arm with Annika's.

"You have a heart of gold, Sweetie." Johanna beamed at her.

"Are you sure you're not an elementary school teacher?" Natalie asked.

Annika laughed. "Nah. I just like books. She looked so sad I thought the poem might cheer her up."

Logan put an arm around her shoulder. "You'll soon learn that Annika is an unlimited fount of literary quotes. She's got a quote for every occasion."

"'There's not a word yet, for old friends who've just met,'" Annika quoted.

"That sounds like something Fred Rogers would have said," Natalie remarked.

"Close. Jim Henson," Annika answered.

Logan squeezed her shoulder. "Smart man."

"That little girl is going to have a hard road ahead of her," Mary Whitaker, Graham's mother, said sadly.

"She won't be traveling it alone. She's got us now," Natalie promised.

After that, the group seemed to be stuck in a melancholy mood. Annika had noticed the instruments on the little stage earlier. "Can anyone play any of those instruments up there?"

"The band that usually plays here is over there," said Jolene pointing to the corner where a group of ladies sat. "Let me see if they'd be willing to play something."

"What do you say to a little freeform karaoke?" Annika asked the group.

Natalie was all for it. "That sounds like fun!"

The band was only too happy to play. "Who's first?" asked the lead singer.

"I'll go if there is a guitar I could borrow," Logan offered.

Annika was stunned. "You play guitar?"

"Little bit. A buddy of mine from the teams taught me some."

"Have at it," one of the band members said, handing him a guitar. They worked together to turn everything on, amps, mikes, and whatever else the instruments needed. Logan strummed a few bars to get a feel for the guitar. Then started to play a few chords before breaking into the chorus of Foreigner's 'Juke Box Hero' making everyone in the restaurant burst into laughter.

"Very funny," Annika groaned, causing more laughter. Logan then leaned over the keyboard to whisper a song suggestion to the band.

Annika was left breathless when he began to sing 'I Wanna Know What Love Is,' another song by Foreigner. She was immediately taken back to high school when the three of them went to see Foreigner in concert. The same concert the t-shirt she slept in came from. She'd heard Logan sing along at the concert but never like this.

His voice swept over her, drifting helplessly on the notes of the song, carried away by the cadence. His soft baritone cradled her, gently rocking all worries away. She let the melody surround her, allowing it to enter her heart, a heart that had been frozen for too long. Each pluck of the guitar's strings also plucked her heartstrings, the vibrations shattering more ice.

Looking around, she could see the effects of the music on the crowd. His song transformed the surroundings. Sadness lifted. Anxieties eased. Anger doused. Souls relaxed as the melody glided like magic.

When the last note was played, the entire restaurant erupted with applause. Annika grinned at Logan when their eyes met. After staring stupidly at each other for too long, he winked then turned to hand the guitar back to the band member. She was still smiling as she watched him strut over to join her. And that's exactly what it was—a strut. He was a man with a destination in mind, confident in his body. Annika could see the members of the band over his shoulder, each one of them watching his ass as he strutted her way. Upon reaching her, he swept her into his arms and treated her to an intense kiss.

Her smile grew to epic proportions after he released her, and she saw the envy in the women on the stage. Logan gazed at her, the gold flecks in his eyes shining. He cupped her face, sweeping his thumb across her lips. "That smile, Sunfire. It does things to me."

"Your music does things to me," she countered, placing a kiss on his jawline. He released a growl before gathering her closer and burying his face in her neck.

"Fuck, Annika. You make me want to find a secluded corner to ravage you," he breathed into her ear, sending goosebumps skittering down her body.

She giggled. "Later," she promised, then blushed when she caught a glimpse of her parents over his shoulder. Johanna was grinning like the Cheshire cat. Thankfully, Jensen hadn't witnessed their public display of affection as he chatted with the other men.

"I'm gonna hold you to that." He pressed his cock against her before stepping back and covertly adjusting himself. Annika giggled again, and he glared at her.

His expression conveyed he was not amused by the mirth she tried to stifle behind her hand. As he sat, he grabbed that hand and pulled her down onto his lap. He held her firmly even as she struggled to go to her own seat. Wrapping his arms around her waist, he placed his chin on her shoulder. Seeing his grin, she relaxed into him to enjoy the next musical act.

Some of the guys jumped up to the stage and tried their version of Bon Jovi's 'Wanted: Dead or Alive.' It wasn't as good as Logan's solo, but they had a blast, and so did the audience. Natalie and Emma agreed to do a song with Annika. They chose 'I Need a Hero' by Bonnie Tyler in honor of the Nighthawks. It was so much fun and did exactly what she'd hoped it would. Everyone was in a jubilant mood as they wound things down and started to trickle out of the restaurant into the brisk night air.

Annika rode home with Logan, who drove her car. They followed her parents through town to the twisting road that would take them up the coast to the lake house. Logan took her hand and placed a kiss on her fingers. "Johanna's right. You do have a heart of gold." She smiled at him, suddenly feeling choked up. "But I about died when you went charging towards that man."

"I wasn't going for him," she argued.

"I know that now. I didn't know that little girl was behind him, so I had no idea what you intended. Scared me to death."

"Sorry, didn't mean to scare the big bad SEAL," she teased.

"Seriously, that was a really sweet thing you did for her."

"I feel sorry for her. I hope her grandparents get custody. They seemed like a really nice couple."

"Since the entire town saw what he did the other night and again tonight, I think their chances are pretty good," remarked Logan.

"By the way, that song?" She waved a hand in front of her face. "Whew! It did things to me that were so not appropriate in a bar full of people."

"Really?" he said, wiggling his eyebrows suggestively. "How 'bout you show me when we're alone?"

"But my parents..."

"Are clear on the other side of the house. I can be quiet if you can."

"You're on!" she replied as they pulled into the driveway behind her parents.

Chapter 13

"A RE YOU READY FOR this, Sunfire?" After three days of getting to know one another again, they were now outside of Grand Rapids at the cemetery. Annika grasped the car's door handle, willing her hand to pull it open. How hard could this be? She'd go to Suzanna's grave, say a few words, then leave. It sounded so easy when laid out like that, but inside there was a riot of emotions erupting, making simple tasks—like opening a car door—much more difficult.

"Yes." She pulled the door latch, thankful her muscles obeyed her command. *Okay, now get out of the car.*

"Do you want me to go with you?"

"Yes." But she was frozen to the seat, and the door was only open a crack as she stared out at the rows of headstones. Logan reached in the back seat and grabbed the bouquet of flowers they'd brought for Suzanna, then climbed out of the car. *See, if he can do it, why can't I?*

Because he's not about to face his biggest failure. She watched as he walked to her side and opened her door, the December chill sweeping through the interior. Reaching in, he grabbed her hand and helped her out of the car straight into his arms.

She distracted herself momentarily by taking him in. He wore dark jeans with a gray sweater that hugged his chest. She could just make out the tiny bird of the Nighthawk logo embroidered over his left pec. To ward off the chill, he was wearing what was quickly becoming her favorite accessory, a dark brown leather jacket. The worn leather matched his eyes and hair perfectly, making her wonder if that was coincidental. His sex appeal in that jacket sent a shiver up her spine every time she saw him in it.

She must have stood motionless for too long, staring at his chest when his warm fingers under her chin urged her to look up at him. She wished she could stay lost in his dark chestnut eyes, not letting the outside world intrude.

"You can do this, Sunfire. And you don't have to do it alone this time. I'm here." Yes, he was here, and she was no longer alone. She'd faced so much alone, but no more. He'd be by her side now.

She took a deep breath. "Okay. I'm ready." They walked hand in hand to Suzanna's grave site, reading the names and dates on the headstones as they passed. Finally, they came to a shiny new headstone. It was a light gray color with Suzanna's name etched into the marble. Below her name was her date of birth and death, far too little time between. Annika gasped as she read the quote on the marble.

Literature is the art of discovering something extraordinary about ordinary people and saying with ordinary words something extraordinary.
— Boris Pasternak

"What is it?" Logan asked when he saw the tears dropping from her eyes.

"That quote. I gave her that quote once. She loved books and words just as much as I. And she could write so splendidly about the simplest things. You wanted to crawl inside her words and spend some time there." She wiped a tear away. That was the best way she knew to describe Suzanna's genius when it came to writing. She hoped someday her parents would get her writing published; the words needed to be shared with the world.

"Okay, how do I do this?" She felt uncertain, at a loss as to what to say, and strangely nervous.

"Just talk. The words will come," he answered.

Annika let go of Logan's hand and kneeled in front of the headstone, ignoring the chill from the ground seeping in. She reached out and touched Suzanna's name in the cold marble. "I'm sorry, Suzanna. I wish I could have been better for you. I tried so hard to fight for you, but I guess God needed you more. I will miss your words. They fed my soul." She couldn't think of anything else to say, so she leaned closer and whispered, "Say hi to my brother for me."

She stood slowly with Logan's help. When he handed her the flowers, she bent to lay them in front of the marble.

"Miss Northrup?" She heard her name as she straightened and turned towards the voice. *Oh, God.* It was Suzanna's family. All of them. Mom, Dad, and her younger sister. She grabbed Logan's hand, not sure if she was ready for this conversation.

"Miss Northrup," Mrs. Hoffsteader said. "Your mother told us you'd be here today. We don't want to intrude, but we needed to see you."

"Of course. What can I do for you?" She used her best parent-teacher conference attitude but could hear the tremor in her voice.

"We've heard ... that is, some of the kids in the classroom that day told us ... that you never left her side."

Of all the things she thought Suzanna's parents had to say to her, this was certainly not one of them. "Yes, I ... I tried."

"You held her hand the entire time?" Mr. Hoffsteader then asked.

"I think so. Some moments are still a little blurry."

"They told us you held her as she ... died."

The sting of sudden tears struck, and Annika fought to keep them back. "Yes," she replied, then she burst. "I'm sorry. I tried. I really did. I tried so hard to get help for her. It just wasn't good enough. I'm so sorry." She squeezed her eyes closed and lowered her head, profound grief and guilt overwhelming her. Warm arms encircled her, on opening her eyes, she saw Mrs. Hoffsteader. The woman had wrapped her in a comforting mother's embrace, and Annika could do nothing but accept it.

"It was good enough," she whispered in Annika's ear. "My Suzanna had someone who loved her by her side when she passed. That's all we could have asked for. You must have been suffering so much with your own injuries, but you wouldn't leave her. They told us you even refused treatment until they had seen to Suzanna. You didn't have to do any of that, but you did. Your mother mentioned your heart of gold, and I, for one, am indebted to you for your care of my daughter with your golden heart." She stepped back and wiped her own tears away, then reached back to her husband, who handed her a small box.

"This was Suzanna's. We gave it to her on her sixteenth birthday. We want you to have it." She handed the box to Annika. Inside was a gold heart necklace carved with a beautifully intricate scrolling pattern.

She looked up at them, stunned. "I can't take this."

"You can, and you will. She would have wanted you to have it. She spoke of you so often and with so much joy. You are the one responsible for opening her up and allowing her to soar. We will forever be grateful for you."

Annika was at a loss for words. Just like Logan and his guilt, she had always assumed that Suzanna's family would blame her. Yet here they were offering a gift. Something that had belonged personally to their daughter. They had given their permission to forgive herself. She looked at the family through misty eyes at a loss for words. This was Suzanna's legacy. They had just given her a truly wonderful gift—their absolution. For the first time since Caleb had entered her classroom all those weeks ago, she felt like she could breathe. She hugged them then, all three of them.

"You're Macey, right?" Annika turned to the teenager, who looked so like Suzanna that it was remarkable.

"Yes," she said quietly.

"Suzanna told me all about you. She was excited that you would get to take my class next year."

Macey smiled. "She never told me that."

"She talked about you all the time. You play soccer, right? Suzanna used to brag about your wins. She was very proud of you."

Macey's eyes grew large. "Really?"

"Really. Have you ever read her poem, 'The Master'? That's about you."

"She wrote one of her poems about me?"

"Absolutely. You were the master on the soccer field. Read it again and look deeper between the lines. You'll see her standing on the sidelines cheering for you."

The girl's eyes filled with tears. Annika took her hand into her own. "I know it's hard right now. I lost my brother when I was Suzanna's age. He was my twin. We'd done everything together for eighteen years."

"I'm sorry. I didn't know that."

"It was hard. Grief can be overwhelming. 'You care so much you feel as though you will bleed to death with the pain of it,'" she quoted.

"I know that one," Macey said excitedly. "That's from *Harry Potter*, right?"

Annika smiled. "You got it. You are well on your way to being a literary genius." She winked, and Macey giggled. "I'm not going to say that the pain will go away. It never really does. I miss my brother every day, but he never really left me. He's always here with me. Sometimes if I'm really quiet, I can still hear him. And if you ever need to talk to someone who's gone through what you are going through, you can call me. Anytime. Okay? Give me your phone." Macey nodded and handed Annika her cell phone for her to enter her contact information.

Macey hugged her. "Are you coming back to school? To work, I mean."

"I don't know. Not for the rest of this school year. I haven't made a decision about the next. I'm sorry."

"Everyone'll miss you."

"That's very sweet of you to say," she said, surprised her voice was hoarse with emotion.

Annika saw Macey steal a glance at Logan, who was chatting with her parents. She felt bad she'd forgotten her manners and hadn't introduced him. Macey leaned closer to Annika and whispered, "Who's that?"

Smiling, Annika whispered back, "That's my boyfriend, Logan. Ever hear of the Nighthawks?"

"Aren't they the ones who rescued Marcus Rayne?"

"Yup. Logan's one of them. He was there that day."

Her eyes went wide in awe. "Seriously?"

"Seriously."

"Cool!"

"Macey," her mother called. "Ready to go?"

Macey gave Annika another hug. "Thanks, Miss Northrup."

"Anytime, Macey." The five of them walked to their cars together. It was a nice day. Even with the chill in the air, the sun was shining, warming her. Annika felt suddenly lighter.

"What are your plans for the rest of the day?" Mrs. Hoffsteader asked her when they reached the cars.

"I have to stop by the school. I need some things from my classroom." Unfortunately, she didn't have a choice. The things she needed were personal to her. She didn't want someone else going through those.

"Have you been back since ..."

"No." And she was dreading it.

"I'm sorry. Do you need help?" Annika was shocked she would offer. She didn't think anyone would want to see where their daughter was killed.

"Thank you, but I have Logan. You guys go out and enjoy the day."

"If you ever need anything, let us know." She gave Annika one final hug. "You are family to us now." Annika was too choked up to reply. They said their goodbyes as Logan held the car door open for her. She kissed him on the cheek before sitting.

Her principal, Scott Macrone, met her at the doors to the school when they arrived. He escorted them to her classroom. "Nobody's been inside except to clean it. Everything should be just as you left it."

"Thank you, Scott," she said as he unlocked her door.

"Come find me when you're done. I have some things to discuss with you."

"Sure. I shouldn't be too long."

He patted her shoulder. "Take all the time you need."

Facing the door she'd never thought she'd open again, she hesitated, her heart pounding in her chest. She reached for Logan's hand while she placed her other hand on the knob. It was like the car door all over again.

Just open the door, you big nimrod. Nothing can hurt you in there anymore.

Logan placed his hand over hers on the knob so that together they turned it. Everything was the same, except everything was different. Someone had indeed cleaned up. Desks were back in their neat rows. Papers and books cleaned up. Backpacks removed.

Annika moved to the little couch at the front of the room and peered over it, half expecting to still see the blood. "It looks like nothing even happened in here."

"This is the couch? Where were you?"

Annika inhaled deeply and let it out slowly. She moved around to the other side and stood in front of the couch that she had squeezed between her desk and the smart board's computer console. She pointed down at the floor. "Here. Strange that there's nothing left."

"I half expected to see something too. Fuck, Annika, I came so close to losing you," he whispered, staring at the floor. "I can't believe I let my own insecurities drive me away from you. I should have been here for you. If you had died, I might never have known. But I wonder if I would have felt it somehow. I've missed so much; it kills me. All the pain you went through over the years, I should have been there for you." The anguish in his eyes nearly unraveled the tight knot she was keeping on her emotions. It killed her to see him in so much pain.

"You're here for me now. That's what is important. Remember? We are letting go of our past mistakes."

He placed his palm against her cheek. "You're right. Sorry. Momentary weakness. Besides, this isn't about me. What do you need?"

"Just your company. I need to get a few things from my desk. Letters and cards and things that some of my students have given me over the years." She went behind her desk and started rummaging through the drawers looking for the folder where she kept all the personal letters she'd received. Finding it in the bottom drawer, she pulled it out and placed it on top of the desk. The inbox she kept on her desk for class assignments caught her eye. She stared at it, remembering. Suzanna had just turned in her latest writing assignment that day, which meant it was probably still in there.

Her hand trembled as she reached for the box. She was nearly frantic as she dug through the assignments, desperate to find Suzanna's. She flipped through the pages, not seeing it. In her haste, some of the pages fell to the floor. With a cry, Annika went to her knees to search, frantically looking for Suzanna's name.

"Sunfire? What's wrong?"

"It has to be here. Where is it? I need to find Suzanna's paper."

Logan was crouched down beside her. He grabbed her hands, forcing her to look at him. His image was watery, panic bringing her tears to the surface.

He held her gaze, squeezing her hands. She focused on the tiny gold flecks in his eyes. "Take a deep breath, Sunfire." She did as directed and took a shaky breath. Then more until she felt the tremors cease. Logan breathed with her, a steadying comfort in her chaos.

When she was once again calm, he wiped a tear from her cheek. "Good. Now, what do you need?"

"Suzanna's last assignment. It's in here somewhere. I need to find it."

Logan looked down at the scattered papers. He gathered a few, then handed her one. "Here it is."

She held it and started to read, unable to control the tremor in her hand again. She gasped, tears blurring her vision. "Oh my God!"

"What is it?" Logan asked, concern thick in his voice.

"Suzanna's last assignment. We were wrapping up a poetry unit. The assignment was to write a poem about the natural world. Suzanna chose the Aurora Borealis. It's beautiful." The words swam in front of her eyes as she tried reading through her tears.

She handed it to Logan with a sad smile. "Christ, you're right. She was a genius with words."

"She was so special. One of the most talented writers I've ever had the privilege of working with." Logan wrapped his arm around her shoulder, kissing her head. Together, they silently read Suzanna's astounding words again. With another kiss on her temple, Logan bent to gather the rest of the papers from the floor. Annika grabbed a few more things then shoved everything, including Suzanna's poem, into the bag she'd left near her desk. Pausing for a moment, she grabbed the rest of the assignments from her inbox; it was time to go. She took one last look before walking out the door with Logan by her side.

She met Scott outside his office. "Can you come with me for a minute? I have something I need to show you."

Curious, she followed him into the auditorium. It was full of people. As soon as they spotted her, they all stood and overwhelmed her with thunderous applause. Stunned, she turned to Scott. "What's all this?"

"All this is for you. Hold on, I'll explain in a minute. Have a seat." He pointed to the front row.

She looked at the seat, seeing her parents were nearby. Behind them and taking up several rows was the Nighthawk family. Then she started to notice the other people. The students who had been with her that day were all in the front. Other students were scattered throughout the audience with their parents. But not just current students, alumni were there as well, going back through her entire career. Overwhelmed, she clung to Logan's hand as she sat. Scott went to the podium, asking for everyone's attention.

"I'd like to thank everyone for coming out today. We are here to honor two of our own. One a dedicated teacher, the other a talented young student who was taken from us far too soon but who will live on in each and every one of us. Suzanna Hoffsteader was a wonderful friend to everyone, with an infectious personality. Let us bow our heads and observe a moment of silence for our fallen friend."

He paused for a moment as the attendees all silently prayed for Suzanna. Silent tears fell from Annika's eyes as she prayed. She was going to miss Suzanna terribly.

"Now, I think her friends, Amy, Tara, and Jen, would like to say something about Suzanna." Three girls stood and went to the podium. They took turns telling special stories about their lost friend. Stories of the ways that she was always there for them, her sunny personality and positive outlook, and her talent in writing. They each cried a little for her, which only showed how much Suzanna was loved. When they were done, they gave the Hoffsteaders hugs. Annika hoped that the three girls would take Macey under their wing and help her deal with her grief. While she could never replace Suzanna in their hearts, developing a friendship with her sister could go a long way toward healing for all of them.

After they found their seats, Scott went back to the podium to speak again. Annika jumped in her seat when he said her name. "Annika Northrup has been a teacher here for eleven years. Hiring her was the best decision we ever made. She has been a valuable asset from the beginning. From her ability to make every student into a Hemmingway or Fitzgerald, to her uncanny way of finding a literary quote for any occasion, Miss Northrup is the epitome of a dedicated teacher." There was more applause, startling Annika once more.

"When tragedy struck our school, Miss Northrup very nearly gave up her own life to save the lives of her students, placing herself in harm's way to protect them. And while we mourn the loss of one of our own, at the same time, we are grateful for Miss Northrup's strength and bravery."

There was more applause as Scott gestured for someone to come to the podium. It was Stephanie Willowby, a student she had her very first year of teaching, eleven years ago. She spoke of the joys and trials they had faced as a class as Annika muddled through that first year. And how she learned that words had power. A power she uses to this day as a journalist. After Stephanie, a few more former students were invited to speak. Even her mentor participated, a fellow teacher who had taken Annika under her wing that first year and showed her the ropes. Sally had retired two years ago but wanted to speak about the teacher with the unnatural habit of spouting great literary quotes.

"I may have been your mentor, teaching you the ins and outs around here, but it was *you* who taught *me*. I never imagined an old stick in the mud like me could learn something new, especially from a fresh out of college, little thing like you, who'd never had her own classroom before. But boy, was I wrong. You taught me that it was still possible to pass on our appreciation for the English language and great works of literature to our students. I'd never heard so many high school students spouting quotes from the great authors in the halls prior to your arrival. So, thank you, Miss Northrup, for bringing the joy of teaching back into my heart." Sally came over to hug Annika as the audience erupted in cheers again. Both women had tears in their eyes.

Scott stepped back to the podium as Sally returned to her seat. "Liam, Sam, can you come up?" Scott asked of the boys who'd helped her that day. *Oh, God.* How was she going to make it through more, especially if Liam and Sam were going to speak? Logan took her hand, and she was grateful for the added support.

Leave it to those two boys to have the whole place roaring with laughter as they shared stories of all the antics they tried to pull behind her back. They always wondered how she knew. Annika pointed at her eyes, then at them, and back at her eyes again. Back and forth a couple of times. She'd constantly done that when she had them in class, letting them know she always had her eyes on them. They gave her a sheepish look as if she'd caught them doing something naughty. Everyone laughed.

When the mirth died down, they turned serious, speaking of that horrible day. They spoke of how, even though she'd been hurt, she still managed to remain their teacher. "She taught us strength, resilience, psychology, and even a bit about medicine when she told us how to try to stop the bleeding. She even threw in a bit of literature for good measure. Once an English teacher, always an English teacher. But most of all, she taught us about bravery." It was so quiet in the auditorium Annika could hear the whoosh of the heat kicking on. The two boys had the attention of the entire audience.

"She taught us bravery in the way she protected us. Risking her own life to keep us safe," Sam said.

"She kept telling Caleb to only look at her. She kept his focus on herself, hoping to shield us," stated Liam. "Every time he'd look at us, she'd force his attention back to her."

"She taught us bravery in the way she was able to get him to put the gun down. Even though she was badly injured herself and must have been in a lot of pain, she listened to *his* pain. She helped him work through it. Kept him talking," Sam broke off then, a little emotional.

Liam took up the story. "She used her love of literature to teach him about love and forgiveness."

"She used her love of words to convince him to do the right thing and let us go," continued Sam, having collected himself.

"But beyond that, she taught us about love."

"It had to have been love because even though he'd done such a horrible thing, she still managed to connect with Caleb and get him to give her the gun."

Liam, his voice cracking a little, continued. "And it was love that kept her by our friend's side, holding her. Giving her the comfort of loving touch as she ... passed." He broke off, too overcome by emotions. He and Suzanna had briefly dated, and it was clear that even though they had no longer been together, he still had feelings for her.

"And it was love that had her forgoing her own medical treatment until Suzanna and the rest of us were taken care of." Sam turned to look at her. "Miss Northrup, we've heard it said about you before that you have a heart of gold. But it goes so much beyond that."

Liam had gathered himself and turned to her as well. "We know that you've taken Suzanna's death pretty hard. We all have. But you always taught us about the positives. You saved us. You saved fifteen lives that day."

"We all have a future because of you," Sam said as the rest of the class joined the boys at the front. "And because of the lessons you taught us that day, the future looks bright."

The auditorium exploded with applause as everyone rose to their feet. Annika, not even bothering to hide her tears anymore, went over and hugged the boys. Then hugged the rest of their classmates. Each one thanked her. Then, there was Macey, standing in for her sister. She gave Annika the longest hug.

Her emotions were overwhelming, leaving her unsure of how much more she could take. Logan came to her and helped her back to her seat, and she clung to his hand, welcoming the added support.

Scott was back at the podium, asking for everybody's attention again. "I know you've probably had enough,

Miss Northrup, but we have one more surprise. And this one is for the entire student body." He gestured to someone at the side of the stage, and the curtain opened to reveal a large movie screen. Clicking a few keys on the laptop in front of him, he brought up a video call. Marcus Rayne smiled out of the screen at them. The kids all hooted and hollered, but Annika was stunned as she listened to him speak.

"Hello, all," he greeted them. "Can everybody see me okay?" There were yeses and nods from the audience members. "Good. I'm sorry I can't be there in person, but as you probably all know, I've been pretty busy with the release of my current movie." He laughed then. "Sorry for the shameless plug. Anyway, my Nighthawk friends told me what you have all been through the last couple of months." Annika looked at Logan who shrugged, just as surprised as she was. "And I'm sorry for everything that has happened to your community.

"As many of you know, I recently got into a bit of trouble while on a hike. A group of brave men came to my rescue. I may play a hero on the big screen, but the Nighthawks are the real deal. True heroes. But then they told me about your teacher and what she did on that terrible day. Miss Northrup is the epitome of heroism, risking her own life to save the lives of her students. And while injured, no less. I'm sorry it even happened at all, but if I ever find myself in a situation like that, I'd want Miss Northrup at my back." The younger students in the audience all cheered.

"Now to the reason for this video chat, and again I'm sorry I couldn't be there in person to announce this, but I have a few surprises for Annandale High School. First, for the classmate and friend that you lost, I've started a non-profit organization in Suzanna's memory. Since I know that schools all across the country are struggling for funding, and most often, the funds they do get go toward improving their technology, I've decided that Suzanna's Books will raise funds to buy good old-fashioned books. Great books, classic books. The kind of books I hear your teacher likes to quote from." Annika blushed as the kids laughed.

"After all, there is nothing like holding a book in your hands and watching as the world created in the pages leaps to life. And the smell of a good book—my favorite." Again, more laughter.

"But I need a little help from you guys. I need a list of the best books you think every school in America needs. From elementary to high school. Put your heads together and get me that list. It doesn't matter how many books are on it. Your principal will give you all the details you need. Furthermore, every year Suzanna's Books will choose one deserving school district in the nation to get the Golden Heart award. It's a monetary award for the district to buy as many books as they can. The first recipient of this award is your very own Annandale school. Each school in your district will receive one hundred thousand dollars. So, choose your books wisely. And more importantly, keep reading!" Everyone was cheering and clapping, amazed that one of the biggest stars in Hollywood would care about their little school in Michigan.

Marcus paused, smiling until everyone had settled down again. "But wait, there's more," Marcus quipped. "In the spring, when the ground thaws, workers will begin construction of a new addition to your high school. Annika's Atrium will be a place for students to sit, relax and read." An image of a beautiful room popped up on the screen. It had floor to ceiling windows and greenery everywhere, as well as seating arrangements all around. It even looked like there was a little pond in the corner. It looked welcoming and comfortable. It would be the perfect place to take a class, a reading garden of sorts. In that atrium, imaginations could soar. And he'd named it after her. Annika was flabbergasted, too stunned to even react. She sat frozen, staring at the image on the screen as tears coursed down her cheeks and wondered why Marcus Rayne had chosen her. And the only conclusion she could come to was because of the Nighthawks. The greatest, most giving group of men and women Annika had ever met.

Marcus's image was back on the screen now. "That's about all I've got for you for now. So, get me that list of books. And remember to keep reading and give your teachers the respect they deserve. After all, I bet Miss Northrup isn't the only teacher in this world who would risk her life for her students. Hey, maybe I should make a movie about that too someday," he joked, winking to the camera before the image went dark.

Scott went to the podium again. "I've taken the liberty of having something made a little early for our new addition." Two students walked to the front carrying a large plaque between them. A close-up image of the plaque showed up on the screen behind them. The words 'Annika's Atrium' were in large typeface in the middle. Below her name were two wonderful quotes by Tolkien.

"It is not the strength of the body that counts, but the strength of the spirit."

"Courage is found in unlikely places."

"A date will be added when we have one for the grand opening of Annika's Atrium. I hope you will all come back to help us celebrate on that day. Thank you all for coming. And thank you, Miss Northrup ... for everything," he said, his voice full of emotion. Annika suddenly grasped the weight her principal must have been feeling since the shooting. She got to her feet and gave him a big hug as the audience erupted in chants of "Speech. Speech."

"You don't have to say anything if you don't feel up to it," Scott told her. "But I think the kids would enjoy hearing what you have to say to all this."

Annika looked to Logan and her parents, all sporting big smiles and nodding. "I'd like to say a few words. Just let me grab something first." She went to the bag that she had put everything into and grabbed Suzanna's poem.

Standing at the podium, Annika waited for the audience to settle, hoping her nerves would settle with them.

There were so many people. So many familiar faces smiling up at her. That gave her the comfort she needed to begin. "I am beyond stunned by all of this. And ever so grateful. 'Even though I have a Very Small Heart, it holds a rather large amount of Gratitude.'"

"Ooh, I know that one!" shouted Sam. "That's from Winnie the Pooh, right?" Everyone laughed.

"That's right, Sam. Gold star for you." More laughter.

"My heart overflows with gratitude at the abundance of love you all have shown Suzanna, myself, and this school today. Thank you." She took a deep breath and began again. "When I was your age," she said, indicating the students from her class that day. "I lost my brother, my twin, in a car accident. There had been three people in that car that day, and the two that survived, myself and a friend, had been helpless to save him. I felt that same helplessness that day in the classroom. I've had a lot of time over the years since losing my brother to learn about grief. And of course, I turned to my books to help me. 'He who feels the deepest grief is best able to experience supreme happiness,'" she quoted.

Another voice in the audience called out. "'Count of Monte Cristo!'"

Annika smiled. "Another gold star." She paused for more laughter. "I've gone through many years of the deepest grief imaginable, but I've learned to find the supreme happiness in the littlest things. Like snowflakes melting on your face. A glorious sunrise. An evening spent with friends." Her gaze landed on her new Nighthawk family. "And of course, a good book. I've started paying attention more. Listening more. I know that my brother is with me ... always. I hear his voice whispering encouragement to me in the winds."

She held up the paper with Suzanna's poem on it. "Before coming in here, I went back into my classroom for the first time. It was just as we'd left it. Which included the latest homework assignments that were still in my inbox." She looked at the students in the front. "And don't think that just because I've been absent that I am not going to grade them all," she told them in her stern teacher voice.

"Oh crap," Sam called out. "I forgot to turn mine in. Can I email it to you, Miss Northrup?"

Annika sighed in exaggerated frustration. "'I might just as well have ordered a tree not to sway in the wind' as to ever get you to turn in an assignment on time."

"Who said that?" Sam asked.

"Part Joseph Conrad, part me," she answered as the audience laughed. "Now, will you stop interrupting me?"

"Sorry, Miss Northrup," he said, not seeming at all sorry. Annika realized how much she'd missed this—bantering with her students. They kept her on her toes.

"As I was saying. I found Suzanna's poem from that assignment. If it's okay with her parents, I'd like to read it to you now," she said, looking at the Hoffsteaders, who nodded. She read the poem to the quiet room, watching and listening as a sort of peace fell over everyone. Suzanna's words had that effect.

"For so long, I had been lost in my grief over my brother, and now in my grief for Suzanna, but after reading this ... Maybe Suzanna was letting me know that I could forgive myself for my perceived failures and let her go; she was going to be okay. So even in our darkest grief, there is always a little bit of light to give us hope. And looking down at all of your faces, I see that hope's light. Sam and Liam, you're right; the future does indeed look bright!"

Everybody cheered once more, and Annika took a moment to drink it all in. The hope for the future as she looked at all those faces. The hope for *her* future as she looked at Logan. For the first time in fifteen years, she found herself excited for what the future might bring her.

"So, thank you, Mr. Macrone, for this great honor. Thank you to my fellow coworkers who came back to this building to ensure our students had that bright future. Thank you to all my students, past and present. Seeing you all here, this is why we teachers do what we do. Thank you to the Nighthawks, who I'm pretty sure had something to do with the Marcus Rayne stuff. Thanks to Marcus Rayne for his generosity. Thank you to my parents for your unwavering support through *everything*! And thanks to Logan Cain for bringing the light back into my life just when I needed it most." She smiled down at Logan, who gave her a wink.

Then she thought of one more thing. "Oh, and to the Hoffsteaders, if you don't get a book of Suzanna's poetry published, I will. The world needs her words!" The cheers and applause from the crowd were deafening. Annika hurried off the stage to the wings, where Logan met her, arms wide. She went directly into them, letting the rest of her tears fall. It had been an overwhelming day, but here in the dark wing of the stage in Logan's arms, she felt comfort.

Logan watched as Annika greeted her students, both past and present, feeling a tremendous pride for her. Each and every one of them greeted her with such love and respect, it spoke volumes for the type of teacher she was. She certainly had taught him a lot just in the last couple of weeks alone. But watching her as he was, he could see the lingering effects of the grief she still felt for Suzanna. It had been an exhaustingly gut-wrenching day for her, and Logan could see she was hanging on by a thread, putting on a brave face for everyone. To the casual observer, she looked to be full of joy, but Logan could see the fatigue beginning to envelop her.

Graham joined Logan in the corner where he was watching Annika and slapped him on the shoulder. "Hell of a woman you've got there."

"That she is," Logan replied.

"You seem so close. Did you two just meet when you rescued her from the bluff?"

"No, I've known her since grade school. I was the friend in the car accident that killed her brother," he confessed.

"Why haven't you brought her around before?"

Logan winced. "I hadn't seen her since the night of the accident," he answered sadly. He would always regret his actions from all those years ago.

"What did you do?"

"What makes you think it was something I did?" Logan asked in an attempt at humor while Graham looked askance at him as if to say *it's always us guys*. He sighed then confessed his greatest regret to his boss. "I ran away."

"Yeah, guys are pretty good at that. I ran because I was afraid of feeling too much too soon at too young an age. It was a mistake I'll regret forever. What was your excuse?" Graham and Natalie had shared a special day together when they were in high school. Having been neighbors for most of their lives, they had grown up together but had gone their separate ways in middle school, different interests dragging them in different directions. Then they watched as a tornado destroyed Graham's house that same day. Natalie helped Graham dig his brother out, not knowing her own sister had been terribly injured. Since his house had been leveled, Graham and his family moved in with his grandmother a few towns away. That was the last time he'd seen Natalie. Until two months ago when she came to him asking for his help in finding two of her students who'd gone missing. They had been apart for twelve years and had reconnected instantly.

"I ran because I thought I'd killed her brother."

Graham looked at him in surprise. "It was a car accident, wasn't it? Why would you think you'd killed him?"

"I was driving," Logan answered simply.

"Did you cause the accident?"

"No. A truck driver was drunk and crossed into our lane. He hit us, sending us down an embankment."

"Doesn't sound like you killed him to me."

"I couldn't get him out in time. There was a fire. I was trying to pull him out when the jeep exploded."

"Fuck, Logan. You are lucky you weren't killed as well. Where was Annika?" Graham looked across the room at her; she was still surrounded by her students, giving hugs and laughs, a ray of pure light in the room. Logan could hear in her laughter the uncanny ability to lighten his heart.

"I'd already pulled her out."

"You saved her?" Logan nodded. "And you think you killed her brother?" Again, Logan nodded. Graham shook his head. "You are more of a dumb fuck than I was."

"Grief makes you do stupid things."

Graham sighed. "I guess I can understand that." Natalie joined them, Graham pulling her close to his side.

"God, Logan," Natalie began. "Your Annika has been through so much. More than anybody should have to face in their life. But look at her." All three of them looked across the room at Annika. She was smiling the smile that made his heart skip a beat. "She looks full of joy! No offense, Graham, but she has to be the strongest person I've ever met."

"Just as strong as you," Graham complimented her.

"Sorry, but no. She's stronger."

"How did we get so lucky to have won the toughest ladies in the world, Logan?" Graham asked.

Logan shrugged. "Pure luck?"

"Nah," Natalie insisted. "Luck had nothing to do with it. It's all the doing of your clever ladies who've managed to teach you the error of your ways," she teased.

"That's it, exactly," Graham kissed her temple. "Thank you for helping me to see the light, Chickadee."

She blushed and batted him away. "So, I take it by the closeness I've seen that she's forgiven you for leaving?" Graham asked.

"Surprisingly, yes."

Graham tilted his head and shot a questioning look at Logan. "Have you forgiven yourself?"

"Not surprisingly, no. But I'm working on it."

"Good," Graham said, clapping him on the back. "Keep working on it. And don't let that one get away."

Logan gazed at her again and smiled. "Never."

Finally, Logan was able to get Annika out of the building. Macey stopped them right outside the front doors. "Miss Northrup!"

"Macey? What's wrong?" The girl looked out of breath.

"Can I see that poem? Suzanna's poem?" she asked.

Logan set the bag down for Annika. She bent to search for the paper. Finding it, she handed it to Macey, who read it quickly. "I don't think this is really about the Aurora at all," Macey remarked, reading it a second time.

"How so? That was the assignment. They had to write about something found in nature."

"Yes, I know. But Suzanna was clever," Macey said with a smile. "You told me her other poem, 'The Master,' was about me, right? I think this one is about you."

"Me?" squeaked Annika. "How do you figure?"

"Look here." Macey pointed to a line in the poem, then read, "'She shines so bright, leading all to her light.' And here. 'She opened the door, permitting my heart to soar.' And 'With the colors of her heart, her wisdom she does impart.' It's all you. Your light. You opened her soul. You taught her to open herself up. You taught her to write. She loved you. And she loved that you allowed her to be herself. Her true self."

Looking stunned, Annika took the poem back from Macey and read through it again. "How did I not notice that?" she wondered. "You're right, Macey, Suzanna was very clever." Annika hugged Macey and promised to email her the poem.

After they said more goodbyes, they made their way across the parking lot. It felt to him like he was practically carrying her to the car, she was that burned out. After she'd stumbled for the third time, he did just that. He swept her up into his arms and carried her the rest of the way. She put up a token protest, then settled into his arms and placed her head on his shoulder, yawning. Logan could hear the other Nighthawks laughing and joking as they made their way to their cars as well. He didn't care that he'd probably be teased for this; he was taking care of his love.

Logan held Annika's hand as they drove down I-196 back to the lake house. The other Nighthawks were not too far behind them. She was quiet, staring out her window. He didn't pressure her to talk about any of it, understanding she needed time to decompress. He'd be here for her if she wanted to talk.

Suddenly, Annika sat up straight. "Oh my God!" she shouted. "Stop the car, Logan! Pull over!"

Chapter 14

"WHAT?" THINKING SHE WAS ill, Logan braked immediately.

"Pull over! Now!" Her hand shot out and grasped his forearm, squeezing in desperation. Logan put on the hazard lights and pulled to the shoulder. Before he could put it in park, she shot out of the car.

"Annika, what ..." he tried to ask, but she was already racing back the way they'd come. Logan ran after her. She stopped when she reached an area with a steep drop-off. Logan looked down and saw what had caught her attention. A car had rolled down the embankment, resting on its slightly flattened roof. Annika started to go down to the car. "Annika, no, stop. It's too steep!"

"We need to get down there. I can hear a baby crying!" Logan heard it too, but they had to do this as safely as possible.

"Let me get my gear. We'll rope down to them. Okay?" He made her look at him. "Stay here. Call nine-one-one. I'll be right back." She nodded as he ran back to the car.

Feeling uncertain about allowing Annika to risk herself, he tried to steady his uneasiness as he adjusted the harness to fit her. By the time he'd gotten the harness on Annika, a few of the Nighthawks were pulling up behind them, jumping into action.

"I need another harness!" Logan yelled. He wasn't about to let Annika go down there by herself. Hell, he shouldn't let her go down there at all.

"Looks pretty unstable, Logan," Graham said as Logan attached the clamp to the rope.

"I know. Let me get down there to assess the situation. Then we'll figure out what to do."

"Sure you want her going down?"

"Try to stop her." He knew there would be no stopping her, especially with kids involved. Logan turned to Annika after checking the ropes and clamps for a third time, "Ready? You understand what you have to do?" She nodded. "Take it nice and easy and follow me down." Watching Annika closely and coaching her when needed, he half rappelled, half walked slowly down to the vehicle. But when they'd reached the car, he could see it was indeed very unstable.

The car had rolled a few times down the embankment and came to rest on its roof. Logan went around the hood to assess exactly how unstable the car was in its precarious position. Several young trees had stopped the vehicle from rolling and sliding any farther, but those could snap from the weight at any moment, causing the car to fall. The Nighthawks were going to have to figure out a way to stabilize the vehicle before they could even think about pulling the family out.

Annika had crouched down by the rear windows. "Hi, Sweetie," she said to whoever was inside. "We're going to get you out of there just as soon as we can."

"O ... Okay," came a tiny voice from inside. Logan glanced in the front seat spotting a man and a woman who were either unconscious or dead, deflated air bags hanging in front of them. There was a baby as well as a small child in the back. Graham had given him a radio which he used to relay information to the team.

Annika was on her hands and knees and about to climb through the window to the kids. "Annika, wait," he called, feeling his heart jump to his throat. "It's too unstable."

"We've got to get to those kids!"

"I know, and we will. Let me get the team down here. Let us do our thing."

She nodded but turned back to talk to the little girl. In no time, Graham, Evan, and Finch had rappelled down while the others stayed up top to get the ropes tied off. Jude's truck, thankfully, had a winch with a steel cable. Since the car was upside down, it was easy to attach the cable to the undercarriage. Then they tied some of their ropes to the car for added security. Logan and Graham were both paramedics and tried to assess the injuries, but the roof had been compressed too much for them to fit through the windows.

"We are going to have to wait for the jaws of life," Graham said.

"I can fit," Annika asserted.

Logan blanched. There was no way he was going to let her put herself in danger. Just the thought of her being at risk tied his gut into knots. "No, it's too dangerous."

"Logan." She placed a hand on his arm, her determination gleaming in her eyes. "I can do this. I have to do this. I have faith in the Nighthawks. You can pull me out if it gets too dangerous."

"I don't know …"

"Emma's not here, so it has to be me. Tell me what I need to do to assess the injuries."

Logan looked into her eyes and sighed, relenting against his better judgement. Time was of the essence; they needed to know what they were dealing with concerning the victims. Annika was the only one who could fit. "Fine. Crawl in there and I'll talk you through it."

She had wiggled halfway through the rear window before he'd even finished. "Hi again, Sweetie," she said to the young girl. "I'm just going to check on your parents real quick. Then we'll see what we can do for you and the baby. Okay?"

While relying on all his SEAL training to compartmentalize his fear for her, Logan told her how to check for a pulse. Both parents were still alive but could have massive internal injuries. Logan asked her to check for blood anywhere. He couldn't do anything at the moment for internal injuries, but if they were bleeding out, they could perhaps do something about that.

"They both have blood on their heads. Cuts on their faces and arms. Airbags seem to have done their job. Maybe some facial injuries from that. Dad looks like he might have a broken nose. Hold on; I'm going to try to climb into the front." He could hear her struggling to get over the seats, his gut tightening with apprehension when the car shuddered with her movement. The baby was still crying, and he hoped that was a good sign.

"Okay, the mom looks like she may have a broken arm or shoulder. Otherwise, no more blood. The dad ... his legs might be hurt. The steering column looks like it's trapping or crushing his legs. No blood oozing, only cuts and scrapes."

"Good, go back and check the kids."

"I'm back, Sweetie. My name is Annika; what's yours?"

"Megan," the tiny voice said.

"What's the baby's name?"

"Chloe."

"Such pretty names you both have. What are your parent's names?"

"Jen and Tom."

"Okay, I'm just going to feel around your arms and legs. See if anything is broken, okay? Does anything hurt?"

"My ... my tummy."

"Can you point to where exactly? Good. Logan," she called out to him, "nothing's broken, I think. She says her chest and stomach hurt."

"Is it near where the seat belt could have caught her?" he asked.

"Yes, that's possible."

"Okay. Check the baby now."

A few moments passed before she called out, "She seems fine but may also be bruised from the car seat harness."

"Okay, why don't you come back out for now? We're trying to figure out a way to get the doors opened." It would be ideal if the team could get them out sooner, but they needed a cutter. And he needed her out of danger.

"I'm good. You guys do what you need to do. I'm going to hang out with my new upside-down friends here for a bit." Logan gritted his jaw, frustrated with her stubbornness. He knew there was no way his Sunfire would leave those children, but that didn't mean he had to be happy about it.

Logan stayed next to the car, ready to pull Annika out at a moment's notice if needed. He knew he should probably help the rest of the team strategize, but he couldn't pull himself from Annika's side. If they had to, the two of them could get the kids out quickly. Hoping the car remained stable until the whole family could be extracted, he listened to Annika chatting with the little girl.

"Do you like being a big sister?"

"It's okay. She doesn't do much yet. Mommy says that will change."

"How old is Chloe?"

"She just had her first birthday."

"Oh, happy birthday, Sweetie." Annika's voice was having a calming effect on the baby; she was no longer screaming her head off. "I was a big sister too. My brother was only five minutes younger than me."

Annika laughed when Megan made a confused sound. "We were twins. I was born first, then him."

"Cool."

"How old are you, Megan?"

"Six."

"Did you start kindergarten yet?"

"Yes."

"How fun. Do you like it?"

"It's good," she answered simply. The girl sounded terrified. Annika was trying her best to take her mind off her fear, but it didn't sound like it was going so well.

"Do you like books?" Logan smiled; of course, she'd ask that. Annika's life *was* books.

"I don't know."

"I love books. Can I tell you about my favorite one?"

"O ... Okay."

"It's about a girl named Anne. She had red hair just like you. Do you like your red hair?"

"It's okay," Megan answered.

"I think it's beautiful. Anne didn't like her red hair too much. Her best friend, Diana, had black hair, and Anne wanted to have hair just like hers. One time, she bought some hair dye, but it wasn't a good kind of dye. It turned her hair green."

Megan laughed. "Mommy dyes her hair, but it never turned green."

"She's very lucky then. Anne had to cut her hair short in order to get all the green out. It was very tragic for her. She loved her long hair. It was probably about as long as yours. Are you sure your name isn't Anne?" Annika teased. "Whenever I read Anne's story, I always picture someone who looks exactly like you."

"Really? What else did Anne do in the story." Logan would never cease to be amazed by how she could capture a child's interest so easily just by talking about books. And it was even more remarkable to alleviate their fears at the same time.

"Well, she was only a little older than you when she was adopted by a brother and sister. They were much older. And neither had married or had kids of their own. They owned a farm, and they needed help. They wanted to adopt a boy to help with the chores on the farm, but there had been a mix-up, and they got Anne instead. It had been the best mistake for all of them."

"They became a family?"

"That's right. And they loved each other very much."

The team rejoined Logan, followed by the first responders who had finally arrived with the jaws of life. It was time to get the little family out of the vehicle. "Annika, we are ready to cut into the car. Can you see if you can get the baby out?"

"Okay. You hear that, Sweetie. My friends are going to get you out of here now. Let's take care of your sister first." After a few minutes, Annika's arms popped out the window holding the baby. Logan took her from Annika's arms and handed her to Graham, who climbed up the incline to the paramedics up top.

"Okay, Sunfire." Logan handed a blanket to Annika. "Spread that over the broken glass if you can. We don't want Megan to get any cuts on the glass." Once that was done with Logan helping as much as he could from outside the vehicle, he said, "Okay, Megan's turn."

"I can't get the seat belt off." Some of the saplings that were helping to hold up the car were starting to give way with loud cracking. Logan heard a tiny squeal of panic from the little girl and Annika's calm reassurance as the car trembled.

"Here. Take my knife." He handed her the same knife she'd given him all those years ago.

"Okay, Megan. Time to rejoin the world of the right side up people." After a moment, Logan heard the clatter of the knife falling as Annika caught Megan. "I've got you, Sweetie. Do you think you can crawl through the window? My friend Logan is out there, ready to take you up the hill. Okay?"

"Okay," squeaked the little girl as the car slipped again. Time was of the essence, and they needed to get the parents out now. And Logan really needed Annika safely out of that car.

A little red head popped out of the window. "Hi, Megan. I'm Logan. You doing okay?"

"Yes." She let him help her out of the window.

"My friend Graham here will take you up top while I help your parents."

"What about her?" Megan pointed to Annika still inside. His trepidation growing, he wondered why she hadn't climbed out right after the girl.

"I'll get her out too. Don't worry. Everyone will get out."

"Hop on." Graham indicated that she should get on his back, piggyback style. "And hold on tight." He climbed up the hill with the girl riding on his back, and the team started with the cutter on the driver's side.

Needing Annika out now, he crouched down to peer inside the car. She had his knife back in her hand and was hunched over the middle console between the two front seats, attempting to cut through the parents' seat belts. The car shuddered again. She froze for a moment and Logan could see the flash of fear in her eyes, but then continued to cut. His heart jumped into his throat; he needed her to get out of there. Now!

"Okay, Annika. That's enough. Time to get out of there!" He had to shout to be heard over the hydraulic sound of the jaws.

"No, I can get the mom too. Just another minute." Logan wasn't surprised she wouldn't come easily, but that didn't help ease the worried knot that she could get hurt. He heard her shifting to the other side of the car, which shook again as more branches cracked. Any movement was causing the vehicle to wobble.

The team had cut into the car enough that they were now working on getting the dad out. They had used another tool, a ram, to try to push the dashboard up enough to get the man's legs out. Graham handed a collar to Logan asking him to pass it to Annika to put on the mom. Logan called out and threw the collar to her. The quicker they could stabilize the parents in the car, the better. Logan understood that, but he wished it weren't Annika who was inside with them. Once the father was out, the car shifted again, and Annika cried out.

"Annika?" He lay flat on the ground to see inside the car, suddenly even more fearful for her.

"I'm fine." But the wobble in her voice worried Logan.

Graham called to her. "We're going to get the mom now. You can crawl out."

"Okay. Just a sec."

The team nearly had the mom out, and still no sign of Annika. The weight of the car was putting stress on the metal of the undercarriage the cable and ropes were attached to. His fear was they wouldn't hold, and the car would tumble down the embankment with Annika trapped inside. The accident that killed Jamie flashed from his memory, momentarily immobilizing him with dread.

"Annika, come on out now," Logan prompted again, desperate for her to be safely on solid ground.

"I'm working on it." Her voice was strained.

"Annika, what are you doing?"

"Trying to reach ... okay. Got it." The car slid again, and she was thrown back against the passenger side rear door. A grunt of pain escaped from her lips.

This was exactly the situation he feared. "I'm coming in."

"I won't argue."

He climbed through the hole they'd made for the parents and over to Annika. She was still in the back-seat area, her back against the passenger side door. "Hey, Sunfire, come here often?"

"No jokes. Just get me out of here." Annika could hear the note of panic in her voice as the car shuddered again.

"Okay. Unhook your rope and grab my hands." She did as he directed with shaking hands. The fear she felt each time the car shook was threatening to immobilize her. When she'd been thrown against the passenger door, she'd been terrified and couldn't move. Her back had hit the doorframe hard. The shuddering of the car had made her stumble into a jagged piece of metal; she could feel the blood sliding down her leg from the cut.

When she was free of the rope, she reached for Logan's hands. His grip firm, he pulled her into the front and clipped her into his rope. Together they climbed out.

He sat her safely away from the car to look her over. "Are you hurt?"

"No, I'm fine." She lied and wasn't entirely sure why. She knew that it had been dangerous to enter the car, but those kids needed someone with them. But now that she was safely out, she couldn't control her shaking as another accident scene crowded her mind.

"Think you can climb out of here with me?"

Annika nodded and, with his help, got unsteadily to her feet. She climbed up the steep hill, Logan directly behind her, ready to catch her should she fall. When they'd finally reached the top and unclipped from the rope, Logan had her in his arms. She was trembling, whether from fear or exhaustion, she couldn't say.

"God, woman. You are going to be the death of me."

"I'm sorry. I couldn't leave them alone in there." She breathed into his neck, attempting to control her shaking.

"I know." He kissed the top of her head, then noticed she had something shoved inside her shirt. "What in the world?"

She grinned and pulled a well-loved stuffed giraffe and a pink blanket out of her shirt. "I couldn't leave these behind."

Logan groaned and rolled his eyes. "Of course not. Heart of gold."

"Annika!" Natalie called. "The mom is awake and asking for you." She flagged Annika over to a waiting ambulance where the mom was sitting up inside. The baby was in her one arm while the other was in a sling. Little Megan was on the bench seat next to her mom. As Annika climbed in to sit beside Megan, Natalie introduced her to the children's mother.

"I have something I think might belong to you." She pulled the giraffe out from behind her back, smiling when the little girl squealed upon seeing her beloved stuffed animal.

"Raffie!" She grabbed the animal and hugged it to her chest.

"And who does this belong to?" Annika held out the blanket, and the baby made a motion trying to reach for it.

"That's Chloe's." Annika handed the blanket to the tiny girl who grabbed it and held it to her face, her thumb in her mouth.

Annika then turned to the woman. "Are you doing okay?"

"Yes, thanks to you and the others," she said, near tears. "I can't thank you enough for what you have done for my girls."

Annika brushed off her gratitude. "They are sweet girls. I'm just glad I spotted your car as we drove by."

"God! I don't know what would have happened if you hadn't." The tears slipped past her defenses now, and Annika placed a comforting hand on her leg.

"You are all safe now. Before you know it, you'll be chasing after your girls again in the backyard."

The mom smiled. "I can't help but wonder why you would crawl into the car like that. Natalie tells me the guys who got me and my husband out are Nighthawks. Are you a Nighthawk too?"

"No. Just a friend."

"Then why ... why would you risk your own life?" She didn't know why she felt such a strong need to get to those children. She just had to do it.

"I don't know. I heard the kids crying, and I figured I could help calm them down."

"You did just that. Megan told me about the story you mentioned to her."

Annika smiled. She loved nothing more than getting children interested in reading. "*Anne of Green Gables*."

"Oh!" the mom said excitedly. "I saw those movies when I was younger and loved them. I never read the book, though."

"You should get a copy and read it with Megan."

"That sounds like a splendid idea. What do you think, Megan?" The little girl nodded with a big grin.

Annika tweaked the girl's nose. "You'll love learning what other silly things Anne gets into."

Megan threw herself into Annika's arms. "Thank you."

"You're very welcome." Annika fought back the sting of tears as the girl's arms squeezed her hard. "Now, you take care of your mom and your sister. Your mom is going to need your help because of her arm."

"I will," she said solemnly.

"I'll let you get to the hospital now. If you ever need anything, the Nighthawks know how to reach me."

"Thanks again!" Logan was waiting for her as she climbed down from the ambulance. Suddenly overwhelmed with exhaustion, she stumbled into his arms.

"Let's get you home." He steered her to the car. The rest of the team, she noticed, had nearly finished packing up the gear they'd used and were heading out as well, leaving the wreck for the other first responders to deal with. Natalie gave Annika a hug as they passed, promising to see her soon. Finally, she was settled into the car, and while Logan drove, she let sleep overtake her.

The next thing she knew, they were home. "Do you want something to eat?" Logan asked once they let themselves inside.

"No. I think I'll just grab a shower."

"Okay, I'm going to make myself a sandwich." He placed a quick kiss on her lips before she turned and went to her bedroom. In the bathroom, she turned the shower on to heat up while looking at her reflection in the mirror, shocked at the state she was in. Her hair was a tangled mess from climbing around the inside of the car. Her eyes looked bloodshot from all the crying she had done that day. And there were dark circles under her eyes.

What's more, her shoulder ached, and her back felt bruised. She took her shirt off and turned to see her back in the mirror. Sure enough, a big bruise had developed across her lower back. Stripping off the rest of her clothes, Annika groaned when she rotated her aching shoulder as she headed to the shower.

She hissed in pain as soon as the water hit the cut on her leg she'd forgotten about. She'd have to make sure to treat it heavily with antibiotic ointment before bandaging it. But that was beyond her abilities at the moment, as was washing herself. Overcome with exhaustion, she stood motionless under the spray.

Logan found her like that a few minutes later. She looked up at him as he entered the shower.

"Christ, Sunfire." He reached out and wiped a tear away; Annika hadn't even known she was crying.

"I'm okay," she insisted. "Just tired. It's been a long day."

"That's for sure." He wrapped his arms around her, and they stood like that for a few moments letting the steam fill up the bathroom. Then Logan grabbed her shampoo and poured some out into his palm. After washing and rinsing her hair, he gathered her tight to him. She could feel his erection against her.

"Sorry," he said sheepishly. "It's the orange scent in your shampoo, does it to me every time." He took her loofah and soaped it up before running it over her body. She winced again from the sting of the soap when he reached the cut on her leg. He saw the slow trickle of blood and went down to his knees for a closer look. The right side of her calf had an inch-long gash. "Why didn't you tell me about this?"

Annika shrugged. "Didn't seem important."

"Fuck, Annika, this needs stitches; of course, it's important." She couldn't miss the note of anger in his voice.

"I ... I'm sorry."

"Let's finish up here and get this taken care of."

Annika blanched. "Please, don't make me go to the hospital." She couldn't face another hospital. Not now. Not with her emotions so raw.

"Annika." He rose to his feet but didn't meet her eyes, his frustration with her palpable.

Her plea was barely audible. She grabbed his hand, forcing him to see her, her eyes pleading with him.

When he finally looked at her, she could see the battle he was fighting. She knew that what she had done for those kids had been risky. She'd heard the fear in his voice as he yelled at her to get out of the car. She couldn't fault him for being angry with her; she had done too much and gotten injured in the process. But she'd do it again if it meant those kids were safe.

Looking deep into her eyes, he sighed, relenting. "Okay, but I need to treat it. I can put a few butterfly bandages on it."

She nodded, grateful for his understanding. Once they finished washing and had dried off, Annika sat on the sink wrapped in a towel while Logan treated her wound. "How did this even happen?"

"I don't know. A piece of metal in the car. I bumped into it when the car shook." She shuddered, remembering the moments of panic each time the car quaked or slid. He looked at her, his eyes haunted, then quickly looked back to her cut. "Logan? What is it?" She was concerned for what she'd seen in his eyes.

"Nothing."

After placing the last butterfly bandage, she tilted his chin up to look into his eyes. "I'm sorry, Logan." She cupped his cheek in her hand. "I know I scared you, and I'm sorry for that."

He sighed heavily. "I can't lose you, Annika. I don't think I'd ever survive." He kissed her palm where it lay against his cheek.

"I'm okay, Logan. Nothing is going to happen to me."

"But when I think about the number of times it's been close; it scares me."

"And how many times did I come close to losing you?" She touched the scar on his cheek. "We can't live in bubbles, Logan."

"I know that. But if anything ever happened to you—"

Annika stopped him. "You *will* survive. And you will live a full and happy life." She paused to draw in a shaky breath. "If there's one thing I've learned over all these years, it's that we can't lose ourselves in that dark place, we can't wallow in our loss and forget to live. Because when we choose the light, when we choose to live, wonderful things can happen. It's moments like this with you that are more precious to me than anything. Even my books," she teased with a wink.

"That is saying a lot." He smiled, then placed his head on her lap, his arms wrapped around her waist. "Natalie is right; you are the strongest woman I know."

"Nah, not strong. Just learned from past mistakes." She ran her fingers through his hair.

"It takes a strong person to learn from their mistakes," he argued.

"Have you learned from your past mistakes?"

"Christ, I hope so."

"You won't get scared and leave me again?"

"Not a chance."

"Then you are just as strong as me." After a moment of running her fingers through his hair, she asked, "Are we done here?"

"Almost." His eyes gleamed with fire as he sat back on his heels and lifted her leg. He placed a kiss just outside her bandage. Then another kiss on the inside of her calf. Then another higher, on the inside of her thigh. And higher still. Annika clutched the edge of the counter as he rested her leg on his shoulder. Then his mouth was on her, teasing and tasting. He ran his hand slowly up her other leg until he reached her apex and slid two fingers inside of her. Annika cried out; her gasp echoed in the tiled bathroom. Together, fingers and tongue worked their magic until she was calling his name. She arched her back and surged into a million tiny starbursts.

Annika sprawled wantonly on the counter, slowly returning to her senses. Logan was placing tiny kisses on her thighs and stomach where the towel had gaped open. She looked down at his dark head. "Logan."

"Mmm?" he muttered, kissing her navel.

"Take me to bed." Logan surged to his feet and picked her up from the counter. Despite her exhaustion, a feeling of supreme contentment settled on her as he carried her into the bedroom. Logan pulled the towel from her before he placed a knee on the bed and laid her in the middle. His towel had been lost somewhere during the journey. He was kissing her then, moving his mouth slowly against hers. Tasting her, savoring her, his mouth devoured hers as his hard body covered her softer curves, pressing her into the mattress. His arms wrapped around her, smashing her into his hard chest, her nipples rasping against him. Craving his touch more than she wanted her next breath, she ached to savor each sensation as the pleasure built.

His lips made a sensual trail down her throat while she ran her hands all over his body. Her fingers found an old scar on his abdomen. Tracing it with her fingers, she wondered why she hadn't noticed it before. Curiosity struck her briefly until his mouth found her breast, then all thoughts fled from her mind except the sensation of what he was doing to her.

When he'd moved back to kissing her lips, Annika decided it was her turn as she surged up and pushed him over to his back. She ran her fingers down his body from his shoulder, over his pecs, and across his abdomen, causing his muscles to twitch as she nibbled on his neck. Reaching lower, she grasped him in her hand, squeezing gently. He groaned and thrust into her hand. She kissed him desperately as she pumped him.

She straddled his hips, her core enveloping him, welcoming him. They both groaned as he slid deep inside her, to the hilt. She stilled for a moment, enjoying the sensation of being stretched by him.

"Annika." His pained groan prompted her to move, slowly at first, hips rocking as she found a rhythm that pleased her. Logan placed his hands on her breasts, his thumbs teasing her nipples, he watched her move over him with an intense fire in his eyes. Pleased with herself for being able to give him as much pleasure as he'd given her, she moved faster. Undulating over and around him, she arched her back, her pleasure at the precipice. He moved one hand down to tease her clit, and that was all it took. One flick of his fingers and she was exploding around him.

He rode with her during her climax, then grabbed her hips and surged up into her several times until he found his own release. Annika collapsed on top of him, breathing heavily. Logan moved her to snuggle into his side, her head on his shoulder. Grabbing the covers, he pulled them up over them.

Chapter 15

Annika was quiet for so long he thought she'd fallen asleep as he held her in his arms. "Can I ask you a question?" she queried into the dark room, startling him.

"Sure."

"Why did you leave the SEALs?"

He laughed. "That's an easy one." She moved her head a little on his shoulder so she could look up at him. "I got tired of being in someone else's country."

"I don't understand. I thought you wanted to protect Americans, kick some terrorist ass. I think that's how you put it."

He smiled, remembering how he and Jamie used to joke about that. "It was. And for a while it was good. I always spent my leave somewhere around here. I'd go camping or rent a cabin. Whatever I could find. I'd rent a boat and spend as much time on the water as I could. About four years ago, while on leave, a mayday went out. A family was in trouble on the river, not far from where I was. Their boat was on fire and sinking, and they were trapped. The bow was on fire, and the family was below in the stern."

"And you didn't hesitate to jump on a burning boat."

"You know me so well." He kissed her briefly before continuing. "I could hear the kids crying, and like you with those kids in the car, I couldn't leave them. There were three of them and their parents. I circled around a few times, trying to find the best way to get them out. My boat, unfortunately, didn't come with a fire extinguisher.

The windows were too thick to break through. There was no way to get to them without going through the fire."

"What did you do?" she gasped.

"The only thing I could do. I raced away a bit, then hit the throttle and sped back as fast as that piece of shit I'd rented could go. When I was close enough, I twisted the wheel hard away from their boat. It created a wave that washed over the boat and put down some of the flames."

Annika looked up at him in stunned disbelief. "Whoa. Impressive! That sounds like something out of a movie."

"Graham thought so. He and his Nighthawks arrived just as I was jumping on their boat. He'd seen the whole maneuver. When I was pulling the first kid out, he offered me a job on the spot."

"Did you take it?"

"It was tempting. But I really loved being a SEAL. I wasn't sure if I was ready to give that up yet."

Annika played with his fingers some more. She was still a hand holder; it was one of the things he loved about her. "What changed?"

"I was sent overseas again. Afghanistan. I hated that place. Some days it felt so hopeless being there. No matter how hard we worked, nothing was going to change for those people. While I knew I was doing good helping to fight for them, I started to feel like there were so many more people I could help in my own country."

"Graham's offer started looking better and better?"

"I called him, asked if he was still interested. When it came time to reup, the decision to get out was a no brainer."

"And the rest is Nighthawk history." She looked up at him again. "I'm glad you found a family with them."

"Me too, but it still felt incomplete. I needed you. I knew that. I was just too chicken to do anything about it."

"Until my mother's meddling."

"I, for one, am very happy your mom meddled."

"Me too." Then she hit him with the question he'd been dreading. "So, tell me, how long have you and my mom had your little secret relationship?"

He gulped. "Umm, she never told you?"

Annika sat up to look at him, the covers slipping to her waist, momentarily distracting him. She was magnificent, with the moonlight playing over her alabaster skin. He wanted to stroke every inch of that soft skin. "No, she never told me. About any of it. How long, Logan?"

"Two years," he admitted.

Her eyes widened, stunned. She turned on the bed to face him, just out of reach. He fought hard to keep his eyes on hers and not wander down to her gorgeous tits. "Two years! You've been talking with her for two years? Why her and not me?" The hurt in her voice twisted his heart.

"I don't know. She emailed me. I hadn't heard from her in probably twelve years. And suddenly, there it was. Mama Jo was not happy with me."

"Good."

Logan smiled. "She yelled at me. I could practically hear her voice berating me through the computer. She told me, in no uncertain terms, that it was time to stop being a toad-spotted barnacle and get my white-livered punk-self home."

Annika laughed. "That sounds like her."

"I bit the bullet and responded. I don't know why. Something just told me to do it."

"Jamie."

He shrugged. "Maybe. I don't know."

"What did you say to her?"

"I told her I was sorry, but I didn't know how."

"Did you really think she was going to leave it at that?"

He shrugged again. "In a way, she kind of did. She didn't ask questions. She didn't put any pressure on me. We exchanged numbers, and she became just another contact on my list. She would text every now and then, just to say hi, ask how I was doing. She never mentioned Jamie. Or you. Nothing from the past."

Annika seemed to ruminate on that. "That sounds so unlike her."

"When I asked her if I could stay at the lake house, I had no idea she had an ulterior motive."

"Yeah, *that* sounds more like her," she quipped.

"I'm glad she did. My only regret is that she didn't meddle sooner."

"She was working with a scared little critter. She didn't want you to bolt again. Slow and steady. That's how you deal with an animal that's full of fear."

He reached for her and pulled her back into his embrace, tickling her sides, where he knew she was most ticklish. She giggled and thrashed until she was out of breath. He took pity on her as she gasped for air and settled her body into his arms again. She went willingly with a deep sigh. "You and your words, Sunfire. They slay me."

A few days after their trip to Annandale, Jansen asked Logan if he could have a tour of the Nighthawk facilities. So, the two men left the women to fend for themselves. Annika decided she needed a run to work out her wonderfully sore muscles from the previous night spent with Logan, blushing even now as she remembered the things he'd done to her. After tightening her shoelaces, she went into the great room, finding her mother in the chair by the window reading a book.

"Have a nice run, Sweetie. Stay away from dogs on the bluff," she teased.

"Very funny, Mom." She thumbed through her playlist after placing her earbuds in her ears and went out the front door. Feeling nostalgic, she found some Foreigner and took off down the road. After a mile or so into her run, she paused to take a sip of water from the bottle she remembered to grab this time. She was feeling good and loose and was thinking of doing another mile before turning to head back. She thought again of Logan and the lovemaking they'd shared. He made her feel things she never even thought possible, and her body still tingled in certain spots. But beyond how he made her feel physically, he made her happy. They were building something good between them and she couldn't wait to discover how far they could go.

Distracted by her thoughts of Logan, she didn't hear the man approaching until he had her locked in a chokehold, a strong arm wrapped around her throat. "Let's see how that Nighthawk feels when he loses his bitch," he hissed. Annika felt something stick her in the neck; then a warm lethargy floated through her body. The dizziness hit as the man dragged her backward towards his truck. The water bottle slipped from her fingers as blackness closed in around her.

Logan was nearly done with the tour of Nighthawk when Jansen's phone rang, and he answered it. "Hey, Johanna. We're nearly done ... What?" Logan was instantly alerted by the note of panic he heard in Jansen's voice. "Hold on." He lowered the phone and put it on speaker. "Say that again."

Logan could hear Johanna's equally panicked voice. "She's not home yet?"

"What do you mean?" Jansen asked.

"Annika went out for a run hours ago. She's still not back. I can't find her anywhere. I drove around to see if I could spot her. She's just gone!"

"You know how sometimes she can lose track of time on her runs."

"Yes, but this feels different," she insisted. "It's been four hours. She's never been out that long before. And after that man the other night ... I'm worried." Logan pulled out his own phone, dialing for Graham.

"Annika's missing," Logan said as soon as Graham answered his phone. "Four hours." He paused, listening to Graham. "I'll text you the address." He hung up and hit the messaging app to give Graham the address to the lake house.

"Johanna?" he said more loudly for her to hear him as the two of them ran for the parking lot. "Graham is mobilizing the team. He's having everybody meet at the lake house. Jansen and I are on our way. Stay inside."

Logan broke quite a few traffic laws as he raced back to the lake house. Every possible scenario raced through his mind as he tried to figure out what happened to her. She wouldn't have gone near the bluff again. He was sure she'd learned her lesson on that front. It was possible she had lost track of time as Jansen had suggested, but he didn't think so. He had a bad feeling deep in his gut, and it revolved around Rob Petersen. They needed to know where that man was. If he were lost in his bottle in his living room, Logan knew he'd breathe a lot easier.

As soon as he shoved the car into park, he was out and running down the road, following Annika's usual route as Jansen went into the house to be with his wife. After about a mile seeing no sign of ... anything, he spotted the water bottle lying on the side of the road. He approached it cautiously, not wanting to disturb any evidence that might be left behind. Swallowing hard, he crouched next to the bottle trying to block the rush of emotions that threatened to pull him under.

There was still some slushy snow that the plows hadn't completely removed from the road, and he spotted marks that looked like something, or someone, was dragged away.

Graham and Ian caught up to him as he crouched by the marks. "What are you thinking?"

Logan pointed to the lines. "I'm thinking she was dragged." He stood and followed the marks. "Tire tracks?"

"Possibly. But those could be anybody's from any time," Ian reasoned.

"True, but I don't think so." Logan pointed to something else lying in the slush. Annika's phone with the earbuds still attached lay there, the screen cracked. And then he spotted the thing that drove an icy fear racing through his veins. A syringe. Logan's heart nearly stopped dead in his chest at the sight of the syringe. Then with a painful jerk, it turned over and began to race out of control. "He's got her."

"My deputies are checking on him." His phone rang then. "Here's one now. You're on speaker."

"No sign of him at his house," the deputy said. "In-laws haven't seen him. Nobody's seen him since you guys put him in that cab the other night. His truck is no longer in Jolene's lot."

"He's got her," Logan repeated. "He threatened her again that night. And that syringe ..." The fear turned into anger. He could still hear Petersen's angry threats from that night after Annika had taken the little girl over to the jukebox. The man had watched her walk away with his daughter with an evil glint in his eye that had set Logan's hackles rising. When he'd muttered, "She should be torn from your life like my Carlie was," Logan had nearly lost it. Graham's hand on his shoulder was the only thing that had held him back. If Annika were hurt or worse ... he couldn't complete that thought. He refused to entertain any notion that didn't involve Annika safe in his arms again.

"Never thought he'd actually do it, though," Graham mused.

"We've got an APB out for him and his truck. Somebody will spot him."

"Okay. Thanks, Ian. Keep us updated," said Graham as they made their way back to the house.

"You too," Ian told them, then told the deputy on the phone to get someone out to the bluff to gather the evidence Annika left behind.

"David's got the maps at the house. He's working on a search pattern," Graham told him.

"She could be anywhere. We don't even know where to start." Where could he have taken her? And if she was inside somewhere, what then? They couldn't search every house in Michigan. Their only hope was for someone to have spotted him and reported it. Otherwise, they were working blind. His lungs felt aflame with the need to roar. Feeling as if each second that ticked by was life or death, he needed to find Annika now.

Anxiety ratcheted up in him. As a SEAL, his missions were well planned out. Information was double-checked and verified, ensuring success. When things went FUBAR, as they inevitably did, they had contingency plans in place to get the objective accomplished and ensure they all went home. But this was different. There was no intel. There was no military drone flying over the area to gather intelligence, with an army of analysts poring over every detail. It felt like an impossibly hopeless mission that went FUBAR from the very beginning.

"Finch will go up in the helicopter. He can cover more ground."

Pulling himself back from his spiraling thoughts, Logan focused on his training. "Good, send Evan with him. He's got the best eyes."

"Agreed." They returned to the house just as Natalie arrived with her father and Graham's parents. "They'll stay with Annika's parents while we work," Graham explained, and Logan was grateful.

With his emotions suddenly lodged in his throat, he fought the sting of tears he felt behind his eyes. "Thanks for coming," he said to them, knowing Graham's parents would take good care of his family which lifted a little bit of the weight he felt on his shoulders.

"Anything for family," Graham's mother answered. Logan's heart swelled. He'd been without family for so long he'd forgotten how it felt. But he knew without a doubt that if he lost Annika, nothing would ever be the same again. She was his family, his heart.

Annika fought her way out of the darkness, her eyes heavy, struggling to remember where she was. She vaguely recalled going for her run, but the rest was blank. She was so tired her eyes drooped, and her head dipped down. With a jerk, she pulled herself out of her stupor. *Come on, Annika, wake up.* She shivered, noticing the air was chilly. Whatever she was sitting on was hard and felt like it was moving slightly. Or maybe she was just dizzy. *Wake up!*

Finally, she was able to blink her surroundings into focus, but all she could see was darkness. Were her eyes even open? She tried to focus on the little stuff instead of the big picture, thinking that would help. Annika tried to lift a hand in front of her face, hoping she could focus on just that, but it wouldn't move. She tried the other hand; her breaths quickened and grew shallow as the reality of her situation started to sink in. She was trapped. Her heart beat harder against her chest as she tried to pull her hands free. When she couldn't move them, she panicked, thrashing her body, trying to break free. She tugged and pulled, not feeling the sting of the ropes slicing into her skin. Suddenly, she stopped her struggles remembering what happened.

Mr. Petersen.

He'd caught her by surprise and stuck her with something. It must have been a pretty powerful drug to have knocked her out for as long as it did since it was nighttime now. She tried to wiggle around, hoping again to loosen her bindings but couldn't move anything except her legs. Looking down her body, she saw an excessive amount of ropes were wrapped around her torso and waist.

The ground below her moved again. Like the motion of a boat. Could she be in a boat? Was that why she was rocking? She tried to focus on what she was sitting on. It looked like some kind of metal. She stretched her fingers out to see if she could feel it, ignoring the burn of the rope on her wrist. It was cold and felt metallic. The aftereffects of the drug were affecting her concentration; Annika couldn't remember what the deck of a boat was made of. *Come on! Focus!*

Turning her head to the side, she tried to see behind her to figure out what she was tied to. Reaching out with her fingers again, she wrapped them around what felt like metal poles. There was a blinking light above her head that caught her attention. The blinking light with an antenna sticking up next to it sat at the top of something rocking behind her. None of this was making sense.

A pain in her leg made her gasp. She stretched her legs out straight to try to relieve the pressure but bumped into more metal in front of her. She looked down in an effort to concentrate on what was below her feet. More metal, a small boat. Her feet hit a bench seat stretched across the width of the boat. From the long hardness behind her, she assumed she was tied to another bench seat.

Sitting up a little taller, willing the nausea away, she peered over the edge of the boat. Water rippled against the hull, so much water, as far as she could see. Something loomed out of the darkness to her right. The clang of metal on metal penetrated her mind. The base of what-ever was hitting her boat was perfectly round. A teepee of metal poles that she noticed earlier rose from the middle. An image was assembling itself in her mind as she stared at the blinking light at the top. No! *That couldn't be right.*

A buoy. The boat was tied to a buoy in the middle of Lake Michigan. Panic threatened to crawl up inside her, but she tamped it down. From what she could remember of buoys, they seemed pretty solid, but she didn't like the way the boat kept scraping and banging against it. The water seemed calm at the moment, so she probably wouldn't tip over and drown; at least, she hoped she wouldn't.

Unless there was a bad storm.

Why did you have to go there! Racking her brain, she tried to remember the weather report. If she recalled it correctly, she thought it was supposed to be clear. Sighing in frustration, she tilted her head back against the seat she was lashed to. What was she going to do? How could she get out of this one? Logan must be frantic by now. And her parents. Oh, God! Her parents. Could they survive losing another child?

One thing was certain; Logan wouldn't stop looking for her. And, she figured, neither would the Nighthawks. They were his family. They would do everything in their power to help Logan. But would they be on time? It was December on the lake. The temperatures were warmer than they had been the previous week, but it was still probably in the mid-forties. How long before she suc-cumbed to hypothermia?

Another certainty she had; Logan would again blame himself for another death. Her heart ached for him. He carried too much guilt with him, and it was unnecessary. He was blameless for everything. She hoped someday he'd be able to forgive himself for everything. Even this.

She opened her eyes and looked at the sky. "Oh!" she exclaimed in awe. The sky was awash with the Aurora

Borealis. A delicate light that hung in fragile curtains. The mesmerizing streaks of light danced across the dark backdrop of God's stage. She'd always wanted to see the Aurora but could never get away from the city lights to see it properly. Here, in the middle of the lake, there was no light pollution. It was stunning!

"Gee, maybe you should have tied yourself to a buoy years ago."

How she wished she had her hands free so she could take pictures with her phone if she even had her phone with her anymore. The colors were amazing. Flickering flames of greens and blues. Then there were the purple and pink accents. So many colors. God was showing off for her tonight. And she was grateful for the distraction from her predicament as the cold penetrated and the trembling started. Teeth chattering, she concentrated solely on the colors blanketing the sky. Of course, she turned to her books. "'In colors of rose and lavender and purple, it moved and pulsed against the night, and the frost-sharpened stars shone through it. What a thing to see at a time when I needed it so badly!'" How had Steinbeck known?

Chapter 16

NEARLY TWELVE HOURS HAD passed since Annika had disappeared. Nobody had reported seeing Petersen or Annika. Logan's hope was waning, but he would never stop looking. Ever. His teammates tried to get him to rest, and Mary shoved some food at him when he stopped by the house for an update since reception was spotty in some of the areas he was searching. Finch had to ground the helicopter when it became too dark to see anything, promising to go back up as soon as it was light enough. But they still had no idea where to start.

In the last few hours, he'd studied everything he could find on Rob Petersen. He knew where he was born, grew up, got married, worked and played. He'd stalked him on social media 'till he knew what his favorite clubs and organizations were, and who he considered friends. The man had been a dedicated employee for Midco engineering and an avid fisherman until his wife died. When he lost her, he lost everything at the bottom of a bottle. Tin Man had spent the day contacting all of Petersen's friends, including his fellow members of the Southwest Michigan Steelheaders, a fisherman's association. But no one had seen much of him since he was laid off.

The maps were spread out in front of him on the kitchen table. He stared at them, hoping for inspiration, but nothing was jumping out at him. They were searching blind.

Just like in Afghanistan when those aid workers had gone missing, kidnapped by a group of Taliban fighters. Logan and a few of his teammates had hung out with them from time to time, enjoying the shared experience of being an American trying to make a difference in a war zone. Hell, he'd even slept with one of them in a moment of weakness. What was her name? Nancy … no Nicki. That was it.

He remembered poring over maps with his CO as he was now, trying to put himself in the Taliban's place. He remembered wondering where the most logical place to have taken them from the school would be. There had been a sense of hopelessness then too. But nothing like the current feeling.

There had been a bit of panic to find them before the worst happened and he remembered being worried for Nicki. But his feelings for her were nowhere near as intense as they were for Annika. He hadn't loved Nicki.

And that's what was making the hollow feeling in his chest so much worse. He was in love with Annika. Always had been. Always will be. That explained why the desperation to find her was more extreme. The outcome for the aid workers had been good. The analysts studying the drone footage had managed to find the hide-out and his SEAL team mounted the rescue operation. Mission accomplished, Nicki went home, and he hadn't heard from her since, both understanding what they had was a momentary fling.

But Annika. Everything was different with Annika. He'd lived so long with the pain and sorrow of knowing what it felt like to live without her. But now he knew what it felt like to love her, and he knew she was his one. The one who understood him and wouldn't let him get away with shit. The one who saw the stains on his soul and wanted him anyway. The one who only had to smile to light up his world. And when she cried, he wanted to tear the world apart to shield her from life's hardships. Even after everything he'd put her through, she had given herself to him willingly. A fact that humbled him and drove him to want to take care of her in every way.

He choked back an anguished sob and dropped his head into his hands. How could he have failed so miserably to protect her? He knew Petersen was unstable and worried that he might snap. And for some reason, Petersen seemed fixated on his relationship with Annika. *Dumbass*, he hissed to himself. How could he have left her alone? How could he have neglected to shield the first and only woman he'd ever loved?

Jamie would be so disappointed in him, a thought that made him hang his head. Nobody had messed with Jamie Northrup's sister, but that was mostly because they feared Jamie's best friend. Logan would have beaten the crap out of anybody who'd tried to hurt Annika. And if he ever got his hands on Petersen ... It wouldn't end well for him.

Annika believed wholeheartedly that her brother had reached out to her a time or two from the great unknown. Maybe ... it couldn't hurt to put it out there and hope the universe was listening. *Where is she, Jamie?* He closed his eyes and listened for a moment. Nothing but the hum of the heat flowing through the vents. *Thanks a lot, man.*

Staring at the maps again, Logan tried to put himself in Petersen's mind. Where was the most logical place for him to have taken her? Logan would have guessed the river where Carlie died, but he'd searched it for hours yesterday, covering miles and miles with no sign of anything. He stood now at the table, overwhelmed by helplessness. He brought his fist down hard on the table in frustration. Johanna, having just entered the room after Jansen had insisted she lay down for a while, saw his frustration and went to him. She stood beside him and wrapped an arm around his waist. He put his arm around her shoulders and hugged her to him.

"It will be okay," she assured him.

"How?"

"I have faith. You'll find her." She seemed so sure. Did she really understand the massive undertaking this shit-storm was? For all he knew, she could be in Canada by now. How do you search for someone without knowing *anything*?

He let out a frustrated breath. "And what if I can't, Mama Jo?"

She smiled at the special name he'd always called her. "You will!"

"But if I can't. I can't lose another person I love. I barely survived losing Jamie. But with Annika ..." he couldn't finish the thought as anguish washed over him. He never wanted to imagine a world without Annika. Even when he had exiled himself from them, he was always comforted by the fact that she was out there, alive and well. If he never found her ... If he never knew what happened to her ... How could he go on?

"I know, kiddo. But don't give up hope. I'm going to make you something to eat." She moved off to the kitchen.

"That's not necessary."

"You need to stay strong ... for her," Johanna insisted.

Graham burst through the front door just as Johanna handed him a plate of toast and coffee. "Ian called," he said breathlessly. "Someone saw a man at the docks with an unconscious woman thrown over his shoulder yester-day. He threw her into a small fishing boat and took off into the lake."

"Petersen doesn't own a boat," Logan remarked.

"No, but he could have borrowed or stolen one. I've got Finch getting the helicopter ready. He's waiting for us."

This was just the break they needed. Now they had somewhere to start. He kissed Johanna's cheek on his way out. "Bring her home!"

"I will," he promised, feeling confident for the first time since Annika had disappeared.

The sun rose with a brilliant display of colors in the east, but Annika almost didn't notice. She was so cold. Sometime during the night, she started cursing the makers of spandex. It was definitely not made for hours in the cold. She had dressed for running in cold weather with a moisture-wicking thermal layer underneath, but after so many hours, it had ceased keeping her warm, the chill permeated the layers. At least she had her thermal hat, gloves, and balaclava to keep the heat from escaping through her head. The fleece-lined windbreaker helped to block some of the biting cold.

Her hands had gone numb hours ago, especially since she'd tried so hard to pull them free. She could feel the dried blood irritating her wrists. Her butt was sore. And there was a pain in her leg that no position would relieve. The rocking motion was not helping anything. The cold was making her so tired; she just wanted to curl up in a ball and sleep. But now that the sun was up, she had to stay alert in case she spotted a passing boat, even though she hadn't quite worked out how she'd flag it down.

Her thoughts turned to Logan once again. She wished, not for the first time, that he was here with her right now so that she could tell him how much she loved him, had always loved him, from the moment they met. These few weeks with him had been the most wonderful time of her life. She wanted more time, didn't want to leave him so soon. Her tears flowed freely. She snorted a laugh as a ridiculous observation occurred to her; of course, her tears flowed, her hands were tied, she couldn't wipe them away. Jeez, she must be losing her mind. If she didn't get out of here soon, she feared she would definitely lose it.

Time. It haunted her. After Jamie, it was "you need time to grieve." After her suicide attempt, it was "you need time to heal." With Caleb and Suzanna, it was "too much time." It'd taken her too long to talk Caleb down, and Suzanna paid for that time with her life. And now, with Logan, it wasn't enough time. It would never be enough time with him. They'd already lost so much time together.

Not knowing if she'd live or die today, her thoughts turned to her attempt to end all the pain. The over-whelming loneliness that led her to such a desperate act.

The spring before the third anniversary of Jamie's death, Annika had just finished finals for the semester and was home at her parent's house for a short break before start-ing another summer semester. After Jamie, she had lost herself in her studies determined to get her bachelor's and master's degrees as quickly as she could. The intense focus she applied to her classes allowed her to escape her pain, and she'd worked her butt off to the detriment of every-thing else. She'd made no friends. She'd dated a few men, slept with a couple, but nothing stuck. They were a poor substitute for the man she really wanted. She was alone. Constantly. For the first eighteen years of her life, she'd never been alone; Jamie had always been there. Then Logan too. And now they were both gone.

She'd written to Logan the week before and had been devastated ... again ... when there was no reply. Thinking she was a fool for loving him so much when he obviously didn't feel the same, she let the depression and grief engulf her. She'd tried so hard to fight all these years, struggled to stay afloat, and find her way in a world without her twin. But her toughest fight was in not dwelling on the man who'd broken her heart, and she was so tired. The fight had completely abandoned her, leaving her desolate.

Alone in her parents' house, she suddenly wondered why she was working so hard. What was the point? No matter how hard she worked, she would never be able to pull herself out of the deep dark hole she was in. She wanted to die. Sitting at her desk, she wrote two letters. One to her parents, which she left on her bed. The other one, the one she'd written to Logan, she'd hid deep in a drawer.

She'd poured everything she'd been feeling into that letter to Logan. Everything. Her love, her hurt, her anger, her grief. She wrote until her hand cramped.

Having nothing else left to do and no hope remaining inside her, she swallowed a few of her mother's muscle relaxers with alcohol until she was numb. Then climbing into the tub, she did the deed on one wrist but hesitated when it came to the other. Something told her to stop, that this wasn't her. She was stronger than this.

That was when her mother found her. Johanna saved her as a voice in her head reassured her that everything would be okay.

After some intense therapy, she'd written that final email to Logan. She needed to say goodbye and let him go if she was ever going to have any kind of future. And she'd been content. Not ecstatically happy, but happy enough with the direction her life had taken. She loved her studies while in college. Then she loved her job. She loved her parents. That was enough.

But now, having Logan back in her life. In her arms ... she didn't want to leave. Time. Again, it was about time. And this time, she didn't want to die.

Chapter 17

LOGAN'S PHONE RANG, AND he used the interface on his headset to answer it while hanging out the side of the helicopter, searching for any sign of Annika. Ian had determined what dock Petersen had set off from and which direction. Even finding the man the boat was borrowed from, who told them it had never been returned to the dock. Unfortunately, it was an older model boat and didn't have a built-in GPS system. Therefore, they had set up a grid pattern starting at the docks. Still, Lake Michigan was big. It would take days to search every inch, even with the help from their newest Nighthawk, Emma, and her Coast Guard friends.

Logan tried to imagine where he could have possibly left her in Lake Michigan. Had she been stashed somewhere along the coast or, god forbid, dumped in the middle of the lake? If it was the latter, there was no way she would survive the freezing temperatures in the water for as long as she'd been missing. *Please, God, don't let that be the case.*

Answering the phone, he tried to understand Johanna through her tears. "Slow down, Mama Jo; I can't understand you."

"There was a note on the mailbox. I ... I think it's from him."

"What does it say?" He pulled his head inside the helicopter so that he could hear her better.

"'Now you know what it feels like to lose someone you care about. Her location will remain locked in my steelhead,'" she read. "But it's weird ... he wrote steel head as one word. Didn't you tell me something about him belonging to that fishing organization? What were they called?"

"The Southwest Michigan Steelheaders."

"It's gotta be a clue, right?" She sounded so hopeful. But steelheads didn't tell him much. He knew they were a type of trout, but that didn't narrow down the search area for them. Suddenly, he remembered something he'd learned in Petersen's background.

"Son of a bitch," he shouted, hoping he was wrong about this suspicion.

"What is it?" Johanna asked.

"Petersen worked as an engineer for Midco. They are responsible for maintaining the lake buoys.

"And he worked hard for years along with his Steelheaders group petitioning lakeside towns in southwest Michigan for the funds to acquire the buoys that monitor marine conditions." Tin Man stated, catching on to the direction Logan's thoughts were headed.

"She's on a buoy," he called out to the other Nighthawks. Graham had his phone out and was searching up coordinates for the buoys. "Thanks, Mama Jo. I'll call you as soon as I find her." He hung up and moved to read Graham's phone, feeling hope fill his chest for the first time since Annika had gone missing.

"Which one should we start with?"

"Maybe start at the bottom and work our way up?" Evan suggested.

But a voice in Logan's head kept saying, *South Haven.* Annika was at the South Haven buoy. Logan was sure of it. "Thanks, Jamie," he whispered. "South Haven. She's there."

"How do you—" Evan began.

Graham stopped him. "Just go with it." Graham knew how to follow his instincts, having known exactly where to look for Natalie when she was in that well. He called the coordinates up to Finch, who turned the helicopter around in a tight circle. While they flew over miles of water, Logan put on his harness and started to grab whatever he thought he might need once they found her.

In no time, they spotted the buoy in the distance. Logan squinted against the sun, trying to see her. She had to be there. Jamie said she was there. He could feel it. He leaned out the side of the helicopter as far as he dared. Was that ... wait ... yes! A dark shape floated on the north side near the buoy. A boat, and she was there.

"She's there!" he called. Finch expertly maneuvered the helicopter into position, hovering over the two objects. Logan never took his eyes off of her. He grew more and more concerned as Finch drifted lower. She wasn't moving. His gut clenched, and fear iced his veins. *She couldn't be dead! Fuck, don't let her be dead.*

Logan hooked himself into the cable that would lower him down. When Graham tapped him on the shoulder, indicating he was ready, Logan swung out of the helicopter sitting in his harness. Slowly, too slowly, Graham lowered him to the boat. There wasn't much room on it, making maneuvering a little difficult, but nothing he couldn't handle. When he got close enough to her, he called her name. She didn't stir. He saw the ropes the son of a bitch had used to lash her to the seat. Her hands were tied behind her back, and her head was slumped onto her chest. The rotor wash from the helicopter was causing waves in the water, making the boat rock harder. The buoy rocked against the boat, the metallic clank making Logan grit his teeth.

Finally, Logan was low enough he could reach her. He placed his feet on either side of her, hoping to steady the rocking of the boat. "Annika," he called again. He tore one glove off with his teeth and felt for a pulse. There! Thready and weak, but there. He breathed a sigh of relief as he pushed her hair off her face, feeling the icy skin of her cheek.

She winced and opened her eyes. "Hi, Sunfire!" Seeing her gorgeous blue eyes, he finally took a deep breath, the first one in nearly twenty-four hours.

"Am I dreaming?"

"Not this time," he answered while taking out his knife. He started to slice through the ropes holding her to the boat. "I'll have you home in no time."

"Can't feel ... anything," she said weakly.

"I know. Just hold on a minute longer."

"'Kay." Her head dropped to her chest again while he hacked through the rope and placed the pieces in a pack strapped to his waist. Evidence. They would need all the evidence they could gather to put Petersen away. He knew Graham was taking pictures for photographic evidence. Once her torso was free, he reached behind her to free her hands. When the rope was off, he brought them gently around to the front and started rubbing her wrists to get the circulation going again. It was then he noticed an old silver scar that stood out from the rope burns on one wrist. He blanched. Suicide? Annika had tried to kill herself. *Why didn't she tell me?*

Because you would have blamed yourself, the voice in his head, the one that sounded an awful lot like Jamie, told him. *She was trying to protect you from yourself, you dipshit.* Oh, you poor stubborn woman.

Moving quickly with ingrained skill, he maneuvered her into a harness and hooked her to him. Once he confirmed she was secure, he gave a thumbs up to Graham, who started the pulley. "I got you, Annika," he said when she started to stir again. "You're going home."

Once in the helicopter, Logan wrapped her in an emergency blanket and sat with her on his lap. Graham started a warm IV for her and treated the rope burns on her wrists. Logan knew he noticed the scars there too, but he wisely didn't say anything about it. With one hand he took out his phone and called Johanna. "Got her. She's safe."

She burst into tears. "Can I talk to her?"

"She's unconscious and hypothermic. She woke up once and saw me. She knows she's safe. We'll meet you at the hospital."

"On our way," she cried before she hung up.

Annika woke slowly, with no idea where she was … again. She was lying on something much softer than she remembered, and she was warmer. But she felt disoriented and confused. She raised a hand to her forehead and saw the white bandages wrapped around her wrists. Panic flooded through her system. *Oh no! Not again.* She couldn't have done it again. Wouldn't have! She sat bolt upright and tried to tear the bandages off. She had to see. She didn't remember doing it this time. She had to see; she needed to know if it was true.

"Not again!" she hissed. "No, no! I didn't!" She was so panicked that she didn't notice Logan until he grabbed both her hands, stopping her from seeing.

"No, Annika. Those need to stay on so you can heal," he informed her gently.

She looked at him, her eyes clouded with tears. "I have to see. I need to know," she insisted. She thought she was better. She hadn't had suicidal thoughts in over a decade. Why now? She was happy. Wasn't she? Had Suzanna's death affected her harder than she thought? It had been rough, but she thought she was dealing with it in the right way. And she had Logan back! She had everything to live for now! So why?

Logan held her hands tightly, but still, she tried to pull away to pry the bandages off. "Annika, look at me," he demanded. The tone in his voice gave her pause. She looked into those dark eyes that were filled with worry.

"Those are there for the injuries the rope caused. Nothing more. You struggled against the ropes, and they hurt your wrists. Do you understand? It's just from the ropes."

She wanted to believe him. She did. But there was still a tiny bit of doubt. She'd fought against the darkness almost every day, especially in the last few months since the shooting. Her parents had hardly left her side since then. Afraid she would succumb to the crushing darkness again. She stared at her wrists in Logan's hands, trying to make sense of everything. Her thoughts were muddled like they were swimming through molasses. "Th … the ropes? I didn't …"

"No, Sunfire. You didn't do anything to yourself except struggle to be free." He placed his hip on the bed next to her and gathered her into his arms, his warmth enveloped her. "You're suffering from hypothermia. That's causing the fuzzy brain. It will clear."

"You found me," she whispered, trying to snuggle deeper into his warmth, wondering if she would ever feel completely warm again.

"I found you." He kissed her head. "I always will."

"I was so scared," she sobbed, the memories of her ordeal suddenly swamping her.

"I know." He hugged her tighter as she cried into his chest. "Me too."

"I was scared, and yet I knew. I knew you'd find me. Jamie," she hiccupped. "Jamie told me you were coming."

"He told me where to find you."

Annika looked up at him, his dark chestnut eyes the most exquisite thing she'd ever seen, even better than the Aurora Borealis. "You finally started listening to him?"

He chuckled softly and kissed her temple. "Yes, I listened. He was very insistent."

"That's Jamie," she stated, smiling as she remembered her stubborn brother. "I miss him, Logan."

"Me too."

At that moment, Annika's parents walked into the room. Johanna cried, running to her daughter's side. "Annika! You're awake!"

"Mom. Daddy." Logan moved off the bed to make room for her parents. Johanna took his place, enfolding Annika in her arms. Jansen went to the other side and hugged both his girls.

Johanna grabbed Annika's face between her hands to study her. "You're really okay?"

Annika knew what her mother meant. She was worried this would set Annika's recovery from the overwhelming depression back. "Yes, Mom. I'm fine." Whatever Johanna saw in her eyes must have convinced her. She dropped her hands to hold Annika's injured ones.

"I'm so glad you are safe," Johanna said as her eyes filled with tears.

"Oh, Mom, don't cry. I'm fine. I'm alive and very happy to be here." She looked around the hospital room. She hated hospitals. "Well, maybe not *here*, exactly. Any idea when I can get out of here?"

"I'll check on that," Logan offered before walking out the door.

"That man is a blessing," Johanna declared. "He never stopped. I've never seen anyone so driven. I still don't think he's had anything to eat. He wouldn't rest until he found you. And it was such a herculean task since they didn't know where to start looking."

Annika remembered being worried about how he'd react. Worried he'd take the blame. "Did he ... did he blame himself?"

Johanna sighed. "He never said, but I think deep down he felt guilty."

"Probably one of the reasons why he worked so hard to find you," Jansen reasoned. "He felt responsible."

"God, Daddy. How do we get him to stop taking the blame for everything?"

"How do we get you to stop feeling guilty over Suzanna?" he countered.

"That's different."

Johanna squeezed her hands. "No, Sweetie, it's not."

Chapter 18

I T WAS NIGHT. LOGAN lay on the hospital bed, Annika in his arms. Jansen had taken Johanna home so they could get some sleep, but the nurses didn't even bother to try to kick him out when visiting hours ended. Annika lay with her head on his chest, sound asleep as he absently ran his still trembling hand through her hair.

The residual fear warred with the relief that was still surging through his system even now that he'd had a moment to unwind, hence the lingering trembling. *Fuck, that had been too close.* He'd nearly lost her. How many times was that going to happen to one person? His little Sunfire had suffered so much.

His other hand was holding one of hers, playing with her fingers. The white bandage caught his eye. He raised her hand and placed his lips on the bandage over her old scar. "Why didn't you tell me?" he whispered. He had to know the story. Had to know what drove her to such a desperate act. Had to know if he was responsible for another one of her hurts.

"It was twelve years ago. I'd put it behind me," she answered, startling him. He hadn't known she was awake to hear his whispered question. Logan sensed that her answer wasn't quite true. He also knew that wasn't really why she didn't tell him.

Fuck, it was his fault. Annika had suffered because of his own cowardice. "Christ, Annika, I'm so sorry."

She sighed. "Logan, please don't. It's not your fault I was feeling weak. We've both made mistakes in the past. The key to life is to learn from them and move on. You usually learn the most from the worst times and the worst mistakes. I learned from mine."

"Can you tell me about it?"

"Are you sure you want to know the whole story?" she countered.

"I need to know." He knew deep down he was responsible, but he needed to hear the words from her lips.

She took a deep breath and began the story of what she called her worst mistake. "A few months before the third anniversary, the spring semester was nearly over. I'd written to you again and waited. I finished up my exams and still waited. I went home for break and still nothing. It suddenly seemed all so worthless. I was busting my butt to get my degrees, but why? I had no friends, no boyfriends. My brother was gone. And you ..."

"I'd left you alone too," he squeezed her just a little tighter. "I never wrote you back."

"Yeah. There was always pain after each letter, but this was different. It'd been so long since Jamie ... I had fought the overwhelming grief and the depression for so long. I was so tired of fighting. It didn't seem worth it anymore. There was nothing to live for any longer." He squeezed his eyes closed, hating hearing those words from her, aware of how much pain he'd caused her.

"What about your parents?" He knew of the close relationship she shared with them and couldn't imagine them leaving her so alone.

"That was the hard part. I knew it would be devastating to them, but I couldn't see past the darkness. I wrote them a letter telling them I was sorry and why I did it. I told them I loved them. I wrote you a letter too."

That surprised him. "Me?"

"I needed to get it out. I had to tell you everything I had been feeling for nearly three years. Even if you never read the letter, I needed to write it."

"I'm sorry, I had to stop reading all your emails. They became too painful. I saved them all, though." He might have been able to do something to help her had he read a letter like that. Maybe it would have woken him up and brought him home to her sooner.

"It wasn't an email. It was a handwritten letter that I hid deep in my desk drawer. I figured my parents would find it someday, but I didn't want them blaming you."

Christ, this woman. He was so not worthy of her. He turned his head and placed his lips on the top of her head that was tucked under his chin. "Still trying to protect me even when you were suffering." He hugged her again then kissed her temple. "Heart of gold."

"Mom found me and got me the help I needed. But I still had one more thing to do to heal completely."

"You had to say goodbye ... to me," he guessed, his gut tightening as he remembered reading that message. "That last email ... the one that nearly broke me." He'd known he would probably lose her because of his cowardly actions that night after the accident, but he'd also held out a glimmer of hope that he could come home to her someday. But after that email, his hope had been shattered. After that, he'd felt just like she had; as if there was no point. Without Annika, even as a distant hope, there had been nothing to live for. He'd gone a bit nuts after that, taking risks that could have gotten him killed. He'd broken his last promise to her.

"I'm sorry. That wasn't my intention. But I had to let you go."

"I understand why now. I wish I had known how much you were suffering."

"What would you have done, Logan?" she wondered. "Would you have dropped everything, your career with the SEALs, to come home? We were still pretty young then. Would you have been able to let go of all your guilt? Would you have been ready?"

He wondered that too. He'd liked to believe that if he'd known what she was going through, he would have gone to her. But was that the Logan of today or the Logan of the past talking. "I don't know."

"I don't know if I would have liked that. I don't know if I would have wanted you coming home out of some sort of warped sense of responsibility, out of guilt. If you had known what I'd done, that would have been why you came back. I wanted you to come to me when you were ready. And from that point on, I was willing to wait."

That surprised him, especially after knowing how much he'd hurt her. Because of that alone, he shouldn't have been worth the wait. "Why would you wait? Why wouldn't you move on like your last letter said you needed to do? I saw you with the Petersen girl. I saw the longing. You could have had a child of your own by now. Probably several. Why waste your life waiting for someone as hopeless as me?"

She smiled a secret sort of smile. "You'll think I'm crazy."

"Try me."

"I've never told anyone this before. Not my therapist. Not even my parents. It was Jamie."

Stunned, he lifted his head to look into her eyes. What did Jamie have to do with her putting off her life to wait for him? "When I was lying in that tub feeling my life slowly slipping away," she continued though he winced, thinking of her precious life disappearing. "Jamie came to me. He told me to hold on. Help was on the way. He also told me that you would find your way home to me. That I just had to wait a little bit longer. Didn't know he meant twelve years," she quipped. "Between Jamie and your Grandma Jean both telling me you'd be coming home. I knew it was true."

"My grandmother?"

"She stayed with me through my recovery. She was there as much as my parents were."

He shook his head. His grandmother had done what he couldn't, what he was too chickenshit to do. "I never knew."

"She passed not long after that. Between her dying words to me and Jamie's, I figured I could be patient. But you certainly took your own sweet time, didn't you?"

"Sorry I'm late. I was busy being an idiot."

"You're forgiven. As long as you don't leave me again." He knew she was trying to mean it as a joke, but he could hear the underlying note of fear in her voice.

He wanted to make that promise to her. He wanted to promise he would always be by her side, but he could feel the guilt and shame from his actions permeating his thoughts. She'd tried to end her life ... because of him.

He'd done that to her.

Him.

He'd driven her to that desperate act. An image of her bleeding in a bathtub entered his mind. He couldn't erase the image. It was all he could see, and it was all his fault. He wasn't sure if he could ever forgive himself for what he'd done.

"Holy shit!" she said, suddenly sitting upright.

Logan sat up to search the room for whatever threat she'd seen. "What? What is it?"

"Jamie," she gasped.

"What about him?" She turned slightly to face him. A look of wonder suddenly on her face.

"After the worst of the grief had subsided, I needed to know why. Why did Jamie have to go? Someone said something to me once about God needing him. I thought that was rubbish at first. But the longer I thought about it, the more I wondered. God always has a plan, right? He must have needed Jamie for something. I comforted myself by thinking that Jamie had an important job to do for God."

He must have looked at her in confusion since she continued, "I know. Too deep. All that God stuff. But it worked for me. He was there, Logan. He was with me in that boat. You said he told you where to find me. Could this have been his important job? Maybe Jamie died so that he could save me someday. But not just today. He also saved me when I ..."

He knew she was talking about the day she'd hurt herself, but he was at a loss for words. It seemed a little far-fetched, but then again, there was that hunch he'd had in the helicopter that she was at the South Haven buoy.

She smiled and snuggled back into his arms. "Weird, right?"

"Yeah. Although it seems pretty extreme to take one life to save another," he mused.

"True. I never said it made sense." She paused for a moment grabbing his hand to play with his fingers again. "Although, you were ready to give your life for his. You risk your life for people you don't even know all the time. How is this any different?"

"That's a good point. I would have done it, you know."

"Done what?"

"Traded my life for his. I didn't want you to live without him. I knew how much you needed him."

She twisted to look at him, placing her palm against his cheek. "Maybe God knew I needed you more. You did just save my life, did you not?" she teased. He grabbed her hand and kissed her palm before tucking her back under his arm.

"Holy shit!" Again, she sat straight up, this time nearly knocking him in the chin with the top of her head. "Maybe it wasn't Jamie. Maybe it was Suzanna."

"What are you talking about?" Logan asked.

"It was there," she started. "When I was trapped out on the lake, I saw the Aurora. For the first time in my life, I saw it. I was terrified, and I was so cold. I didn't know if I'd live; if I'd be found in time. It was so dark how could anyone have possibly spotted me there?"

She turned on the bed to look up at him, her knotted hair falling over her shoulders. "And I worried about you."

"Me? Why me?"

"If I died—if you never found me, I knew you'd blame yourself. Again. I didn't want you to live the rest of your life buried under that kind of guilt, especially because it wasn't your fault. I remember closing my eyes and praying for more time. I wanted more time with you. We just found our way back to each other. I wasn't ready to give that up yet. Then I opened my eyes and there it was, in all its glory. It was so bright. So beautiful. And I just knew."

"What did you know," he wondered.

"That I would have the time I wanted with you. That I would soon be in your arms again." She lay her cheek on his chest and wrapped one arm across his stomach, hugging him tightly. "Don't get me wrong; I was still terrified. But seeing those lights, it was like someone was sending me a message. Jamie. Or maybe it was Suzanna. Remember her poem? Maybe they were both there in those lights. Jamie knew how I'd always wanted to see them. It may sound crazy, but I believe he sent them to me. He let me know I wasn't alone."

"Nothing concerning Jamie seems crazy to me anymore. If anyone could have sent the Aurora to you, it would have been him." He still wasn't sure he completely believed in what Annika was talking about, but if it brought her peace and comfort, he wasn't going to argue. She deserved all the peace and comfort she could get after what he'd put her through.

A day later, Annika was happy to be out of the hospital, but sad her parents were leaving. "Really, Mom. You don't have to leave."

"You and Logan need time together. And you don't need your old parents hovering over you," she explained.

"You're not old."

Johanna patted her daughter's hand. "Heart of gold." Annika sat on the bed in her parent's room, watching her mother pack. How many times had she done exactly this growing up? Anytime they went anywhere, she'd sit and watch her mother while they talked, just like now.

Johanna placed the sweater she had just folded into the suitcase. "He knows everything?" she asked.

Annika rolled her eyes. "Yes, Mom. He knows everything."

"Good. But I have one more thing I need to tell both of you," she confessed, zipping up the suitcase. Annika grabbed it before her mother could, placing it on its wheels on the floor. She was curious about what her mother could possibly have to tell them.

Johanna walked out into the great room and asked Logan and Annika to sit on the couch. She stood in front of them nervously wringing her hands.

"Are you sure you want to do this?" Jansen asked her.

"It's time they knew."

"Mom," Annika started, suddenly concerned. Had her mother been hiding an illness from her. Was she okay? "You're scaring me. What is it?" Logan reached over and grasped her hand.

"I never told you what we learned that night after the accident. About Jamie."

"What about Jamie?" Annika asked.

She was wringing her hands again. "You remember he'd had all those heart problems when he was younger?" They both nodded. Annika remembered the days and weeks they'd spent in hospitals trying to fix his heart.

Logan seemed to grasp what she was trying to say to them. "Are you trying to tell us—"

"Yes," she interrupted, tears in her eyes. "Logan, it wouldn't have mattered if you had managed to pull him out of the car. He was already gone. His heart gave out."

Annika gasped. Logan ran his fingers through his hair in complete shock. "Oh my god," Annika wheezed. She was breathing hard. Scared she might hyperventilate, she struggled to slow her breathing. She could feel Logan breathing beside her, his arm wrapped around her shoulders as if he sensed she needed aid. All this time ... there was that word again. Time.

Annika stood and started pacing in front of the big windows that overlooked the lake. All that wasted time. If her parents had only been honest with them from the beginning, would things have been different?

Oh, God! All the grief, the depression, the *suicide!* Had it all been unnecessary? Could she have had the last fifteen years with Logan? He would have been by her side through the grief. They would have helped each other. Neither one of them would have had to be alone through it all. She wouldn't have felt so lost, so hopeless. Never would she have surrendered to that desperate act of suicide.

But what good did it do to dwell on all she lost. There was nothing she could do to change the past. She had a chance now to be happy. A chance to have everything she'd always dreamed of having. With Logan.

They'd all made so many mistakes. But maybe, just maybe, it was time to look forward. Tomorrow *is* a new day with no mistakes in it. *Thank you, Anne of Green Gables.* It was time to move forward. Sure, they could think of the past and remember it fondly. Learn from past mistakes but keep moving forward. One step at a time.

Annika turned around to find her mother on the couch next to Logan. She had one of his hands in hers. "I know what you are thinking," she was saying to him. "That if you had known about Jamie all those years ago, things might have been so different. And that might be true. We'll never know. But I never imagined you'd cut yourself off from us so completely. I understood the first couple of weeks; you were grieving, you needed time. I could never have imagined you'd need fifteen years.

"We should have told you both from the beginning. We thought at the time what difference would it make for you to know how he died. It was a mistake. If we had known then why you'd cut yourself off from us, we might have made a different decision. We never felt you were responsible so we never imagined you would blame yourself. We never dreamed you would think you caused his death. Now, it's my turn to take some of the blame. All the years of hardships you both went through ... I am so sorry ..." She broke off on a sob.

"No, Mom." Everyone turned to look at her. "It's time to stop. No more accepting blame. No more guilt for past mistakes. Tomorrow is a new day for all of us. Let's all start living. It's what Jamie would have wanted for us." She didn't realize she was crying until Logan came to her and wiped a tear off her cheek. "God, Logan. Remember how much zest for life he had? How could we have forgotten that? We've done such a disservice to his memory. That needs to stop. Here and now. It's time to live like Jamie did."

He placed his palm against her cheek. Annika closed her eyes and leaned into its warmth. She saw the depths of his feelings for her in his eyes, but also something else. Some unnamed emotion that scared her a little. He leaned down and kissed her forehead as Annika threw herself into his arms, too overwhelmed with emotion to say anything coherent.

She looked at her parents. Johanna, of course, was crying. Even Jansen eyes looked watery. "Mom," she held her hand out to Johanna, who grabbed it like it was a lifeline. "While I wish you had told us all those years ago, I understand why you didn't. I'm glad you finally told us the truth. And now we can move on and start creating new memories."

"You, Sweetie, have a heart of gold!" Johanna cried through her tears.

Jansen had his camera bag in his hand. "Okay, everyone. Time to begin those new memories, starting with a new family portrait. So, dry your eyes, ladies, and go stand in front of the tree."

Jansen set the camera up on the tripod and set the timer. Then stood with the rest of his family in front of the tree. The four of them had their arms around each other's shoulders. A cohesive unit. Then came the silly candids, which they had a good laugh over.

"One more," Johanna said. "Of just the two of you." Annika stood with Logan. Their arms wrapped around each other, big silly grins on their faces. "Perfect."

But Annika wasn't so sure that was true. Logan's smile seemed stunted, not quite reaching his eyes. Trepidation tingled in her spine. Logan's mind was somewhere else, somewhere unpleasant, and she had no idea what was wrong.

Chapter 19

T HE NIGHTMARE CAME AGAIN in the middle of the night. Logan jerked awake and glanced over at Annika curled up in a ball, her back to him. Hoping not to wake her, Logan carefully extracted his arm from under her and eased off the bed. Naked, he padded to the bathroom. He grabbed a cup and filled it with water, his hands shaking slightly as he brought the cup to his lips. Disgusted with his weakness, he put the cup down and placed both hands flat on either side of the sink, breathing heavily as he stared down into the basin.

He thought about the nightmare. He'd hoped that being with Annika would have chased the nightmares away for good, but it just changed them. Before, it had been about Jamie and his guilt. Now, they were centered on Annika and the very real possibility that he could lose her, and it would be his fault. In his head, he knew that it was highly unlikely anything would happen to her. But he couldn't get the image of her attempt at suicide out of his head; his nightmares were torturing him with it.

A pain in his chest hit him as an image from the nightmare that had woken him popped into his head. Annika hurt and bleeding. Her life slipping away. But ever since learning of her suicide attempt, that was all he could see, Annika bleeding. But this time, the nightmare was worse. As she lay bleeding, he stood over her, holding the knife, blood dripping down his arm. It didn't take a psychologist to analyze that dream to tell him what it meant.

Despite what Annika had told him, he couldn't help but blame himself. He'd made a mess of both their lives. And for what? Johanna's confession about Jamie's cause of death had hit him hard. Learning that if he had gotten Jamie out, it wouldn't have mattered, did nothing to ease the tangled knot in his gut. Knowing his best friend had already been gone before he could get him out of the burning car did not lessen the guilt he felt. But it wasn't about Jamie anymore. It was about Annika and the things his actions had driven her to do.

Fuck. And now there was Petersen to contend with. He'd taken Annika because of Logan's actions. Or, in this case, his inactions. He'd failed to save Petersen's wife. It was that failure that had driven Petersen to fixate on him, and by extension, Annika.

Christ. He stared unseeing at his reflection in the mirror. His failure had put Annika in danger. She'd nearly died ... again. By his count that's four. Four times he'd nearly lost her. And even if the shooting hadn't been his fault, he still blamed himself for the other three. And Petersen was still out there, still a danger to Annika because of him. His gut kept warning him that something was coming, and it scared him to death.

"Logan?" Annika called out from the bed.

"I'm here." Shoving his hands through his hair to try to tame the areas where his fingers had messed it up, he gave himself one last glance in the mirror before turning and heading back to the bed. She rolled into him as he settled himself under the covers.

"Are you okay?" she asked.

"I'm fine, Sunfire." He kissed her forehead.

"Logan?"

"Mmm?"

"How did you get this?" she asked, tracing the scar on his abdomen. He flinched. "I'm sorry. You don't have to tell me. I was just curious." She removed her hand from the scar and lay quietly.

"I didn't keep my promise," he confessed.

She tilted her head back to look at him. "What promise?"

"The one I made to you that summer at the lake." He could see the confusion in her eyes. "I was in a bad place after Jamie. I pushed myself hard through boot camp. Then even harder through BUD/S training to be a SEAL. Once I'd accomplished that, I kept pushing myself. I took risks and broke my promise." He watched as understanding replaced the confusion in her eyes.

"I remember now. I asked you to be careful and not to take any risks. I was so afraid something would happen to you."

"That's right." He looked away from her blue gaze, not quite being able to meet her in the eye.

"And you did ... take risks, I mean?"

He nodded, staring at the darkness outside the window. "Those years ... looking back on them now, I guess I didn't care if I lived or died. I had lost everything that ever mattered to me. I didn't care what happened to me. It made me good at what I did but at a horrible cost."

"Tell me, Logan. What happened?"

He sighed. "So many things. So many stupid chances. So many scars."

"Take them one at a time." She touched the two scars on his face. "How did these happen?"

"Debris from a building that was hit by a mortar shell. I was too close, trying to flush out enemy combatants we had been searching for. I nearly had them when they fired that mortar." Annika pushed herself up and kissed the two scars.

"And this one?" She pointed to the small gash in his left shoulder.

"Bullet graze from enemy fire. I got in the way of a terrorist trying to kill us. I can't share more than that." She nodded then placed her lips over the scar.

She pointed to one on his right bicep. "I had a disagreement with some barbed wire."

"A disagreement?"

"Yeah, it was in my way and didn't take too kindly to me cutting it and its buddies so that my team and I could pass." She chuckled and kissed the mark.

"Okay, now the big one." She traced the scar on his abdomen. "This one looks pretty serious." He looked down at the ugly jagged scar. That was also the one he regretted the most. The one that had come when he'd taken the biggest risk.

"Knife wound."

"You were stabbed? Can you tell me about it?" He could tell she was shocked, but he'd been rather lucky as a SEAL that he'd never been shot, except for the graze, like so many others had been. The knife wound had been his worst injury and it happened shortly before he'd left the SEALs.

"I can't tell you too many of the details, but since it was all over the news at the time, I can tell you some. A group of aid workers had been captured by a Taliban group that was trying to assert themselves in the region."

"Wait, I remember that. They were building something for the community, right?"

"A school. Nicki and her team ..."

"Nicki?"

Uh-oh. "She ... umm ..." He so didn't want to tell her about that mistake. "Umm ..." he stuttered again and could feel his cheeks heat.

Annika laughed, cupping his cheek with her hand. "Logan, it's okay. We both have a past. I certainly wasn't a virgin when we first slept together."

The thought of Annika with any other man was not something he had ever considered, and he didn't like it. But he hadn't been a monk during their time apart, so who was he to judge. Even still, he worked to tamp down his anger at the thought of another man touching her.

"My team and a few of those aid workers hung out together on some nights. She was a drunken mistake, and we both knew it." He lowered his head shamefully, unable to meet her eyes. He'd made a lot of drunken mistakes in the last fifteen years. But that night with Nicki was one of the worst. He didn't exactly treat her with the respect she deserved the next day. He would always regret his actions concerning her. He'd known as soon as he'd gotten her into bed, she was a mistake. She wasn't what he'd wanted.

She kissed him briefly on the lips. "It's okay that you have a past, Logan."

He kissed her too and squeezed her a little tighter to him. "So, tell me about this." She pointed to the scar again.

"When the aid workers disappeared nobody saw anything, and nobody knew where they were taken. We pulled all our resources to find them. Finally, we tracked them to a grouping of caves the Taliban were hiding in. My team was tasked with the rescue."

"I'd heard a SEAL team got them out. I always wondered if you had been there."

"We worked our way through the system of caves and tunnels, immobilizing enemy combatants. I was in the lead. I was always in the lead. Always willing to take the risk. We found the aid workers grouped together in one of the caves. They had been roughed up pretty bad. Nicki was ... not good." Logan felt the anger rush through him as it did every time he thought about what had happened to her. She'd been broken and bloody, obviously raped several times. When he'd spotted her laying there in the dirt, clothes torn and ratty, hair matted, half starved, he'd felt an intense rage take over his body. He'd crouched down beside her, and her eyes widened when she recognized him. He could see the relief flood through her, and she cried.

Being the team medic, he treated as many of her extensive injuries as he could as quickly as possible. The other members of her group were not as badly injured as she. He'd learned later that she'd fought them fiercely and had been punished in the most horrendous ways possible. Nicki had been strong, full of life, but the woman lying in the dirt was unrecognizable. They had broken her.

"How awful for her," Annika remarked, her voice full of compassion. "Is she ... did she survive?"

"Yes. But I'm pretty sure it was a long road to recovery for her."

"I'm sorry for her, but that doesn't explain how you were stabbed."

"She reacted badly after spotting one of the terrorists who was trying to sneak away. I just knew ..." As he'd treated her injuries, she had looked over his shoulder and shrank back in fear. Logan had glanced back and spotted a man in the usual Afghan clothing and turban trying to sneak out of a tunnel his team hadn't spotted yet. Seeing the fear in Nicki's eyes, Logan knew that he was the one who'd broken her. The rage took over. He charged the man before the rest of his team was even aware of his presence. The rage had blinded him, and he hadn't seen the knife until it was too late.

"You knew he was the one who'd hurt her."

He nodded, still feeling shame for losing control the way he had. "I went after him and didn't see the knife. I was just so angry. Tired of dealing with these assholes who have no qualms about doing unspeakable, horrible things to women. I just reacted, badly, as it turns out. I didn't even feel the knife. My teammates had to pull me off of him before I killed him."

She was quiet for a moment as she studied the scar. "I don't know much about anatomy, but this looks like it could be a dangerous spot to get stabbed."

"Yeah, I got lucky. A few inches in either direction and the blade could have done some serious damage to organs."

She leaned over and placed her lips over that scar as she did all the others. Unable to face her compassion because of the shame he felt for his actions, he pushed her gently away from him and sat up. He had his feet on the floor and was about to get up when Annika stopped him. She wrapped her arms around him from behind and laid her head on the back of his shoulder. He dropped his head, feeling unworthy of her care.

"I'm sorry, Annika," he choked out.

"You have nothing to be sorry for, Logan. You were doing your job. You saved that woman and the others. That's all that matters."

"I've broken every promise I'd ever made to you."

"I knew when I asked you for those promises that they were unrealistic and unreasonable. I knew that there was no way you could keep a promise like that. Life is unpredictable."

"Yes, but I was reckless. I never should have gone after him like that. Never should have let my emotions get the better of me. I was trained better than that," he sighed. "I was just so tired of dealing with assholes like that all the time. So tired of that place. So tired of fighting. I lost control."

"I bet, given the chance, any one of your teammates would have loved to have a piece of him as well," she remarked.

"It was irresponsible. I put my team at risk, and I put that aid group at risk. Instead of extracting the hostages quickly, we had to stop and tend to my injuries. Any number of things could have gone wrong then."

"That could have happened to any of you at any time. Did you get the hostages out?"

"Yes."

"Did your teammates have to carry your body out?"

"No."

"Then it sounds like a successful mission," she reasoned. "And if I remember the news reports, that SEAL team were heralded as heroes. So, stop being so hard on yourself." She gave him a little slap on the shoulder as a reprimand.

Logan grabbed her and pulled her around him until she was sprawled across his lap. "Heart of gold. How can you always be so forgiving?"

"It takes less energy to forgive than to live in regret."

"Wise woman," he said before he leaned over and kissed her. He held her tight, her head resting against his chest. He sensed something was bothering her as she went quiet and still. "What's the matter?" He raised her chin to see the sadness in her eyes.

"I was just thinking ... If you had died then, would I have even known?"

"Yes. After Grandma Jean died, I changed my next of kin notification to you and your parents." Her eyes met his in shock. "I knew that no matter how mad you all might have been with me, you would have taken care of me. It gave me comfort knowing that even though I was alone in life, I wouldn't have been alone in death."

"Oh, Logan, you were never alone in life. We were always here. Always praying for you." Overwhelmed with emotions, he held her tightly to his chest, his worry over his issues pushed aside for the moment.

Chapter 20

T HE ALERT OF AN incoming text on Logan's phone sounded just as he was sliding his hand up under Annika's shirt. They were making out like teenagers again in the armchair, even down to the light petting they were enjoying. It was another memory in this chair that would stay with him forever.

Reluctantly, Logan broke the kiss and pulled the phone out of his pocket. "I'm sorry. I have to take this. I never know when the team will be called out."

"I understand," she said, but Logan saw the worry in her eyes.

He read the text. "It's Graham. He needs me for this one. Is that okay?" He wasn't sure how she'd feel about him leaving her alone. This was all still so new for them.

"Of course, it's okay, Logan. It's your job, and you're needed." She looked suddenly nervous, and the guilt hit him again that there was nothing he could do to ease her worries.

"I don't know how long I'll be. Don't wait up." He stood and leaned down to give her a brief kiss before walking away. He couldn't help but look back at her one more time before grabbing his pack and opening the door. She still sat in the chair, staring out the window biting her fingernail, her fear evident. He felt a pang as once again he was causing her pain.

"Sorry to pull you away," Graham apologized again as Logan piloted the RIB downriver. "But we need your frogman skills for this one."

"Don't apologize. I'm happy to help. And, oh yeah, it's my job." Graham had briefed the team at the dock. Boaters in distress and taking on water. But they received an update en route.

"The water levels are high from the recent snows," Graham explained. "The boat has sunk completely. The passengers are trapped in the cabin in a pocket of air. No idea how much longer they will have that pocket."

"Why didn't they try to get out?" Jude asked.

"From what I understand, something happened to the door in the cabin, and they couldn't open it. I have a present for you, Logan." Graham picked up a bag at his feet and unzipped it holding it open for Logan to see inside.

Logan smiled. The bag held just enough plastic explosives for him to create a small underwater detonation to blow the door open if necessary. No wonder his SEAL skills were needed.

Logan gestured for Finch to take the helm so that he could get his scuba gear ready. He and Jude stripped down to their skivvies to don their wetsuits. After pulling the zipper up the back, he knelt to check his equipment. Jude did the same. Ascertaining that the tank and hoses were all in excellent condition, he proceeded to don the gear. Logan then did the rest of the safety checks, made sure he had good airflow, checked the regulator and gauges. Then checked his dive light. It was going to be murky down there, he needed to make sure the light was in proper working condition. Then he checked the spare gear they would be taking with them to get the passengers out of their submerged boat.

Taking the bag of C4, he began to assemble what he needed to blow the door, grateful to have something to take his mind off of his worries about Annika.

When Graham gave them the minute warning, he and Jude sat on the platform at the stern. Logan strapped on his fins, pulled his hood up, and put his mask in place. One more check of the regulator, and he was ready. As they approached, Logan could just make out the top of the boat. It had indeed sunk quickly from the first mayday call. Receiving a tap on the shoulder from Graham, the signal to go, Logan and Jude pushed themselves off the RIB and sunk below the surface. Logan let the water engulf his body as he floated deeper. He was in his element under the water and enjoyed the quiet peacefulness. He was at ease, even though he couldn't see jack shit.

Flipping on his dive light, Logan made his way to the boat. It was a medium cabin cruiser. He pictured the boat in his mind, finding the entrance to the cabin. The closer they got, the more he could make out of the boat. The stern was facing them; the door to the cabin was right in front of them. They swam past the bench seating and located the door. Sure enough, the thing was jammed. Reaching into his dive bag, he pulled out the plastic explosive, placing just enough to blast open the door.

Once inside, they spotted the passengers in the rapidly shrinking pocket of air in the corner. Two of them. A man and a woman. Mid-twenties, he guessed. He surfaced near them and took out his regulator. He introduced himself and Jude to the couple and explained how they were going to get them out of there. Since Logan could hold his breath for a fairly long time thanks to his SEAL training, he decided to forgo the extra gear for the woman and let her use his regulator. He could tuck her under one arm and have her out in no time. Jude, meanwhile, was adjusting the gear on the man.

Logan asked the woman if she was ready and, at her nod, indicated that she put the regulator in place. Taking a few deep breaths, he filled his lungs with air and dropped underwater again. In no time, he had the woman out the door of the cabin and was making his way to the surface, knowing his team would see the bubbles and know exactly where they were going to be. The RIB was there as soon as they emerged, and Graham and Evan pulled the woman up into the boat. Logan waited in the water for Jude and the man to assist them.

As soon as everybody was aboard, Finch turned the boat and raced to the nearest public dock where an ambulance would be waiting. Graham, meanwhile, was checking the couple over, determining they were slightly hypothermic after being in the chilly water for so long. But they would recover quickly as soon as they were under some warming blankets. All in all, one of the easier rescues he'd been on.

Upon arriving back at the Nighthawk's facilities and stowing their gear, Logan headed to his room in the barracks to grab a few things. When he opened the door, he noticed an envelope on his bed. Picking it up, he read the sticky note that was on it.

"Found this in Annika's old room and thought you should read it." It was signed Papa J.

Logan opened the envelope and pulled out the letter. The corner of his lips lifted in a tiny smile upon seeing her familiar handwriting. But as he began reading, the smile died an agonizing death. This was the letter she said she'd written to him before she'd attempted suicide, and reading it tore his heart to shreds. Sinking to the floor, his back against the door, he read through it again. And then a third time, needing to punish himself with her words.

Logan,

Nobody tells you about the little things disappearing. I stepped into Jamie's room, and it was so quiet and empty that it hurt. His smell had faded. His clothes had been donated. His body sprays, and other toiletries no longer clutter the bathroom counter. It's a disappearing act that takes place over time, slowly, until one day you open your eyes to reality. He's really gone.

Then there is you. You did not live in our house, so there is no slow fading of your existence. You vanished. Tore the band-aid off too quickly, causing the wound to open up again until I bled out. And I am left with only a t-shirt to try to staunch the flow.

For the longest time, I sustained myself on anger. An anger I detested because it was directed at you, my favorite person. You cut me open, slashed my heart to ribbons, then I got put back together wrong. There's no healing from that. No balm that can soothe the pain. And the anger can no longer sustain.

I once read about a wasting grief. Days and nights full of despair that turn into months, then years, as time disappears, just like those we loved. And those of us left behind waste away in our grief.

I could have loved you, but never got the chance to see where we could go. The moments of pure bliss filled with laughter that we shared once sustained me. But now, the emptiness I feel seems to go on endlessly. I am defeated by the struggle to endure.

My wish for you is to keep living for both of us. Chase after your dreams. Find love. Experience all there is to encounter. And do not grieve, for I will exist forever in the memories and experiences we once shared.

"I will not say: do not weep; for not all tears are an evil."
J.R.R. Tolkien

Annika

Logan let the letter slip from his finger, watching as it floated to the floor. Lowering his head, he wept. He'd broken his girl. He did not deserve her forgiveness. He was not worthy of her love.

Three of the four attempts on her life had been his fault. The car accident, the attempt at suicide, and Petersen; he was responsible for them all. Hell, might as well blame the fourth one on him as well; he deserved no less. Not knowing if he could face her, he hid.

Hid from his shame. Hid from his guilt. And hid from the only woman he'd ever loved.

<h1 style="text-align:center">Chapter 21</h1>

ANNIKA WAS GRATEFUL TO Natalie and Maddie for letting her hang with them. It had been two days since she'd last seen Logan. He'd texted her after his mission to say there were some things he'd needed to take care of at the Nighthawks facilities that would take a few days, and that was the last time she'd heard from him.

She'd tried to contact him several times, just to check in, but with each unanswered text, her abandonment issues reared their ugly head. He couldn't have left her again. He wouldn't. But a tiny voice in the back of her mind said he most definitely had. She hated that voice. It was the same voice that prompted her into her desperate act a decade ago.

Needing a distraction from that voice, she contacted Natalie, who invited her to dinner at her duplex. She was making the circuit around the living room, looking at all of Natalie's amazing artwork. The one over her fireplace was magnificent. It depicted the lake from the shore with a storm brewing in the distance and painted in such a way that Annika could almost feel the breeze in her face.

"Natalie, this is stunning."

Natalie joined her at the fireplace. "Thank you. It's the spot that Graham and I spent the afternoon at before the tornado." Natalie and Maddie had told Annika the whole story. How Graham had picked Natalie up from the side of the road when they were in high school after Maddie kicked her out of the car, then spent the rest of the day with her. He even offered to give her a first kiss, just like she'd requested of Logan all those years ago. Annika knew some things about the tornado that struck their town that day, having seen the 20/20 interview Graham had given, but she had no idea Natalie was the friend who'd helped Graham dig out his brother from his demolished house. And she'd had no idea that Maddie had been injured then, eventually losing her leg. She'd noticed Maddie's slight limp but never would have guessed it was because she was wearing a prosthetic.

"This is a real place? It's so beautiful."

"Want to see more?"

"Absolutely."

Natalie took her to her studio on the third floor of the duplex she shared with Maddie. That, in and of itself, was fascinating to Annika as well. They bought the duplex together, each turning their half into their own space. She would have loved to do that with Jamie.

The paintings were equally as stunning as the ones hanging in the living room. Natalie, it seemed, preferred to work with birds as her subject. They were everywhere. All different shapes and sizes. A current project sat on an easel in the center of the room. In it was a chickadee perched on a branch staring into the sky, watching a larger bird with a white stripe on each wing. The details she'd painted in the feathers was amazing. Even the light around the birds was remarkable. They looked as if they could jump off the canvas and fly away.

Annika's eye was drawn to another painting in the corner. This was another chickadee but deformed, twisted ... broken. Its beak open as if crying out in pain or fear. A dark swirling vortex made up the background. Sudden tears clouded her vision. It was as if Natalie had painted how she'd felt right before she'd made that suicide attempt. A quote from August Wilson popped into her head. "Confront the dark parts of yourself, and work to banish them with illumination and forgiveness. Your willingness to wrestle with your demons will cause your angels to sing." She'd spent so many years wrestling with her demon but in recent years, she felt confident her angels were singing.

Natalie, having observed Annika's reaction to the painting, said, "I wanted you to know, Graham saw your scars on your wrist." Annika paused in the process of swiping a tear away, suddenly fearful her new friends would judge her for her moment of weakness. "Don't worry," she rushed on to assure her. "No one else knows except for Maddie. I only wanted to say something because I've been there."

"You have?"

"Yes. I was a freshman in high school. The school weirdo. The artist. My parents had rejected me. My classmates avoided me. It was a very lonely time."

"You two seem close."

"We are now, but back then, we were like oil and water. Polar opposites. I wondered why it was even worth it. I found my mother's sleeping pills, and I'd taken four of them before stopping myself. I didn't want to die. I liked who I was. And if other people couldn't accept me as I was, then screw them. I just wanted you to know I understand that kind of darkness."

Annika looked away. "It was a long time ago."

"So was mine. But it never completely goes away."

"No, I guess it doesn't."

"No, it doesn't," Maddie agreed.

Natalie stared at her in shock. "You too?"

"Yeah, me too."

"Why didn't you ever tell me?"

"I'm not sure," Maddie admitted. "I guess I felt as the bigger sister I should lead by example. I didn't want you to worry more than you already were about me. It was just a fleeting thought in college."

"What stopped you?" Natalie wondered.

"Surprisingly ... David."

"David?" Natalie squeaked. "You talked to David all the way back in college?"

"I ran into him on campus once. I looked up as I was making my way across campus, and there he was. He recognized me and smiled. You know that smile of his, the one that looks like he has a secret joke to share. He was happy to see me. He walked with me for a while, and we chatted. He didn't try to do the thing that most people tend to do when with someone in a wheelchair. He didn't try to push me. He just walked beside me. It was ... refreshing."

"That sounds like David," Natalie mused.

"He asked if he could take me out for coffee. I had to get to class, so we agreed to meet up the next day. Talking to him was like chatting with a best friend. It had been a long time since I had a good friend. No offense, Natalie."

"None taken. I know what you mean."

"He told me I looked more beautiful than he remembered. Do you know how long it had been since anyone had said anything like that to me? I know it seems superficial, but when you grow up hearing it all the time, and then you lose it ... you lose a part of yourself. After that, we talked all the time. I even tutored him in his math classes. And we've kept in touch over the years. I've never told him what he did for me. He saved my life just by caring. By being himself."

"You've been in touch with him all these years? Why didn't you say anything?"

"You always got so sad when any of us mentioned any of the Whitakers; I figured there was a reason for that. I didn't think you'd be happy that I was talking with David."

"Just how close are you and David?"

Maddie blushed, a pretty pink color flooding her cheeks. "We're just friends."

"But you wish for more?" Annika speculated.

Maddie sighed. "Umm, no. It's not like that. He's like a brother to me. Besides, he's so much younger than me."

Natalie snorted. "It's only three years. That's nothing."

"I know. I enjoy spending time with him; I'm just not sure if I want more with him."

Natalie stared at her sister closely. "There's something you're not telling me."

Maddie looked away. "I don't know what you're talking about."

"There's someone else, isn't there?"

"Natalie, drop it. There is nothing going on between David and me, and there is nobody else."

They were silent for a moment, each lost in their own thoughts. "Funny how we both kept the most important things about ourselves from each other. And I thought we had grown so close over these years," Natalie mused.

"We *are* close, Natalie. I guess we were just trying to protect each other. Either that or we have a lot to learn about being sisters."

"My brother and I didn't always tell each other everything. And we were twins. We were very close but still kept some of the most important things about ourselves from each other. I guess that's just normal sibling behavior," Annika said. "'Sisterhood and brotherhood is a condition people have to work at.' Maya Angelou."

The sisters laughed. "Of course, you have a quote," Natalie teased. "How about we make a pact? If any one of us feels like we are slipping, if we feel lost, we call each other."

"I'd like that. I haven't had much luck making female friends," she confessed. "I'd like to have friends like you guys to talk to."

"Okay, girls," Natalie said. "Let's go put together something for dinner."

The three of them had a lot of laughs making dinner together. Annika suddenly realized how much she'd missed moments like these. She and her boys, Logan and Jamie, had this same type of relationship. She never realized how special it was until it was all gone. She felt sudden tears well; Natalie noticed and questioned her about it.

"I'm sorry," she apologized. "It's just that I haven't had a moment like this since my brother died."

"I was sorry to hear about that. I can't imagine what that has been like for you."

"How long ago was his death?" Maddie asked.

"Fifteen years," she answered as a tear slipped. "I miss him every day."

"Well, you have us as sisters now," Natalie told her. Annika had never heard anything more lovely than that. Natalie and Maddie gave her a big hug at the same time, and Annika felt like she had finally found true friends. *Kindred spirits*, as her once favorite book character used to say.

Logan was in a hell of his own making. He'd spent the last two days hiding and avoiding. He'd sequestered himself inside his room at the Nighthawk barracks. The letter lay on his dresser, taunting him. Her words forever etched into his brain, torturing him. "*I could have loved you,*" played over and over again in his mind. Followed closely by the words that gutted him the most. "*You cut me open, slashed my heart to ribbons, then put me back together wrong.*"

Fuck. He was an asshole. The absolute worst person on the face of the planet. He was a big, bad SEAL and a Nighthawk, but here he was, hiding like a coward. Full of shame and regret.

Three of four. That thought had taken root in his mind, and wouldn't let go. When the texts from Annika that he couldn't bring himself to answer began to torture him, he escaped his room for the gym. There, he pushed his body hard, hoping to banish the thoughts. But they taunted him still.

He lifted weights to Annika's words, "*Cut me open. Slashed my heart,*" engraved on the barbells, becoming heavier with each rep.

He ran on the treadmill, and her words, "*Could have loved you,*" chased him.

Graham found him running from the latter. "What the fuck are you doing?"

Logan slowed the treadmill as the other Nighthawks that were using the gym facilities stopped what they were doing to stare at them. He grabbed his towel and wiped the sweat from his face and neck, using the time to think of an answer that wouldn't get his ass reamed. He knew this confrontation was inevitable, but he'd been too lost in Annika's words to figure out how he was going to respond to his boss.

"What?" *Fuck.* Even he could hear how pathetic that was.

"You've been ghosting around here for the last two days when you have that stunningly brave woman waiting for you. So again, I say, what the fuck are you doing?"

Logan glanced around him, taking time to form his answer. Emma and David had stopped climbing the wall and now stood at the edge of the mats staring at him; Emma's stare more of a glare. Finch had frozen mid-lift, and Jude, his spotter, hovered over him with his jaw dropped. Tin Man, still wet and in a towel, had come running from the locker room at Graham's bellow. And Evan, on his way out the door, paused to watch the train wreck that was Logan Cain.

"Umm ..." *Shit.* Even more pathetic.

Graham threw his hands up in the air. They smacked loudly in the too-quiet gym as they came back down against his legs. "I knew I should have required therapy for you shitheads. You're fucking up again, aren't you? Running from the best thing to ever come back to you because ... Why? You're scared? Christ, don't make the same mistakes I made. But it's too late for that, isn't it? You've been here for days, which means she's been alone. I bet you haven't even answered her texts." Logan lowered his chin, his shame palpable as Graham started pacing and ranting.

"Go home. Go back to your girl. It was obvious to all of us how much you love each other. She forgave your sorry ass the last time you pulled this shit. You planning on staying away for another fifteen years? I don't think she'll give you a third chance. So again, what the fuck are you doing?"

"Three of four," Logan mumbled.

"Come again?"

Logan lifted his head and met his boss's angry gaze head-on. "Three of the four times she's nearly died have been my fault."

"What the hell are you talking about?"

Logan could sense everybody moving closer to listen. "First, there was the car accident that killed her brother, my best friend. I had been distracted by her because I was a horndog. She had given me a goodbye kiss, and it was all I could think about. I was looking at her in the rearview mirror when she screamed. If I hadn't been distracted, maybe I could have prevented the accident."

"That's—" Logan held up a hand to stop whatever Graham was going to say.

"The second time was also my fault. I'd disappeared from her life, leaving her alone in her grief. She fought for years to fight her depression until she couldn't anymore.

"You can't know that's because of you," Emma said softly.

"I can, and I do. Her father found the letter she wrote to me before ..." His voice cracked, and he attempted to clear it to continue. "And I quote, 'You cut me open, slashed my heart to ribbons, then put me back together wrong.'"

"Fuck," Finch cursed.

"I bet that's not all she wrote," said Emma.

He turned to her. "What?"

"I said, I bet that's not all she wrote. What else did her letter say?"

"She talked about her grief for Jamie, how we both disappeared from her life. Her anger at me."

"What else?"

"She wished me to live life, love, follow my dreams and crap like that."

"What else?" *Fuck.* Why wouldn't Emma leave this alone? She stepped closer to him when he didn't answer. "What else, Logan?"

"She said she could have loved me," he finally shouted. "Not that she *did* love me, only that she 'could have.'"

"That's because you didn't give her the chance, just like now. You could have her love. A second chance at her love, and you're fucking it up." Emma certainly didn't mince words. The Amazon warrior was fierce when she needed to be.

"What's the third one?" Evan asked.

"Petersen." It was all Logan needed to say. They had all been there for it. Knew the agony Logan had gone through searching for her. They'd all seen how very nearly she'd come to dying.

"Why are men such idiots?" Emma muttered.

"Hey, we're not all idiots. Some of us learn from our mistakes. Look at the boss man here. He fucked up then fixed it," Finch defended.

Graham stopped pacing directly in front of Logan. Reaching out, he smacked him on the back of the head. "Oww," Logan cried, rubbing a hand over the back of his head.

"First of all, she might have been angry at you when she hurt herself, but I'm sure that was not the only thing she was feeling. She was probably under a lot of stress. She was in college then, right?" Logan nodded when Graham paused. "College can be stressful. And she may have never dealt with her grief properly. All those mitigating factors combined drove her to what she did. But she survived.

And look at her now. What does her mom say? Heart of gold. She survived, and she thrived.

"Secondly, that accident could have happened to anybody. You guys were just in the wrong place at the wrong time. Even if you hadn't been distracted by that lovely girl, and who could blame you, you probably wouldn't have been able to avoid the accident. And from what I hear, you pulled her out of the car. You saved her life.

"And third, the only person to blame for what Petersen did to Annika is Petersen himself. Was it difficult to experience? Absolutely. Was the fear for her overwhelming? Most definitely. Should it have never happened? Undeniably. But she survived. She survived again because of you. You saved her."

Graham paused, letting his words sink in. "Now, the way I see it, you have two choices. You can either let your insecurities and fears drive you away from the best thing in your life. Or you can come home with me and get your woman back."

"It would help if you apologized to her for abandoning her for the last couple of days too," needled Emma. He winced, knowing it had been an asshole move but unable to think past his guilt.

Logan thought about the last fifteen years without her and how dark and lonely his life had been. Then he thought about the last few weeks he'd spent with Annika and how her smile alone brought him so much light and love. There really was no contest.

"What are we waiting for?" The Nighthawks cheered at Logan's answer.

Graham clapped Logan on the shoulder. "Right, let's go. She's at the duplex with Natalie and Maddie."

Chapter 22

GRAHAM PULLED THE TRUCK into the driveway just as the women were hugging goodbye on the porch. Climbing out on the passenger side, Logan made his way around the front of the truck, unable to take his eyes off of Annika. She spotted him and gifted him with a smile that made his heart skip a beat. His steps faltered, amazed at seeing no hesitancy in her smile, and for the first time in days, he felt like he could finally take a deep breath. Unable to take his eyes off that smile, he watched as she ran down the steps and threw herself into his arms, burying her face in his neck.

"Hey, Sunfire," he murmured into her hair.

"Hi."

The orange scent in her hair surrounded him as he inhaled deeply. "I'm such an ass. I am so sorry."

"I know. And I forgive you."

"Fuck, I do not deserve you."

"Nonsense," she admonished as tears started to slide down her cheeks.

"Hey, no tears. We are done with that."

"What if they are happy tears?"

"Those are acceptable, I guess, but I still hate seeing you cry." She gifted him with another of her bright smiles, and his heart felt lighter.

He'd just cupped her cheeks to kiss her when something caught his eye on the right. A glint of metal, a movement of shadow. Acting purely on instinct, he quickly pushed Annika behind him, blocking her from the unseen threat. He heard a loud blast and felt a searing pain in his abdomen. Hearing Annika scream, his instincts told him to move, to get her to safety, but his body wouldn't obey. Instead, he fell to the ground. He could hear Graham and David shoving the other women back inside the house. Annika though, was by his side, pushing down on his stomach.

Fuck, that hurt.

Another movement behind Annika had him trying to rise, to shield her again. But he couldn't move.

Annika looked over her shoulder and gasped. She got to her feet and moved to stand in front of Logan, blocking him from the shooter's view. She had her hands raised in front of her, elbows slightly bent, the glint of something dark and shiny covering her hands.

"Mr. Petersen!" she yelled. "Stop!"

"Annika! Get back," Logan heard Graham call. She ignored him, her focus completely on the man with the gun.

"Mr. Petersen," she tried again. "You don't want to do this." She was inching slowly forward, closer to the bastard who'd kidnapped her. Logan felt his heart in his throat as he watched the woman he loved face down a crazed gunman.

"Annika," he moaned. He needed to protect her, but his body wouldn't obey his commands. He tried to roll to his side to push himself up, agony erupted from his abdomen, making his vision blur at the edges. Gritting his teeth, he fought to stay conscious. There was danger, and he needed to stop it.

"Put down the gun, Mr. Petersen. You are not a killer."

Fuck, Annika. Please stop. He wanted to get up. The need to whisk her away from yet another person holding a gun on her consumed him. He wanted to protect her from that and had vowed to himself to always keep her safe. But, once again, he hadn't acted quickly enough. He should have charged the guy when he first saw the movement. For days he had felt that something was coming, that this thing with Petersen was not over. He was kicking himself for becoming sloppy since leaving the SEALs; he should have been more vigilant. He'd been careless and incompetent, and now it might be too late. He was going to lose Annika ... again. And he was helpless to stop it.

"No!" Petersen cried. "This is the only way!" There were sirens in the distance, growing closer. Then he felt pain again as Graham pressed on his stomach. Hard. Something niggled at his brain, confused as to why he was in so much pain. He looked down at himself and saw the red of his blood staining his shirt.

Fuck. He'd been shot. He looked at Annika's hands that were still raised and saw blood. He was having trouble thinking straight, pain overcrowding his senses. He wondered whose blood that was and worried she'd been shot too.

Think. Remember your training. How much blood had he lost already? How much time did he have left? *Annika.* He had to get to Annika. Protect her. He couldn't lose her again. Not now. Not ever!

"No, Mr. Petersen. It's not the only way." She was arguing with him, trying to reason with a crazy man. He tried to get to his feet again, but Graham held him down.

"Stay down, Logan," he insisted.

But Annika was in danger. She needed him. "Annika," he croaked, trying to make Graham understand. He couldn't just lay here. Annika had been shot, twice, and she still managed to talk her shooter down. Why couldn't he move? Why was he having so much trouble breathing? If she could do all she did that day in that classroom, why couldn't he? "Help Annika," he pleaded with Graham. Why wouldn't Graham help her? Why wasn't he doing anything?

"Trust her," Graham ordered. "Let her do her thing. She's got this."

"But ... I promised. To ... keep her ... safe," he wheezed between ragged gasps.

"She will be. David and I won't let anything happen to her," promised Graham. Logan could just make out David sidling up closer to Annika, bracing himself to charge Petersen if needed.

Ian McClintock and his fellow deputies arrived then with sirens blaring, the tires screeching to a halt. They jumped out of their cruisers; guns trained on Petersen. Annika stepped to the left, between the deputies and Petersen. Logan groaned. She was now between the cops and Petersen. What in the world was she thinking?

"No! Stay back!" Annika screamed, holding her hands up to ward off the deputies. The cavalry was here, she needed to let them take Petersen down.

With her back turned to him, she didn't notice Petersen approach until he'd grabbed her, and Logan was helpless to stop it. Petersen pulled her back against his front, his arm wrapping around her neck, gun held to her side. Her eyes went wide, and her body froze.

This wasn't happening. His worst nightmare played out right in front of him. And this time it most definitely would be his fault. Barely able to breathe and unable to get up off the ground, he couldn't shield her. He was going to lose her, and he was helpless to stop it.

"Annika," Logan tried to yell for her, his voice barely a whisper as he gasped for air. She ignored him.

"Mr. Petersen. Do you remember me from Jolene's the other night?" She started talking to him like they were meeting for coffee or some such shit. Her voice wavered slightly, but she spoke clearly to the man holding her hostage.

"I met your daughter, Rachel, there that night. She's the sweetest little girl. So full of life and joy. I always wanted children. A daughter just like your Rachel." Logan watched as Petersen's body language relaxed a margin. She had his attention. Completely focused on her and her words, the arm holding the gun lowered a tiny bit.

"Can you tell me, Mr. Petersen, I've always wanted to know, what was it like when Rachel was born?"

"What?" Petersen asked. He shook his head and his arm around her throat loosened. Annika took advantage of his loosened hold and spun around to face him. Logan groaned, seeing the same sudden move she'd used during her first confrontation with Petersen. The risk she'd taken that night in Jolene's had made him so angry. He'd let his fear overcome his common sense and said some nasty things to her that night. But that had led to their first night together, and he wouldn't change that for anything in the world.

Petersen was momentarily shocked by her change in position but rallied and raised the gun again, this time pointing upward toward her chest.

"Rachel. What was it like to hold your baby daughter for the first time?" She kept saying Rachel's name. He figured she was hoping to remind Petersen, to get him to put the gun down for the sake of his daughter.

She was so close to him, and Logan was in agony seeing the gun mere inches from her. Logan felt the panic build in intensity, afraid the gun would go off again.

Petersen's eyes darted around, from her to the deputies to Logan, and the panic in them was evident. "Eyes on me, Mr. Petersen," Annika shouted in her stern teacher voice. His eyes shot back to her. "Look at me! Only me. Look at me and tell me what it was like to hold Rachel for the first time?" He looked down; his attention completely focused on her. "What were you feeling when you first saw her?"

"It was ... it was like nothing I'd ever experienced before. She was so little. So completely dependent on me." The corners of his lips tilted up in a small smile.

"Why did you choose Rachel for her name?"

"It was Carlie's idea. She'd read that name in a book somewhere."

"Carlie must have been overjoyed as well to meet her new baby girl."

"She was. She always wanted a girl." Shockingly, the man smiled as he thought of his wife, the gun trembling in his hand. The strobe light effect from the rotating beacons on top of the police cars had an eerie effect on that smile.

"Mr. Petersen. How do you think Carlie would feel about what you are doing right now to that little girl? To Rachel."

"I ... what? I ..." he stuttered.

"Think back to those first days you and your wife had with Rachel. I bet you both had big plans for her future. You probably wanted to give her the world."

"I ... yes. We wanted to give her everything."

"What kind of world are you giving Rachel right now?" There was confusion etched into his features. It was clear he didn't understand or couldn't comprehend in his maddened state what she was trying to convey. "Do you want her to live the rest of her life in a world where her daddy, the first man she ever loved, is a murderer? Or do you want her to live in a world where her daddy made a mistake but worked hard to fix it? To make amends so that he can return to his baby."

"I ... don't know," he muttered. The gun wavered in his hand, slipping lower.

"Yes, you do, Mr. Petersen. You want to give me the gun. You want to teach that precious little girl of yours that there is still good in this world. That you loved her enough to give up the gun and start making amends for your mistakes. She will forgive you if you give me the gun. Carlie will forgive you. But only if you give me the gun."

"I ... I have to ..."

"Did Carlie love you?" she asked, interrupting whatever illogical thought he had.

"What? Yes, of course, she did."

"And did you love her?"

"With everything I had."

"That sounds like a true love, Mr. Petersen," Annika said with a sad smile. "Do you really want to taint that love? If you do this ... if you take away someone else's love, you will destroy Carlie's love. You will dishonor that precious gift of love you shared with Carlie with one despicable act."

"I have to do this *for* Carlie," he mumbled.

"No, Mr. Petersen. Carlie would never have asked this of you. Especially knowing you have a child that is completely dependent on you. I understand your grief, Mr. Petersen. I do. I lost my brother. My twin! He was the most important person in my life. I understand how the grief takes over everything, how you can't see past the agony and pain of the grief; it's all consuming. I, too, tried to take a life because of my grief. I thought it was the only way to end the pain. But the life I tried to take was my own."

Petersen looked at the gun in his hand. He turned it slightly towards himself. "Maybe ... the only way out ..." Fuck. Were they all going to witness this man's suicide?

"Eyes, Mr. Petersen!" Annika shouted again. "Look at me!" He tore his gaze from the weapon, a look of pure agony in his eyes. "I survived, Mr. Petersen. And I am so thankful every day that I was unsuccessful in my attempt. It would have been a great disservice to my brother's memory had I succeeded in killing myself. He was so full of life, as is your Rachel. As I'm sure your Carlie was as well. My brother would never want his legacy to be my death. And Carlie would not want her husband to become a murderer for her legacy. She would not want your death either. She would not want her daughter to be left all alone in a world as dark as that." Annika reached out and placed her hand over his on the gun. There was an audible gasp from everyone. Logan's heart felt like it was about to be torn out of his chest.

"Let go of the gun, Mr. Petersen. For Rachel. For Carlie." Miraculously he let go. One finger at a time. Annika grabbed hold of it and held it away from her. Then she stunned everyone by throwing her other arm around Petersen's neck and pulling him in for a hug. He placed his head on her shoulder, sobbing, his grief tangible. Annika held him as the deputies closed in, and Ian grabbed the gun from her hand.

"You have to go now, Mr. Petersen. But I promise you this; Rachel will not be alone. She has her grandparents who love her very much. And she has me now. And I come with an extended Nighthawk family. She will be waiting for you when you are better."

Petersen nodded to her as two deputies grabbed his arms and put him in cuffs. Before Logan could blink, Annika was kneeling beside him. She'd picked up his hand and placed it against her face. He tried to bring her into focus, but it was getting more and more difficult. "My Sunfire," he rasped.

"Stay with me, Logan." She was crying, the tears falling freely down her cheeks. "Don't leave me again."

"I'm sorry, Annika." He tried to reach up with his other hand to touch her face, but his muscles wouldn't obey. She caught his hand and brought it to her lips, her tears falling on his fingers. "I love you."

"I know. I love you too," she sobbed. He smiled at her, content for the first time in fifteen years. He could just make out Annika's voice calling out for him as his world went dark.

Hours later, Annika paced the hospital waiting room as they operated on Logan. Waiting for someone to tell her if he was alive or dead, the entire extended Nighthawk family was with her. She was grateful for their presence while lost in her own thoughts as she paced.

Ian and another deputy had already interviewed her about the incident. They also offered her a job as their hostage negotiator, but there was no way she ever wanted to do anything like that again. Twice was enough for her.

After Natalie forced her into a bathroom to try to wash as much of Logan's blood off her hands as she could, she'd called her parents, who were racing to Lake Haven. But at the moment, she was left alone with her thoughts, unable to get the image of Logan's blood on her hands out of her mind. A terrifying thought repeating itself over and over haunted her; what if he died? The answers searing through her thoughts frightened her. Jamie's death had been devastating, but it was Logan's abandonment that affected her the hardest. Her parents had been helpless to see her suffering, especially after she'd tried to end that pain. And now Logan was suffering, and she was helpless to save him.

But if Logan died now as she feared he might, she didn't know if she was strong enough to keep on fighting without him. It worried her to think the darkness would take hold again. She looked over at Natalie, who seemed to understand exactly where her thoughts were going. She jumped out of her seat and grabbed Annika's hands.

"He *will* be okay!" she insisted.

"But what if ..." Tears overwhelmed her, cutting off her ability to voice her fears.

"You will survive. But you won't have to worry about that. He will be okay. He's strong. And he knows you are waiting for him. He's got too much to live for. He won't give up. And neither will you!"

Annika nodded, and they hugged. Her parents burst into the waiting room then and thought the worst upon seeing Annika's tears. "Oh God!" cried Johanna. "He's not ..."

"No, Mom, we don't know anything yet." She hugged her parents, and her mother's sigh of relief was short-lived as the doctor came in.

"Who is Logan Cain's family?" he asked.

"We are," the room called out as a whole.

"All of you?"

"Please," Annika begged. "Tell us. Is he okay?" She held her breath, waiting for his answer.

"The bullet entered his abdomen, perforated his lung, and lodged itself against a rib. We repaired the damage, but his injuries were severe. He will need to stay in the ICU for a few days."

"But he's alive?" Annika needed to hear the words, to understand what the doctor was telling them.

"Yes. I expect he'll make a full recovery." He smiled at her, and Annika felt her knees give out. If her parents hadn't been holding her, she probably would have collapsed to the floor.

"Can we see him?" Johanna asked.

"Maybe just one of you for now. He needs his rest."

"Go give him our love, Sweetie," Johanna told her daughter.

Annika followed the doctor down the hall but hesitated at the door when she saw him in the bed hooked up to all manner of machines. He was deathly pale and somehow seemed smaller. It was a shock to see the once vibrant man reduced to this. Annika forced her feet to move, and she went to sit next to him. She lifted the hand that didn't have all the wires sticking out of it to her lips. *Please, Jamie*, she prayed. *Tell me, will he really be okay?* She held her breath, waiting for a reply. Any sign that would give her the reassurance she desperately needed. She closed her eyes and concentrated on listening.

"Sunfire." The whispered nickname came from the bed. Annika's eyes flew open to see Logan looking at her. He opened the fingers of the hand she was holding and brushed her cheek lightly. "My Sunfire," he whispered. "No tears, remember?"

"Happy tears," she cried. "I love you, Logan."

He smiled as his eyes drifted closed again. "Love you, Sunfire."

Chapter 23

TWO DAYS LATER, ANNIKA tossed and turned on the recliner the nurses had wheeled in for her, her scattered dreams making it impossible to sleep. Jamie was there in her dreams as always, as was the car accident. Logan featured prominently in her nightmares. In them, she'd be sitting by his hospital bed, and he'd vanish. Over and over again, she'd have this dream until the fear of losing him followed her even while awake. She couldn't sleep. She couldn't eat. She was in a constant state of worry that Logan was going to disappear.

Giving up on sleep, Annika stood and went to sit in the chair next to Logan. She placed his hand in hers and put her head down on the bed next to their joined hands, listening to his breathing. Johanna found her like that a few hours later.

"Annika." She gently placed a hand on her shoulder, and when Annika looked up, her mother gasped. "Oh, Sweetie. You look beat. Why don't you go home for a while? Get something to eat. Get some rest."

Annika shook her head. "I can't,"

"Sure you can. I'll stay with Logan," Johanna insisted.

"No, I need to stay. I can't leave." She could hear the panic in her own voice, and she was sure her mother could hear it too.

"Annika? What is it?" she asked, concern for her daughter in her voice. "Why can't you leave?"

Annika felt like she was on the verge of madness. How could she explain her waking nightmare to her mother? How could she explain that she feared he'd disappear if she left?

She just shook her head, unable to voice her fears. Johanna crouched down beside her. "Sweetie, you need rest too. You are not going to do Logan any good if you collapse."

"I know, Mom." She pinched her lips together, desperate to keep the panic at bay.

Johanna searched her eyes. "You look scared to death. You're so pale. Sweetie, what is it? Logan's going to be fine, you know that. So what has you so scared?"

The tears slipped past her defenses. With all-consuming anguish, she cried out her fears. "I can't leave him, Mom. If I leave, I'm afraid he'll vanish. I'm so scared he'll disappear. I can't sleep. My dreams are filled with him disappearing. I feel like I'm losing my mind."

Johanna pulled another chair over and placed it next to Annika's, then gathered her into her arms. "Sweetie, you are not losing your mind. I think I know why you have this fear." Annika looked at the sweet compassion on her mother's face. "You are afraid that Logan will vanish because that is what happened after Jamie's death."

Annika gasped. The memory smacking her full in the face. "I left the hospital and went home to change."

"And by the time we got back to see Logan ..."

"He was gone," she whispered.

Johanna smoothed Annika's hair back from her face. "You fear that it will happen again. He loves you, Annika."

"He loved me back then, too," she reasoned.

"But this is different. You've both come so far, overcome so much to find each other again. He's not going to give up what he's found with you for anything in the world."

"But he almost did when he placed himself between me and the gunman." She still couldn't believe he'd done that. He could have been killed.

"He was protecting you," insisted Johanna. "And from what I hear, you did the same when you stepped between him and that man."

Annika could see in Johanna's eyes how hearing what she'd done had scared her mom. "I'm sorry, Mom. I just acted on instinct."

"And so was Logan. He did exactly what he'd promised us he would do all those years ago when he told us he was going to join the Navy. He protected you."

"Oh God, Mom! I was so scared. If I'd lost him again ... I don't know if ..."

"Shh," Johanna said, hugging her daughter close to her again. "You didn't lose him, and you never will."

They held each other quietly for a time. "Go home, Annika," Johanna urged. "Get some rest. I promise you he's not going anywhere. Even if I have to tie him down."

"You'll call me as soon as he wakes up?" she asked, needing more reassurance.

"Of course. Now go." Annika stood and leaned over Logan to kiss his cheek, then did the bravest thing she'd ever done. She turned her back on him and left the room.

Logan opened his eyes as soon as he heard the door click shut. "I really messed up when it came to her, didn't I, Mama Jo?" He'd heard every word of their conversation. The fear and panic in Annika's voice breaking his heart. He'd had no idea that his leaving the hospital all those years ago without saying goodbye caused a fear that rooted itself deep inside her.

"Yes, you did, Kiddo. But you have the rest of your life to make it up to her. And sacrificing your own life for hers is a good start," she teased with a wink. "Just don't make a habit of it."

"Did you know how much she'd been struggling back then? Back when she tried to ..." He couldn't say the words.

"I knew she was still grieving for both of you. But she'd been so full of joy, since the moment she was born. I could never have imagined that the girl I knew who was like light itself could possibly go *there*. I didn't think the light had completely gone out."

"I read the letter Papa J found. She'd written it just before she made the attempt." Johanna gasped.

"I'm so sorry. We had no idea that letter was from that time. We'd just found it behind a drawer in her desk. It had your name on it. If we had known what the letter was about, we would have burned it."

Logan tried to sit up higher in the bed, wincing in pain. Johanna brought another pillow over to him and placed it behind him. "No, I needed to read it. I needed to know what she was going through. I needed to understand how my actions had affected her, to come to grips with my mistakes. I'm ashamed to say I nearly made the biggest mistake of my life after reading it, but my boss straightened me out. Still, it wasn't easy reading her words."

"Yeah, it wasn't so easy experiencing that in person either," Johanna said sadly, and he felt a pang in his heart for what they'd all gone through.

"I'm sorry you had to go through that."

"She fought hard after that. You should have seen her. She was determined to recover and move on. I'd never been so proud," she whispered.

"She told me Jamie came to her." Johanna seemed surprised by that information. He wondered why Annika had never told her.

"Really? She never said anything to me about it."

"Knowing her, she was probably worried you'd think she was crazy."

"True. That sounds like her." She sighed. "Did she tell you what he said to her?"

"He came to her just after she'd ... done it. When she was in the tub. He told her to hold on, that help was coming. I guess he meant you. She said you found her." Johanna nodded, tears in her eyes. "I'm sorry, Mama Jo; I can't imagine what that must have been like for you."

"I won't lie, it was scary as hell. But we survived."

"Jamie also told her that she needed to be patient just a little bit longer. That I was going to find my way back to her."

Johanna's eyes grew wide with wonder. "Really?"

He nodded then paused remembering Annika had told him his grandmother had said something similar to her before she died. "Thank you for what you did for my grandmother," he suddenly felt compelled to say, feeling ashamed he hadn't paid more attention to the old woman who'd raised him.

She waved off his gratitude. "It's what family does." And for Johanna, it was as simple as that.

"Thank you, Mama Jo," he said, squeezing her hand. "Thank you for reaching out again and being so patient with me."

"Thank you for finally answering me."

"I'm sorry it took me so long."

"Why did you finally answer?"

He shrugged, a mistake that sent pain radiating through his body. "I don't know, really. I guess I just thought I was making all these drastic changes in my life, quitting the teams, joining Nighthawk, moving back here; it was time to fix the mistakes of the past. I just didn't know how to begin."

"I'm proud of you, Kiddo. You've accomplished some great things in your life. And you did it all alone. That must have taken a lot of strength of character. I'm happy that you achieved your goal and became a SEAL, but I think I'm more proud of the work you do for the Nighthawks."

That pleased him to no end, but he became pensive as he wondered if he should continue with the Nighthawks. Or if he should give it up for Annika. "The job can be dangerous. I'm not exactly sure if I should continue or not. If something were to happen to me, Annika would be alone again." He was growing tired, could feel the exhaustion approaching fast. He had a long way to go to be back to his old self if a simple conversation exhausted him.

"I think that is a conversation you are going to have to have with Annika," Johanna stated.

Yes, he'd have to talk to her. He could quit the team for her, but if he weren't a Nighthawk anymore, what was he? Who was he? He didn't have an answer, but he knew that he didn't want to leave Annika alone again.

Johanna patted his hand. "Stop thinking so much and rest. I'll be here when you wake again."

"Yes, Ma'am," he said as his eyes drifted closed.

It was a week later, and Christmas day was upon them. They had a lot to be thankful for this Christmas. Logan was home, having been released from the hospital the day before. Waking up next to Annika on Christmas morning had been one of the greatest joys of his life. She still looked exhausted and worried, but at least she was sleeping now. He would work to bring the rest of her light back. She'd been far too dim this past week.

At the moment, they were in their usual spot on the big armchair. Logan was strumming absently on the guitar Annika had given him while she read beside him. They had enjoyed a lovely Christmas together as a family. Logan didn't realize how much he'd missed that. Growing up, the Northrups had always included him in their traditions. And even after all these years, nothing had changed except for their missing brother. They'd lit a candle for him and placed it in the window. In that moment, Logan felt the loss deeply. But then they'd put their sadness aside and celebrated Christmas as a family. Logan had been stunned that they had gifts for him. He'd asked both Annika and Mama Jo to pick up a few items he'd wanted to give them since he was stuck in the hospital. The biggest gift still sitting in his pocket, waiting for just the right moment.

After a huge Christmas dinner with all the fixings, Annika's parents decided it was time for them to go back home. They missed their own beds, they claimed, but Logan knew they were giving him and Annika time alone together, and he'd waited to give her his gift. He set the guitar down on the floor next to the chair and reached in his pocket to pull out the little box, then placed it in her lap.

"What's this?"

"Just one more gift for you."

"Logan, you've spoiled me enough today."

"Just open it, Sunfire."

She pulled on the ribbon then took the lid off the little box. Inside was a velvet jeweler's box. Annika looked at him over her shoulder in surprise. He knew what she was thinking, and he hoped she wouldn't be disappointed.

She shook the velvet box out and opened it gasping when she saw what was inside. "Oh, Logan! It's beautiful." In the box lay a necklace he'd commissioned for her after she'd gone missing. The necklace held a gemstone called labradorite. It was carved in such a way as to bring out its brilliant colors. Blues and greens swirled around each other. An intricate scrollwork in gold surrounded the gemstone. Annika studied the colors in the gemstone. "Is this ...?"

"It's the Aurora." He took the necklace out of the box and secured it around her neck. She held the gem in her hand, moving it from side to side, letting it catch the light.

"It's perfect," she whispered. She shifted to face him and gave him a kiss. "I love you."

He kissed her as well. "I love you. Thank you for accepting me back into your heart."

"You never left," she confessed. "I fell in love with the boy who gave me rainbows in the fifth grade, and it's only grown from there."

"Your words ... what they do to me." He kissed her again, longer and deeper this time.

Now was as good a time as any to have that discussion about his job, so taking a deep breath, he plunged right in. "There's something I need to talk to you about." She raised one questioning brow. "I don't ever want to be apart from you again."

She smiled. "I don't either."

"Good," He paused, unsure why he was hesitating. He'd do anything for Annika. He could do this. "When you return to school, I've decided to tender my resignation with Nighthawk to join you there." She looked stunned. "It's the right thing to do if I want to be with you ..." Her lips tilted upward with a smile as she placed a finger over his lips to stop him.

"Logan, you don't have to do that. I'm not going back to Annandale. I just don't think I could ever feel safe teaching there again."

"But you love teaching. I've seen you interact with the kids, Rachel, the girl from the car accident, Macey, and the students in your class who obviously love you. Sunfire, you were born to be a teacher and are an exceptional at it. You can't give that up."

"I'm not going to. I haven't had a chance to tell you yet. I ran into Miss Letty a few days ago. She's friends with the dean of the college here. They have an opening for a Literature professor starting next school year. I meet with them after the New Year. Miss Letty's assured me they only want me."

"Annika! That's wonderful! I'm so happy for you." He hugged her, his joy for her overflowing.

"So you don't have to quit the Nighthawks."

"But it's dangerous work. I think I still should quit. If anything ever happened to me on a rescue, you'd be alone again."

Annika shook her head. "No, Logan. I won't be alone. I'll have your extended Nighthawk family."

"But ..."

"No buts. I would never ask you to give up the job you love."

"But the danger, Annika," he still insisted.

"If anybody should understand the unpredictability of life, it should be us. You never know what might happen. It's dangerous to cross a street, but that doesn't stop us if we need to get to the other side. Is it dangerous to rescue people who need help? I imagine sometimes it can be, but that doesn't mean you should ignore the call. You are a born hero. It's part of who you are. It's part of what I love about you. Please don't give up that part of your life. And don't ask me to ask you to do it because I never will."

Logan lightly ran his fingers down her cheek. "You are too good for me, Sunfire."

She smiled that wonderful smile that filled his heart with joy. "No, Logan, I am just right for you."

Epilogue

Marcus

BREATHING A SIGH OF relief, Marcus parked his rental in the Nighthawks' lot. He was finally away from LA and all the ridiculousness of his celebrity life. Opening his car door, he took a deep breath of pure Michigan air, happy to be back and ready to work hard.

Looking around, he noticed the lot was nearly empty. Only one car remained besides his own. He knew the Nighthawks probably wouldn't be here since it was New Year's Eve, but he'd hoped to run into some of them.

Hearing the squeak of a door open, he looked up to see a tall woman step out of the building in front of him. He remembered seeing her that night at Jolene's when he'd made the deal with Graham to make a movie about the Nighthawks. He remembered she took his breath away. She hadn't noticed him yet, so he took advantage of her distraction to study her.

She was taller than the average woman but would be a perfect complement to his six-foot-four stature. Her brown hair was cut short and accented her sharp cheekbones. Black leggings covered her long legs, and a forest green sweater hugged her curves. She shivered and he smiled. It was cold out, but she wasn't wearing a coat; no wonder she was shivering.

She finally noticed him and stopped in the center of a halo of light from a lamppost. Startled, she looked up at him, and he felt lost in her deep brown eyes. She still took his breath away.

"Umm ... hi, Mr. Rayne," she said in a smooth voice that settled over him like a warm blanket. "Were we expecting you?"

"It's Marcus, please," he replied. "And I was in the area and was hoping to catch up with Graham and the others."

"Oh, well, everyone is at a New Year's party at Logan and Annika's place. I was just headed there myself if you'd like to join me."

He was surprised at the offer but pleased she'd included him. He smiled his best movie star smile, which for some reason, made her narrow her eyes. He nearly laughed out loud. *Figures she wouldn't fall for my LA charm.* "If you're sure they won't mind."

"Not at all. Besides, I'm sure Graham will be *thrilled* to see you," she replied, her tone dripping with sarcasm. Marcus knew how much Graham hated the attention that his rescue had brought him and his Nighthawks, and his team took great joy in teasing their boss about it every chance they got.

"Well then, let's not keep him waiting." He stepped towards her car, opening the door for her when she unlocked it. "I'll follow behind you if that's all right."

She ducked her head as she passed him and sat in her seat, swinging her long legs into the car.

He bent down to meet her eyes, one arm on the roof, the other still on the door. "I met a lot of you that night a few months ago. You'll have to forgive me for not remembering your name."

She blushed, a fascinating rosy glow coloring her sharp cheekbones. "I'm sorry, it's Emma."

He smiled and watched as her blush darkened. "It's a pleasure to meet you, Emma." Then he stepped back and shut her door.

Emma. Her name wrapped itself around his heart. When she smiled through the windshield at him, he felt that organ clench tightly in his chest. He had been anticipating the enjoyment of working with the Nighthawks and learning their skills, but now, he had more to look forward to.

New Year's Eve had arrived, and since Logan was still recuperating, they'd decided to have everybody out to the lake house instead of going to Jolene's. And Jolene being who she is, decided she would bring all the food from her restaurant, claiming they could do without her for one night. Annika listened to her hum to herself as she flitted about the kitchen, preparing everything as she and the other women waited nearby to do her bidding when needed.

"Where is Emma with the rest of the food? I thought she'd be here by now," Jolene lamented. "I need those other ingredients."

There was a knock on the door just then, and Annika moved to answer it. "That must be Emma now."

Annika pulled the door open to find that indeed Emma had arrived, arms laden with supplies. "Emma! Good. Jolene's been frantic," she winked. "Come in. Here let me take ..." It was then Annika noticed Emma wasn't alone. Marcus Rayne stood behind her, his arms equally loaded with boxes.

"Sorry about this, Annika," Emma said.

"No, It's okay. Come in. Both of you." She stood back to let them enter then took a box from Emma. "You can put that stuff over there." Annika indicated the island in the kitchen.

"Emma! It's about time," Jolene began, then she saw Marcus. "Holy shit!"

"Mr. Rayne," Annika began after he'd put down the boxes. "While you will always be welcome in my house because of your generosity for my students, I have to ask, what are you doing here?"

"Sorry to just barge in here like this. I was looking for Graham and the team. Emma told me you'd all be here. I hope you don't mind," he stated.

"Not at all. Like I said, you are always welcome. Here, let me take your coat. Can I get either of you a drink?"

Graham entered then. "Annika, Logan asked me to ask you ..." he broke off when he spotted the only other male in the kitchen. "Marcus?"

"I know ... What the hell am I doing here?" he supplied. "I needed to talk to you."

"Ever hear of a phone," groused Graham.

"Graham!" Natalie admonished. "Don't be rude."

"Sorry," Graham mumbled.

"I know I should have called. It's just ..." he broke off and sighed. "I had such a nice time with you all last month at Jolene's. I had some time to myself for a change, so I just thought ..."

"Well, if that's not the sweetest thing ever," Jolene exclaimed. "Bless your heart."

"Come on, Mr. Rayne. Let's get you something to drink." Annika decided to accept the movie star as a friend.

"No need to go to any fuss. And call me Marcus."

"All right." She grabbed a beer and held it up for him to see, he nodded, accepting the bottle after she'd popped the top. "Seriously though, Marcus, I'm glad I can thank you in person for everything you've done for Suzanna and my students. It was ... remarkable."

"Nah," he replied. "What you did in that classroom was remarkable."

"You think that was incredible; you should have seen her two weeks ago," Natalie muttered.

"I heard about that too," he informed them. "Shit, Graham. Are all the women you know such amazing warriors?"

Graham smiled and placed an arm around Natalie's waist. "Absolutely!"

"Okay, so Natalie and Annika I know. And Miss Jolene of the heavenly burgers, of course."

"She's a master chef," Emma praised, then caught Jolene's glare. "What? You are."

"Not anymore," Jolene mumbled.

Natalie interjected then, pulling Maddie closer to her. "This is my sister Maddie."

He shook her hand. "Maddie. Let me guess; you can swim across Lake Michigan in one breath."

She laughed. "Not unless I can change this out for some kind of bionic flipper," she said, lifting her pant leg slightly to reveal her prosthetic.

"Fascinating. Titanium?"

"Yup," Maddie replied.

"Lose a fight with a shark?" he teased.

"Nope. Tornado."

"No shit!" he exclaimed. "Wait, tornado?" He looked at Graham and Natalie. "Your tornado?" They nodded. "Wow, the story gets deeper." Graham looked like he was about to protest Marcus revealing Maddie's story to the world, but Natalie held him back. "So, you're the warrior princess of the group," he said to Maddie, making her blush.

"And, Emma, my knight in shining armor who saved me from an exceedingly long, lonely night. What's your story?"

"Emma's the newest Nighthawk," Natalie answered.

"And an expert climber." Maddie supplied.

"Oh, and did we mention she also fences?" Jolene supplied.

"No shit?" Marcus exclaimed again.

"No shit," Jolene answered.

"Is there anything you can't do, Emma?" he asked.

"Dance."

Marcus gave a bark of laughter. "Maybe you just haven't had the right partner yet," he said with a wink, and Emma blushed. Marcus reached out to shake Emma's hand. "Another fascinating warrior woman." He placed his other hand over their joined ones and stared at her for a moment, seemingly reluctant to let her go.

David came into the kitchen. "We're starving. What's taking so long?" Then after spotting Marcus, he said, "Oh." He leaned out of the archway to yell to the guys in the other room. "Hey, guys! We're losing the women to the movie star!" Within seconds, the kitchen had filled up with the rest of the Nighthawks.

Logan, who was technically the host along with Annika, stepped forward to shake Marcus's hand. "Nice to see you, Marcus."

"Logan! Damn good to see you up and around. No lasting effects?"

"Nope. I'll be back in fighting shape in no time." Logan walked over to Annika and took her hand. "Can't thank you enough for what you did for Annika and Suzanna," Logan said gratefully.

"Hell of a woman you got there, Logan," Marcus said with a wink for Annika.

"Couldn't agree more. 'Though she be but little, she is fierce.'"

"Ah, I see she's got you quoting now as well. And Shakespeare too, good choice," Marcus teased. "But I bet your fierce Annika has a better quote she's just itching to share."

Annika felt the blush heat her cheeks. "I must admit one did pop into my head. Something from Ariana Dancu. 'She made broken look beautiful, and strong look invincible. She walked with the universe on her shoulders and made it look like a pair of wings.'"

Everyone was silent, as the words hung in the air around them, until Jolene gasped. "That was beautiful. I'm gonna enjoy having you around, Annika. I've learned so much already." Everybody laughed and Logan gathered her into his arms. When his lips touched her forehead and held there, she closed her eyes, reveling in his love.

"You are a fount of literary brilliances and I look forward to garnering more renowned wisdom from you." Marcus looked around at all the curious faces. "I know you are all wondering why I'm here. Well ..."

"Nuh-uh," Jolene cried. "Not until after we eat! Everybody who is not cooking, out!" Everybody laughed. The men all wandered out of the kitchen except for Marcus.

"Can I help?" he offered.

"Aww, bless your heart, but no. I've got this down to a science. Go out and enjoy a beer with the boys." She shooed him out into the other room.

Later, after everyone had their fill of Jolene's splendid food, Marcus stood to address the group. He pulled a flash drive out of his jeans pocket and placed it on the table in front of him. "Rough draft," he said. Marcus had been after Graham for months asking to make a movie about him and his Nighthawks. It was only last month that Graham had agreed with a few stipulations. The Nighthawks would have final say on the script. A Nighthawk would act as technical director during filming. And most importantly, Marcus Rayne would go through all the training the Nighthawks could teach him.

"Go easy on me," Marcus continued. "It's my first try at scriptwriting."

Everybody stared at the tiny device sitting on the table. "Who's going to read it first?" Natalie wondered.

Graham turned to Annika. "What do you say, Annika?"

"Me?" She was stunned he'd ask her to read it first. After all, she was the newest member of their group and didn't know much about search and rescue.

"You're our word guru. Have at it."

"If you're sure," she looked uncertainly around the group. All were nodding their heads. "All righty then. I guess I'll go first."

"Perfect. Next order of business. February first, I will be available to start my training."

"Good," Graham said. "Emma will be your training instructor."

"What?" Emma exclaimed.

Marcus looked at Emma, a curiously fascinating expression of pleasure on his face. "Perfect."

Read on for an excerpt from Emma's Element Book 2 in the Nighthawk Search and Rescue Series

Visit Spotify for Annika's Playlist
https://tinyurl.com/AnnikaSpotify

Also By

Nighthawk Search and Rescue Series
Nadia's Nemesis (Free Prequel)
Natalie's Nighthawk (Book 1)
Annika's Aurora (Book 2)
Emma's Element (Book 3)
Sutton's Shadow (Book 4)
Hollynn's Horizon (Book 5)
Sophie's Song (Book 6)
Jolene's Justice (Book 7 Coming Soon)

Acknowledgments

Dear Reader,

Thank you so much for allowing me to tell this story that means so much to me. I appreciate you taking the time out of your life and offering a piece of yourself to these words and these pages.

Did you enjoy Logan and Annika's story?

People are often hesitant to try new books or new authors. Honest reviews of my books help bring them to the attention of other readers and encourage them to make that leap and give it a try. If you've enjoyed this book, I'd be eternally grateful if you could spend just a few minutes leaving a review on any or all of the following sites to help this story find the readers who would enjoy it. Goodreads, Bookbub, Amazon. Even the short reviews really make an impact.

I would also like to acknowledge the following without who this book would not be possible.

Laetitia Treseng of Little Tweaks, whose advice and prodding has gone a long way to fluff up this story.

Jenni Bara, beta reader extraordinaire. I look forward to reading your third book as well.

My family, who more often than not leave me alone long enough so that I can commune with the voices in my head.

About the Author

Amanda Zook has been an avid romance reader since middle school when she delved into Gone with the Wind and has finally decided to liberate the stories that live in her head. After growing up in the Sweetest Place on Earth (Hershey, Pennsylvania) she attended college at a small liberal arts school majoring in English (what can you do with an English degree?). She met the love of her life there and followed him to the Jersey Shore (no, not the MTV reality show) where they lived for the first 20 years of their marriage, before moving halfway across the country. Amanda now lives in the Southwest corner of the mitten state on the shores of Lake Michigan (no sharks, no salt, no problem).

She is a wife, a mother of teenage twin girls and can now add published author to her list of achievements.

You can find her on Facebook, join her reader's group, Amanda Zook Books, Instagram , and TikTok.

Visit her website for all the latest news and sign up for her newsletter for freebies. www.amandazook.com

Kron'ael flew as if hit by a wrecking ball, and again a pleased Cheshire grin spread over James' face. Now he knew his powers would work here, and on top of it he had the exorcism song of his friends tearing this place down brick by brick around the demon's ears.

He reached out with his mind and grabbed the demon preparing to slam him into the stone floor, but the demon was fast and rolled away flinging out black orbs. James decided he didn't want to know what they did and threw up a quick shield while jumping behind the closest pillar.

He threw sword sharp blades of fire and crossed the room from one pillar to another. The answer was thousands of tiny darts jabbing into his side and leg. He cringed in pain as he leaned against the pillar and pulled out the most annoying ones. He expected them to be something crazy and explode after a few seconds or maybe they were covered in poison.

"Can't do anything about that now." He said to himself as he used the power to grab the top of a column and pull it down on the demon's head. He knew Kron'ael was too fast to catch with the old falling column trick so he followed it up by making the floor as slick as possible to try and cause him to fall while jumping away from the column. Unfortunately he'd forgotten about the wings. Instead of dodging like any normal person would, the demon simply took to the air and started tossing anything he could think of down on James' head. This provided a problem and an opportunity. He quickly tossed up a shield but focused the majority of his power on grabbing the flying monster and yanking him into the stone wall as hard as possible.

A lovely series of cracks in the wall were his reward and James tried to follow it up with a good lightning blast to the face, but by the time he got to where he thought the demon would be nothing was there. As he frantically looked around, massive arms wrapped him in a crushing bear hug.

"I wanted to bleed your emotions for years," the demon breathed into his ear, "but I will have to settle for simply killing you."

James whipped his head back trying to connect with something breakable and kicked down at the demon's feet at the same time. A loud crack preceded the demon's arms releasing him and James rolled away amazed at the result. More cracks echoed off the stone walls and his brain went momentarily crazy trying to figure out what was happening. It decided the best plan was to roll away a bit to make sure nothing was going to kill him immediately then figure out where the sounds were coming from.

He stopped his roll at the base of the broken pillar and looked around. Kron'ael was slowly being forced backward by two people swinging clubs. The only thought James could get a hold of was a resounding, what? After a few seconds he realized the two he'd left downstairs were wielding their newly holy chair legs like baseball bats. Small explosions popped each time they struck the retreating demon, and James decided to take full advantage of the changed situation before the demon regained his wits enough to deal with the teens.

He sent a pulse of force at the back of Kron'ael's knees followed by another from the opposite direction at his chest, knocking him to the floor. The two teens started screaming and continued to pummel him. James decided the only way to get a good shot at the prostrate demon was from above.

He dug his fingers into the stonework of the pillar and pulled. The power filled motion tossed him to the ceiling where he grabbed on as if it were styrofoam. Lifting his legs up until his feet were pushed flat against the roof he let go and kicked off straight at the chest of the demon. Twisting in the air James did his best cartoon superhero elbow drop. He fueled it with truth, belief, power, and most importantly a lot of extra mass and gravity. A loud crunch greeted his landing and he rolled to the side in the off hand chance one of the teens was over-exuberant and decided to keep swinging even though his head was in the way.

The demon's form had broken into shards of darkness and James knew they needed to take care of them before they ran back together like a bad replay of the liquid metal Terminator.

He started stomping the pieces and noted with admiration that he didn't need to tell Grace and Mitch to start smashing. They took to it with amazing gusto. He guessed they'd decided to get what measure of revenge they could and came up the stairs ready to hit anything in swinging range. He wasn't sure how mentally stable they were at this point, but it would have to wait till after the evil demon from Hell was dealt with.

Out of the corner of his eye James noticed a movement and turning he saw a piece of shadow, white eyes blazing, flick out a razor sharp tentacle and cut a line in the air. Multiple things dawned on him like a twin sunrise.

First the demon was trying to escape again like he had in the church and the second realization followed quick on the back of it. If he was trying to make a doorway to Hell this wasn't really Hell, which meant it had just been Kron'ael's personal version of Hell. At that mind bending thought so many questions banged around his head that he decided the best choice at the moment was to destroy the monster then ponder the philosophical ramifications of people's personal Hells at a later, safer, date.

Worried his mental effort would slip on a trip into Hell James decided to actually grab the demon. He was surprised when two pairs of hands grabbed his clothes and pulled. Looking quickly over his shoulder he was greeted with the determined faces of emotionally broken and revenge fueled teenagers trying to help him.

Hell has a gravitational force all its own, and once you're caught not much can resist the pull. After a few moments of struggle three people and one demon fell through the doorway and rolled in a heap down hard, gray stairs. Not wanting to lose the initiative James rolled to his feet as quickly as possible and pulled a flaming sword from his imagination.

Spinning he saw a small twisted human-like shape trying to run down the stairs. Without putting more than the necessary reflexive thought into it James threw the sword end over end. It tumbled in flames, reflecting firelight off the stone wall of the tower of Hell. The stooped little demon dodged and the sword missed him and stuck quivering in the wall. As he turned to continue his escape down the stairs he was met immediately with a chair leg to the side of his head. Crumpling to the ground he curled into a ball and moaned.

James walked down the steps toward him, closing his eyes for the last few steps to search for any traps or tricks. Below him, in the strange colors of truth, lay a wrinkled little thing marked with cancerous growths and oozing sores. Empathy made him hesitate on the last step but the fresh memories of Grace and Mitch being tormented pushed him on. He wasn't sure he wanted to know what'd happened to Ray. Using the power to craft chains he wrapped them around the demon and bolted them to the wall.

Sitting down on the steps he looked back up at the two teens then out over the desolate plains of Hell. The energy went out of him, and the force of exhaustion felt like it would crush him. It was over. Not totally because they were still sitting on the stairway to Hell. But in a simple way it was over. The long chase through the United States followed by the trek through Purgatory, losing his hand, and everything that had happened on the tower had left him feeling empty and poured out. Looking up at Grace and Mitch he felt like crying and the only thing he could think to say was, "To be honest, I'm not quite sure what to do now."

A look of shock crossed the teen's faces, and Grace came down two steps toward him, "But how do we get home? I thought once we got that," she paused and waved a hand at the demon, "thing it would all be over."

James nodded. He understood exactly what she was saying, and truth be told he was hoping something would show up and fill him in on all the details. Like why he was chosen to do all this, and if that juggler really was who he thought he was, why didn't he just take care of this mess himself? Most pressing, however, was how to get out of here.

Staring out over Hell at the slight glint of distant gates he said, "This is Hell. Out there," he pointed, "is Purgatory. This," he patted the stone step he was sitting on, "is a tower that doesn't really exist, at least according to a conversation I had with the Devil."

He heard a noise and turned to look up the stairs not really caring at this point what it was. "And that," he pointed and the teens looked behind them, "is a really big raven I met on the way up here while looking for you."

The raven flapped its wings, drifted down to land a few steps closer, and cocked its head at him. James returned the favor and cocked his head at the raven. A sound like a stick running over a hollow log came from the raven's throat and James smiled. "Well, I think I've figured some of it out."

The raven answered by hopping closer to the chained demon.

James sighed and gave a small nod, "Yes, I think I'll leave him to you. I'm not really sure what to do with him anyway. It's not like I need to send him back to Hell." He chuckled at that. "I guess Ren's exorcism worked didn't it?"

The raven hopped past him and with a flutter landed on the demon's head. A shudder ran through what was left of Kron'ael, the thing James had formerly thought of as the Darkness, and for a moment their eyes met. James smiled and didn't feel bad at all for hoping whatever happened to the ugly little demon would take a very long time.

He released the chains and with a caw and a flap of wings the raven carried the demon out over the plains of Hell. In a moment quicker than it should have been the two were nothing more than a speck on the horizon.

"But," Grace was standing over him and when James looked up to see what she was going to say all she could do was wave her hands at the bleak landscape.

Brushing himself off James realized he was still wearing the black robes of the students from a college he never even learned the name of. "Hell," he turned to look at them, "let's get out of here."

He picked up the chair leg Grace had thrown at Kron'ael and traced a door on the gray stone wall. As he did, he knew the door would work because, after all, Hell was something you brought with you, and if that was true, then no matter how hard it was, there was always a way out. He tossed the chair leg to Grace, reached out, grabbed the edge of the new door, and pulled.

www.ingramcontent.com/pod-product-compliance
Lightning Source LLC
Chambersburg PA
CBHW010345220726
48290CB00016B/2636

9 781960 564016